# STRIKING DOWN SCOUNDRELS

## JERRY D. HARRISON

STRIKING DOWN SCOUNDRELS by Jerry D. Harrison
www.JerryDHarrisonauthor.com

Published by Jerry D. Harrison through
BelieversPress
6820 West 115th Street
Bloomington, MN 55438

Edited by Snapdragon Group Editorial Services
Cover design by Dugan Design Group
Interior design by Jeff Gerke Typesetting
Printed by Bethany Press International in the United States of America

International Standard Book Number (ISBN): 978-0-578-05301-1

# PROLOGUE

His highness emerged from the tall double doors on the third level of the white stucco Government House. He felt splendid in his new uniform, which was white with gold braid trimmed with quarter-inch red ribbon everywhere the tailor could manage to sew it. His matching military visor hat was also splendid, but uncomfortable because it fit so tightly on the emperor's large head, a head proportionate to the emperor's huge body. The emperor was certain his dress conveyed his unquestioned standing as head of state of this African country, a country long known to Europeans for its violence, disease and poverty.

The emperor raised his chin slightly as he thought of the French diplomat whom he had kept waiting at the foot of a massive flight of stairs, stairs that the emperor would soon descend in his magnificent attire. The French had requested this meeting concerning trade matters. In particular, the French wished for lower tariffs for certain automobiles and specific foodstuffs. When the emperor had earlier received the request for the meeting, he had set certain goals for it. If all went well, when the Frenchman returned home with the lower tariffs, the emperor would have access to a new line of credit in a particular French bank, which he would immediately use to fund his personal retirement program. In his country, a head of state must prepare for a sudden departure from office. International trade, and the bribes collected in

1

its process, offered a lucrative flow of funds for any dictator determined to put his personal needs before those of his country.

The enormous man moved slowly across the veranda to the top of the stairs. There he paused to look over his assembled officials and the French diplomat. Once the applause began, he would slowly begin his descent. He would not hurry. He would enjoy having the Frenchman wait for him.

At the bottom of the stairs, the Frenchman stood looking straight ahead with the expressionless face of a career diplomat. He was thinking how much silliness he must endure in order to sell a few cars and vegetables. He was an agent of his nation's commerce, a trade diplomat. He could wait all day if he must in order to make this sale. He could even tolerate the verbal abuse from this tyrant because in the end the bribe would be placed, the sale made, and the diplomat would return home to France.

The Frenchman sympathized with the subjects of this obese despot, knowing they suffered greatly from his tyranny and stupidity. But they had suffered under every leader in the fifteen-plus years following the nation's independence in the early 1960s, and would probably suffer even if they had no head of state. Although he would stay as long as necessary to conclude the agreement, the diplomat would be pleased to soon leave this dark spot of poverty and brutality.

Through an open third-floor window in the nation's only clean hotel across the street from the Government House, a middle-aged American watched the proceedings through old field glasses. He saw the smirk on the face of the emperor as he approached the stairs. He noticed how the man lifted his chin and delayed at the top of the stairs until the crowd's applause reached an appropriate level.

The American slightly moved his fingers on the field glasses as the emperor started his first downward step. He then watched the emperor's leading leg collapse at the knee, causing the fat tyrant to topple forward, missing the next several steps but crushing the new hat and the head in it on the edge of the seventh step down. The speed of descent increased as the emperor tumbled the equivalent of two flights of stairs. Nobody was close enough, big enough, nor brave enough to stop the fall, and the emperor couldn't.

A very dead emperor with a twisted neck and bleeding head landed at the feet of the Frenchman. There would be no trade discussions that day.

The American showed no emotion to what he had witnessed when he said softly, "Now, that's a sudden fall from power. It couldn't have happened to a more deservin' fellow." The American slipped his field glasses into his leather bag, latched it, and moved from the room, hoping to leave this hot, dirty country on the noon mail boat.

# CHAPTER 1

The Ozark View Retirement Center sits atop a limestone bluff overlooking Table Rock Lake southwest of Branson, Missouri only a few miles north of Arkansas. Eighty-five individual cottages strung along the edge of the bluff provide an expansive view of the lake and surrounding wooded hills. Near the midpoint of this array and slightly back from the bluff sits the Central Building, which appears to be a magnified cottage and houses a dining room, recreation rooms and offices. A flower garden between the bluff and the covered patio of the Central Building encloses a small swimming pool, two hot tubs and four fountains. A medical building, a skilled nursing facility, and an assisted living center sit across the parking area, away from the bluff. All cottages and other Ozark View buildings are clad with grayish-white clapboard approximately the color of the surrounding limestone, and are trimmed and roofed in oak-leaf green. Although the straight lines of the homes contrast with the soft lines of limestone and forest, the cottages almost appear to have been created with the bluff.

On covered patios of each Ozark View cottage, an eighteen-inch-diameter thermometer with bold black numerals and red pointer dutifully displays the current outside temperature. On Friday, April 30, 2004, at 10:00 A.M., those thermometers all read 74 degrees. A gentle breeze blew from the south. Oak trees boasted new leaves. Dogwoods displayed white and pink blossoms. It was springtime. Most Ozark View residents were outside.

"Scoundrels! Somebody oughtta strike 'em dead!"

Roy Cole raised his eyes from the dominoes on the table in front of him. "Huh? Who're you talking about?" Roy followed Abe Brown's gaze down the line of cottages. "You're not talking about Ann's family are you? They're just helping Ann move to her daughter's home."

"Of course I'm not talkin' about Ann's family! I'm talkin' about the scoundrels that wiped out Ann's savings so that she can't afford to live here anymore! Those scoundrels should be shot dead!"

"I thought she lost her money in one of those corporate meltdowns. A utility company, I think."

"It was Middle North Public Service. Mid-North was a utility company servin' northern Midwestern states until a bunch of sneaky thieves got control of it. They made Mid-North a corporate wild animal. They used the cash flow from the utility business to invest in everything from grand scale emu farmin' in Australia to drillin' for water in the Sahara Desert. If not crooked, the ventures were at least stupid. The scoundrels should each be shot twice, once for theft, and once for stupidity."

"You follow financial stuff better than I do. All I know is that Mid-North went bankrupt when one or two of its big investments didn't do well."

"It was more than one or two. In the house I've got a magazine article about it. I'll go get it. You need to know more about the Mid-North scam so that we don't have to watch your family move you out of here some day. I need to take a couple of pills, anyway."

"In Kansas, I had a friend like Walt who sold insurance. My money is mostly in annuities with Plain States Mutual."

Abe slid his chair away from the table, used both arms to help himself rise, and tottered slightly before he began a shuffle under the covered walkway toward his cottage next door. "You better hope scoundrels like those that got Ann's company don't get that insurance company. I'll be right back, so to speak."

Walter Wilson, sitting across from Roy, had also been watching Ann Walker's son-in-law and grandson carry furniture and boxes to the small rental truck parked at the curb in front of Ann's cottage. Walt looked toward Abe's back, and called after his short, stooped friend, "Ann probably wouldn't approve of what you're suggesting for her malefactors."

"I meant what I said! Somebody oughtta' strike 'em down!"

Don Stone, who had been adding the domino scores, spoke softly about Ann's plight and Abe's anger. "It's sad. Ann's husband, Warren, was a field engineer at Mid-North for his entire career. Warren and Ann faithfully set aside money in Mid-North stock in the company's thrift plan, what we now call a 401K plan. When he died, Warren thought Ann would be comfortable for the rest of her life. But somehow, a little group of self-serving jerks got control of Mid-North, ruined it, and erased all the faithful employees' life savings. Hundreds of people are facing the same situation Ann is facing. I agree with Abe. Someone should shoot the scoundrels!" He shifted in his seat and looked over his wire-framed reading glasses to better see the moving activity. "It's easy for me to say, though. I won't be striking down any scoundrels even if I knew who to strike."

Walt nodded, "Yeah, we're just four old guys sitting here with little to do, and no way to do it if we wanted to."

Roy challenged his big blond-haired friend. "I think you're understating our condition, Walt. Our little foursome does a lot. We travel every second or third month in Abe's motor home. Each of us, except for Abe, travels to see family three or four times a year. We golf, except for Abe. We fish, we go to the shows in Branson, and now we're planning an Alaskan cruise. We're pretty active considering three of us are over seventy years old, and Abe is over eighty-five."

"Yeah, we're active, but we aren't out there solving the world's problems. Maybe we could be, but we'd rather sit here and let other people deal with the big issues."

Don finished tallying the domino score, and pushed the tablet to the center of the table, turning it as he did so. "I don't know that I've ever solved one of the world's problems. Maybe, in a small way I helped. I fed a lot of hungry people in my restaurants."

Roy glanced at the tablet as he addressed Don's point. "And when you were running those restaurants, you made sure the food was prepared tastefully in sanitary conditions, and served efficiently for a reasonable price. People counted on you to provide that food and service day after day. You did. But who's counting on you today other than your buddies here who need you to lose at dominoes to boost our egos?"

Don grinned. "I'm glad I make you guys feel better about yourselves."

Roy nodded, and returned the focus to Abe's declaration. "Abe's plenty upset about what happened to Ann. He sounded willing to shoot the scoundrels that brought down Mid-North."

"He might be willing," Walt agreed. "We don't know much about Abe's background, and if he ever would have considered shooting someone. We know he's a man of action even with his physical limitations. But I don't think he'll jump on his little scooter with a rifle strapped over his shoulder, and ride off to wherever the scoundrels are. He wouldn't get out of Missouri with his arthritis and heart condition."

"His heart blockage is getting worse," Roy cautioned.

Don looked over his glasses toward Abe's house. "Yep, and he still has a big issue to take care of."

Walt also looked at Abe's house. "He says he's done it, but I think he's diligently avoided the issue."

Roy agreed, "He's always been in control, and he's unwilling to release it."

"Common deterrent," Don said as he shifted his attention back to the moving activity. "It looks like Ann's family is about through. As soon as Abe gets back, we need to walk over there to tell Ann good-bye."

Roy looked, too. "She's just moving to Neosho. That's only seventy or eighty miles away as the crow flies. We'll see her from time to time."

"Yeah, well all of us are too old to be flying on crows," Walt lamented. "We'll have to drive the winding roads. I'll bet we don't see Ann much."

Don proposed, "Let's take Abe's motor home to visit Ann next month. I'll fix my lasagna, which she really likes. We can reheat it in the motor home's little oven, and eat in that pretty park by the big spring in Neosho."

Roy wiped his eye. "Yes, we should do that, but I like seeing Ann every day. She can brighten the gloomiest of days. Somebody really should do in the rats that caused this."

The slamming of Abe's door and the shuffle of his feet drew the threesome's attention.

"I thought you said you would be right back," Roy called.

"In my condition, and at my age, 'right back' is a figure of speech." Abe ducked his head to look through the upper lenses of his trifocal eyeglasses, which were large and framed in gun-metal gray. He saw Ann's grandson throw extra moving pads into the back of the van. "I see Ann's family is about finished."

Walt arose from his chair." Yeah, we've been waiting for you to go say our good-byes."

"Then y'all shouldn't read this article before we go. You'd be too mad to be civil. Believe it or not, I've calmed down from what I felt when I first read it."

# CHAPTER 2

Abe was quiet, and his friends noticed. Ruth Birch and Cyn Smith had joined Ann, Abe, Don, Walt and Roy along with Ann's daughter, son-in-law and grandson at a long table along the edge of Ozark View's dining room. The friends had shared laughter and tears during lunch, and were aware that Ann must soon leave. Nobody wanted to initiate the departure. They continued talking to delay the impending separation.

To himself, Abe recalled the first time he had seen Ann Walker in the Ozark View dining room. He had estimated her big smile and large twinkling eyes to be twice the size of those of other ladies housed in such a petite five-foot frame. Her hair was a natural salt-and-pepper mix of black and gray, short and combed back on the sides of her head. Her skin was white, her small hands were lean, and her fingernails were short without polish. He guessed her to be an honest, happy person that he wanted to be his friend. He had confirmed his original assessment each day during the four years he had known her, and had found that she could brighten the darkest of days. He liked talking to her even if he didn't feel like talking to anyone else. He would miss her. He hated the people that had hurt her.

At Walt's suggestion, Abe had refrained from haranguing about the scoundrels. Perhaps because of this restraint, he remained silent, thinking. He was planning. The first phase of his plan was simply to gather more information. He could do that himself. For the second phase, which required travel, Abe would need the help of his men friends, but he knew they would not approve of his plan. He would have to get their cooperation without their knowledge. In the old days, he would have smirked at the thought of gaining anyone's unwitting cooperation. But now Abe regretted his need to covertly use his friends.

Abe looked at Walt, Roy and Don. No, they would not approve. All were Christians, and tried to live their faith. Not one could be told of his plans. But these buddies could help him without knowing they were doing so.

Ann interrupted Abe's thoughts. "I'm worried about you, Abe. After I'm gone who is going to insist you brighten up on those cold wet days when your arthritis hurts so much?"

"I'll have to interview potential new residents. I'll insist on someone with a happy, giving personality. We're going to miss you around here, Ann." This was the most loving statement any of the group had ever heard from Abe.

Ann smiled broadly as tears began flowing down each cheek. She abruptly stood, and in a breaking voice said, "That's it. I have to go now. If I don't, I'll cry all the way to Neosho."

All stood. Ann, Cyn and Ruth led the group from the dining room toward Ann's car and the rental truck, now fully packed. Along the way, Ann hugged other residents and staff, finally reaching her car where she again hugged her closest friends. Ann's daughter would drive Ann's car while the son-in-law would drive the rental truck with the grandson sitting tall in the passenger seat. Ann's family drove her away. Ann was gone. It hurt.

Cyn sighed deeply and spoke first, referring to her husband of thirty years who had died four years earlier. "When Steve was with me and I was sad like I am now, I would snuggle up against him. He would hold me, and I would cry. He was like an oversized teddy bear. Right now I miss both Ann and Steve." She wiped her tears. "I'm going to my cottage, plop down on my chaise lounge, and cry myself to sleep."

All agreed that the best thing they could do was what they normally did right after lunch each day, nap. The friends quietly headed to their homes.

Abe had no intention of sleeping. Ann's situation had brought up from his past an attitude of contempt he had not experienced in years. Greed, corruption and fraud enraged him. He wanted to act, to right a wrong. At the least, he wanted to deliver consequences to those who had harmed so many people. He would try, even though he might be too old, too tired and too sick. So be it. Abe Brown would try. He thought of the expression "I'll die trying!" The expression might literally apply to this endeavor.

Abe needed information. He would start with simple Internet searches on the computer in his cottage. But Abe knew better than to do all of his research from his home computer and Internet address. He had a plan for that, too.

From its inception, Abe had welcomed the Internet, and had quickly learned to use it well. He had always embraced new technology, and had begun using personal computers when they first appeared in the late 1970s. He had remained a student of technology until he sold his business and retired when he was eighty years old.

Frequent lessons from two young men in Hong Kong had taught Abe more than he should know about computers and the Internet. They had taught him to hack supposedly secure systems, a skill that had proven very helpful during Abe's last few years in business. However, Abe had not seen his instructors since he had retired and disappeared from his former life. He knew computer security had improved, and could only hope his skills were still useful.

# CHAPTER 3

The mid-afternoon hush at Ozark View was broken by the sound of Abe's shiny black Stella. The Stella is a quiet motor scooter and Abe made no unnecessary noise, but any sound was enough to break the near-silence at Ozark View. Abe left quickly, taking the fastest route to the oldest part of Branson, avoiding 76 Country Boulevard, also known as "The Strip," where April tourist traffic moved at a speed just faster than a good walking pace.

Abe's destination was an Internet café located in downtown Branson. The café, which had flourished with Branson's emergence as a music and entertainment center, was always busy, especially during tourist season. Nobody there would notice a quiet old man wearing non-descript shirt, trousers and broad-brimmed hat. Only his stooped posture and shuffle might be recognizable to a truly observant person.

From news articles, Abe knew the identities of three known perpetrators of the Mid-North collapse, and suspected there were others. He would concentrate his research on the three known conspirators, gathering information about each of them, and would be alert for clues of additional thieves. Abe signed onto the Internet with a user ID that could not be traced to his current name.

Abe began with Edward L. Harm who had been President at Mid-North from 1998 until it fell in 2003. He had learned from a magazine article that Harm was an avid golfer, playing most often at his club near his home in Connecticut. It took Abe only about four minutes to hack the simple computing network of the Glistening Spring Golf Club. He learned that members of Glistening Spring paid more to belong to the club than even many rich people pay for their homes. He also discovered a wealth of photos, aerial photos, drawings, and maps of the course. Abe could use this information.

According to member billing and pro-shop records, Ed Harm was very active at Glistening Spring. He entertained lavishly, habitually played golf on Tuesdays and Thursdays, and played irregularly on Friday and Sunday mornings. Harm's regular foursome had standing 10:10 A.M. tee times for Tuesdays and Thursdays, and consistently completed each round in slightly less than four hours.

Abe studied the course layout. He compared aerial shots to layout drawings, looking for an accessible point overlooking a tee or green close to the perimeter of Glistening Spring's property. He found only one spot near the course from which he might observe play. On an aerial photo, Abe saw a road following the edge of a hill near the 12th green, which was elevated in the northwest corner of the club's property. He spotted a narrow turnout on a curve in the road, which looked to be higher than the green and not too distant. The spot might offer a clear view of the green if trees did not block the line of sight. Abe looked for recent photos. He found a June 2003 photo taken from the southeast that clearly showed the 12th green, an automobile on the road above, and no trees between. Abe had found a place to work.

Abe spent more time perusing the Glistening Spring network, and found Glistening Spring rules forbade slow play, banned cell phones and other electrical devices, and required all players to use carts. He reviewed the overall course layout, noting distances and par for each hole. He then calculated that Harm's foursome starting at 10:10 A.M. would be at the twelfth hole about 12:30 P.M. Abe had determined a time to work.

Abe also hacked into the computers of two of Ed Harm's luncheon clubs in New York City, but learned the man did not consistently use the clubs. Only Harm's golf outings seemed useful to Abe's plan.

His fingers hurt, but Abe continued to work the keyboard, resolving to take extra pain medication as soon as he returned home. He turned his attention to Fred Fogg, who had resigned as Chief Financial Officer of Mid-North shortly before it collapsed, and who was clearly instrumental in plundering the company.

Abe hacked the network of Fogg's country club on Long Island, New York. He found Fogg used his country club mostly for entertainment. Fogg golfed sporadically, recording inconsistent scores.

Abe then searched for behavior patterns in Fogg's records at two downtown clubs frequented by financial people, but he drew a blank. He determined Fogg was inconsistent in everything he did, which seemed to him to be inconsistent with the stereotype of financial officers.

Abe opened his folder and reviewed several articles torn from magazines and newspapers. He noticed a photo he had only glanced at earlier which showed Fogg dashing across heavy traffic on Pine Street in New York's financial district. The caption stated that Fogg, age forty-five, made this dash from his office building at exactly twelve-forty every day to meet associates in the bar and grill across the street. Fogg was quoted, "The thrill of dashing through traffic is good training for dashing through the risks of the financial world. It sharpens one's timing."

From what Abe could find, nothing else was consistent in Fred Fogg's behavior. Okay, the lunch dash or the bar would have to do.

His hands were killing him. Abe signed off the system, gathered his folders and, still wearing his hat, headed for the coffee bar. There he rewarded himself with a seven-inch round cinnamon roll and a cup of thick Colombian coffee. Abe reflected that for most of his life he would not have allowed himself such a treat. But, with the end near, why not indulge one's self? Eating like a harvest hand might even speed the end to his constant pain. Abe continued to lose weight in spite of his eating habits. His moment-to-moment effort to breathe burned more energy than he took in, even with extra sweets and large meals.

As he slowly ate and drank, Abe rested his fingers, purposely relaxing them as best he could in order to reduce the immediate pain. He had one more scoundrel to investigate.

So far, he had found two small clues as to the existence of a fourth conspirator, but Abe was a long way from identifying any such fourth person. He would keep looking, but in the meantime, he would concentrate on the three.

Abe shuffled back to the computer he had been using, and signed on. He sought information about the third person involved, Gus Whitby, who had been Executive Vice President of Diversified Business for Mid-North. It was through these "diversified businesses" such as the ill-conceived emu farms and Sahara water drilling, that the scoundrels siphoned money out of Mid-North. The only question was whether the scoundrels had stolen the money or had simply squandered it.

Abe learned Whitby had three homes, but primarily resided in a mansion in Chevy Chase, Maryland. He quickly hacked Whitby's personal computer, which confirmed that Whitby was always in Chevy Chase for the Greater Washington Professional Golf Classic. Abe pondered this, and his temptation. The 2004 Golf Classic was fast approaching. There were extra risks in doing his work at a golf tournament, but the tournament seemed to be the best place to deal with this third target. Abe would have to develop a tight plan.

Abe wanted to search more, but his hands hurt and he knew tourist traffic would soon snarl Branson streets during the dinner hour. He should start back to Ozark View. If only he didn't hurt so much! He imagined his hands slipping from his scooter's throttle and brake levers, causing a crash that would kill him. If he didn't harm anyone else, that would be acceptable.

# CHAPTER 4

Ruth Birch sat very still on Don Brown's lakeside patio, staring across Table Rock Lake. She was wearing her standard daily attire, navy warm-ups recently ordered from a stylish travel clothier. Her fingernails were trimmed and polished. Her hair was the same light brown and the same shoulder length as it had been for the past twenty years, though the color was now enhanced from time to time in the Ozark View beauty salon. Ruth was thin, and her shoulders slumped slightly as she sat.

"Ruth, how about a refill?"

"Thanks, Don. Yes, I enjoy your delicious coffee on a beautiful day overlooking a beautiful lake. I'm trying to be cheerful, but I just want to cry. I hate that Ann had to move. She and I were close. She was one of the first people I met when I moved here. We helped each other grieve over the deaths of our husbands. We traveled together. Our traveling days are over, too. If it weren't for her kids, Ann would have trouble surviving now."

"I share your sadness, but know that we're spoiled with our nice little spot on the world. In most of the world, there is no such thing as retirement, Social Security, 401K plans, or other provisions to provide for people when they are old. In most places, people just work until they die. And, by the way, people in many countries tend to die young."

"You haven't helped me, Don. You've given me something else to be sad about."

"Count your blessings. Be charitable and kind to everyone, including yourself."

"Yes, sir, and thanks for the good coffee. In the terms of the TV commercial, 'Your coffee has a stout, rich flavor without being harsh.'"

"This coffee is a carryover from my restaurant days. I buy it from the little beverage company that serviced my restaurants. I was once its biggest customer. Now, I'm its smallest."

"I'm tempted to ask you to order some coffee for me. But I won't. I'll just look forward to a treat when I'm at your house."

"Anytime you want coffee, Ruth, either in liquid form or as grounds, just let me know."

"Thanks. Where are the others? I heard Abe's motor scooter earlier. From the sound, I guessed he was leaving, but I didn't look outside."

"I looked out of my window when he left. He looked like a man on a mission."

"Has he come back?"

Don shook his head. "I don't think so."

"He was more upset by Ann's situation than any of us. He normally covers his feelings, but at lunch you could read sadness and anger all over him."

"He's been upset since he learned how badly Ann was affected by the Mid-North collapse. He's an astute investor. He knows the financial markets and its players. He showed us an article this morning which he feels accurately encapsulates everything he's read about the Mid-North debacle. He's mad that a good company was ruined, and that those responsible haven't been thrown into a deep dark dungeon."

"Don, I don't know enough about Mid-North to know whether to be mad, sad or what."

"Abe is mostly mad. He can name the people who are responsible, and can list their offences. He's very compassionate when folks are hurt, and completely unforgiving of those who harm others."

"He offered to pay Ann's Ozark View bills until she recovers her losses by the class action lawsuit that is sure to come. But Ann was advised by her son-in-law, a banker, that those class action cases rarely produce anything of value for the small investor. They mostly only enrich the law firm that puts together the suit."

"Abe knows about such lawsuits, Ruth, and he knows that Ann is unlikely to recover any of her losses. He would never say so, but Abe is wealthy, and could pay Ann's bills forever."

"She doesn't think it's appropriate for him to pay her bills."

"I don't think he has given up, Ruth. He may ask her again."

"He says the perpetrators of Mid-North are scoundrels, sneaky cowardly thieves, and that someone should shoot them."

"He was so mad today that he would have shot them on the spot, had they been within range. But Abe is old and weak. He won't shoot anybody."

"Don, here comes Cyn. Pour another cup. She doesn't awaken well without coffee."

Cyn, short for Cynthia, waved at Don and Ruth, swept her hand outward across the view, took a deep breath and smiled as she approached Don's patio. She exclaimed, "I just want to etch that view into my memory so that when I can't see it every day, I can remember each beautiful detail."

Ruth looked at her short, slightly overweight friend who had tight curls of red hair on her head and freckles covering her face, neck and arms. "Cyn, tell us what you see while Don pours your coffee."

"I see an expanse of water shaped something like a hand with the fingers spread apart. Between each finger is an elongated mound of green, separated from the blue water by grayish white lines of lime-stone. Spotted amongst the green trees on those mounds are miniature buildings, miniature when viewed from here, but not in reality. Those little buildings are homes, shops, boat docks, and barns of active living people, a few of whom I personally know and the rest of whom I would like to meet. On the water are little bugs moving at different speeds making wakes as would be made by the boats that they really are." Cyn paused. "Enough, I want coffee. Thank you, Don."

"You're welcome. If you concentrate on that line of limestone, you'll see slight changes as waves tweak the lower edge, and blowing tree branches adjust the upper edge."

"I'm a boat-watcher," Ruth said. "I love to watch pontoon boats creep across the lake or explore the shoreline. I often try to guess who is on each boat and what their relationship is. Sometimes I use my binoculars for a closer look. Even then, though, I can only learn so much about the boaters. I've been observing long enough now that I know the regulars and the strangers."

"Are there more regulars or strangers?" asked Don.

"Strangers, by two to one."

"That makes sense. This is a recreational lake. People travel long distances to visit Branson and Table Rock. More are coming every year."

"Shall I start our standing discussion as to whether that's good or bad?" Ruth asked.

Cyn shook her head. "No, remember we're all move-ins here. Besides, I want to talk about Abe. He is intensely upset about Ann."

Don reported Abe's departure on his Stella. "Intense is a good description of his aura when he rode off. He looked neither left nor right, but directly down the road."

"Are you talking about Abe?" It was Walt, who, with Roy, had approached without notice. Walt was carrying an eight-inch dark green paper plate covered with a navy blue napkin. "I brought us some celery and carrots from the main building." He placed the plate on the table and removed the napkin.

"To me, your celery and carrots look like scrumptious oatmeal raisin and chocolate chip cookies. They perfectly complement Don's delicious coffee." Cyn said this as she reached for the smallest oatmeal raisin.

"Well, to guys like Roy and me, they have to be celery and carrots in order for us to eat them without guilt."

"You guys don't understand guilt," Ruth countered as she, too, reached for a cookie.

"I know I feel guilty that I can afford to live here, but Ann no longer can," Roy replied.

Don nodded, "Roy, we've been talking about that and about Abe's reaction."

Roy raised his head and opened his eyes wide. "He was livid, and after I read the article he gave me, I was livid, too. But Abe can't let go of it."

Cyn asked, "What do you four know about Abe? He's never said much about himself when we've talked. I don't even know how long he's been at Ozark View."

Ruth, who had been at Ozark View longer than any of the group answered. "Abe has been here about four years, maybe a little more. The first six months, he would barely talk to anybody. He seemed to examine and analyze everybody before he decided to be friendly to particular people, namely Ann, me, eventually the rest of you, and a few others."

Walt leaned back in his chair after lifting a second cookie from the plate. "Abe is guarded as to what he says about himself and his background. About all I know is that for most of his life he lived in Houston where he owned an import/export business. I say he lived in Houston, but I think he really lived in hotels around the world, and only alighted in Houston once a month or so. When I've asked him what he imported and exported, he said 'everything at one time or another.' I don't know exactly what an importer and exporter does anyway."

Don smiled, "I asked him that once, and his response was 'Whatever it took to make a buck.' I asked if he took ownership of goods, or simply handled material for someone else. He said 'Yes. ' I've asked him other similar questions, and he always has given me vague answers."

Roy added, "I've gotten that kind of response when I've asked him about his family."

Ruth raised a hand as she dealt with the remains of a cookie. "I've inquired about his family, one time bluntly asking, 'Abe, were you ever married.' He only answered 'No,' and offered no additional information." Ruth reached for another cookie.

Walt speculated, "In his import/export business, he might have gotten involved with unsavory activity or people. Abe might be in a witness protection program, or something."

Don shrugged. "'Or something' is a scary idea. He might be hiding from law enforcement agencies."

"Maybe it's something less spectacular," Ruth suggested. "For example, I'm living at Ozark View to hide from the noise of grandchildren at my kids' homes."

"Ruth, you just told us Abe said he was never married. How would he have grandkids?" Roy asked.

"I didn't say he had grandkids. I said he might be hiding from something innocent like I hide from the noise of my grandkids."

Walt abruptly stood, stepped to the edge of the patio and looked between houses toward the parking lot. "Speaking of noise and Abe, I think I hear the hum of a friendly, stylish motor scooter. Wow, he looks like a man possessed by purpose."

Ruth shuddered, "I should think his arthritis would keep him from riding that scooter."

Don agreed, "Me too. He doesn't want to drive a car any longer because he might suddenly die and run through a school crossing or something. He says he can ride the scooter because he can just step on, sit there with his feet resting on the scooter's floor, and not worry about anybody other than himself if he crashes. He told me the toughest part of riding is using his arthritic hands to operate the bike."

Roy took another cookie, leaving two on the plate. "When we went to Minnesota in his motor home last year, he took his scooter for a ride around a big lake while Walt, Don and I played golf. When we got back, we found Abe soaking his hands in hot water. He had tears in his eyes. He told us that he had just kept motoring, and hadn't rested his hands all the way around the lake."

"Does he ever drive his motor home?" Ruth asked.

Don shook his head. "No. His concern about injuring somebody if he crashes is multiplied for the motor home. Walt does most of the driving. Roy can drive for a while if somebody talks to him to keep his blood pressure medicine and road boredom from putting him to sleep. I drive a little, but my bad knees hurt too much after a while. We mostly rely on Walt."

Walt assured his friends. "Well, it's fine with me. I like to drive that motor home. I feel like I'm driving a cross country bus. Besides, we each take our turn doing the things we do best, or the things the others of us can't do anymore."

"There seems to be more of that latter group as time passes," Roy mused.

"Back to Abe," Ruth injected. "I know he's upset. I wonder what he's up to. Do you think he'll tell us at dinner?"

Don answered, "If he's at dinner he might or might not tell us, and he may not even be at dinner. You know in the past when he concentrated that genius mind of his on some matter, he wouldn't come to the dining hall for several days, but would stay in his cottage in front of his computer. He'll let us know when he wants us to know."

Cyn looked toward Abe's house. "*If* he wants us to know."

# CHAPTER 5

"If you do, I'm leaving! I hated those things when I was a kid!" Roy was responding to Ruth's suggestion that they wrap the Ozark View flagpole and have a Maypole celebration.

Ruth leaned back, raised her arms over her head. "Oh, I loved Maypoles when I was a child and when I taught. Only a few little boys ever objected."

"I'll bet most of 'em hated May Poles. Prancing around some pole like we cared whether it was spring, or May, or whatever . . . it was the pits. The colors were always sissy, too."

Ruth thoughtfully asked, "What would you rather do in spring when you were a child, Roy?"

"Easy, play baseball."

"Didn't you like to dance?"

"No."

"You dance nicely now."

"That's because I can't play baseball anymore. But you've never seen me dance around any dang Maypole."

"You're going to hurt someone's feelings, Roy. Be careful," Cyn cautioned.

Walt saved Roy from his discord with Ruth. "Hey, look. Here comes our missing buddy. He looks like he was up most of the night."

Don looked toward the breakfast buffet line. "I think Abe was still awake when I went to bed at one-thirty. I started reading a new book last night, and couldn't put it down until my eyes were too tired to read more. I stepped outside just before I went to bed, and noticed Abe's lights were still on."

"Y'all are looking at me as if you've never seen an old man push his breakfast tray." Abe spoke to his friends as he pushed a tray trolley cart that many Ozark View residents used to transport their meal trays along the buffet line to their tables.

Walt moved his eyes between Abe's tray and Abe's face. "Well, we didn't see you last night at dinner or cards. Since yesterday noon, you haven't come out of your house except to go somewhere on your scooter. When Don asked about you last evening, you simply grunted that you were 'fine.' What's going on?"

"I'm thinkin' about something, and you know how I get when I'm thinkin'."

Cyn joined in Walt's inquiry. "The last time you got into such a mood, you were planning a trip for you four guys to Florida. That trip appealed to me, too, but you guys didn't invite any ladies. What are you planning now?"

"New England. Mid-Atlantic. You know me. When I get upset, I plan a trip. An escape trip, I guess. I'm still upset by Ann's situation. I gotta get outta here." Abe eased into his chair as he spoke.

Roy inventoried Abe's breakfast tray. "Your tray looks like you're compensating for missing dinner last night. Are you planning to miss lunch, too?"

"I'm hungry, and I was up late plannin' and hurtin'. I used the computer too long yesterday and last night. My arthritis was killin' me. I finally knocked myself out with some stuff I have left over from my Houston doctor."

Ruth showed sympathy. "Are you in pain today, too?"

"Yes."

"And when are you thinking of making this trip?" Don asked.

"As soon as possible. I want to get out of here. It's too early to go to northern New England, but we could go to Connecticut or Rhode Island. I need some time with my financial people and attorneys in New York City. Then, we could catch the Greater Washington Open Golf Tournament at Chevy Chase, Maryland. Trip should take almost three weeks. By the time we get home, I may be settled down from the Ann thing."

Cyn objected. "It's not fair. When Ann left, Ruth and I lost one of our best friends, too. You're not inviting us."

"Sorry, Cyn. I don't do co-ed trips. The bus won't accommodate it." Abe always called his motor home "the bus." "Maybe you two could fly to Washington to see the tournament with us."

"I wouldn't drive to Springfield to see a golf tournament, but I'll invite Ruth to go with me to Saint Augustine to soak up some sun. We'll get away, too. What do you say Ruth?"

"If I can schedule it around my doctor appointments, I'd love to go."

"That takes care of the ladies. What about you guys? Can you be ready to go within a week or less?" Abe looked at Walt, Roy and Don.

Roy nodded. "I have a treadmill test scheduled for this coming Thursday. I'll be ready after that if I don't die during the test."

Abe looked at Walt. "You're the main driver, Walt. Are you in?"

"Yes. I have nothing for a month or so."

"Don?"

"Yes, but I have to be back before June third. I'm going to visit the kids then. I guess we should take our golf clubs?"

Abe's "yes," was muffled by egg in his mouth. After a few seconds, he added, "A long time ago I traveled in the area we're going to. The area has several pretty courses y'all can play. I'll take my Stella, and enjoy the great scenic roads while you guys hit the little round ball."

"I don't think of New York City as being a place to play golf. Are you going to putt down Broadway, or something?" Ruth asked behind a smile.

Abe did not return the smile, but explained, "On either side of the New York-Connecticut state line are some of the most exclusive courses in the country. And, on Long Island, there's a great public golf park with five courses that has hosted the U.S. Open and other tournaments."

Cyn shivered. "Abe, you're not going to ride that Stella into Manhattan from Long Island, are you."

"No. My financial management firm will provide a limo."

Don nodded, "Good, I certainly don't suggest the train and subway considering your arthritis. In appreciation that you'll provide the motor home and gasoline for our trip, if your financial advisor doesn't provide a limo, your traveling companions could chip in for one."

Abe shook his head, saying, "Y'all can keep your money in your pocket. We can count on the financial people." Abe looked at Roy. "Roy, can we assume you survive your treadmill test, and plan to leave Friday morning?"

"Yes."

"Good. I'll schedule tee times for the first few stops. We'll be flexible after that, and develop a plan while we're traveling."

"Are we going to take the full rig?" Walt asked.

Abe nodded vigorously as he swallowed more eggs. "Yes. You'll need a car. I'll need the Stella. We'll have your golf bags, and other stuff. I always like to have the big tool chest. Yes. We'll take the full rig. You're not scared of heavy traffic and tight turns are you, Walt?"

"Yes, but reasonable fear helps prevent accidents."

"You're drivin'."

# CHAPTER 6

Roy did not die on the treadmill on Thursday; he returned to Ozark View before Walt and Abe arrived with the motor home, or bus, as Abe called it. The bus was a seven-year-old, thirty-five-foot-long Road Lynx. Abe had bought the Road Lynx from a country music group that had opened a Branson theatre and retired from the road. As originally configured, the Road Lynx could sleep six. Abe had the bus modified by a motor home dealer in Springfield so that it could "comfortably accommodate four men and no women."

Abe's modifications primarily involved tearing out tiny bedrooms at the rear of the Road Lynx in order to build one large dormitory with upper and lower beds against opposite walls. Between the bunks at the back of the vehicle was a short stairway and platform complete with banisters so that those on the top beds could enter and exit their bunks without fear of falling and without bothering the men in the lower bunks. The lower bunks and top bunks were also independently supported, which minimized transfer of motion between them. The platform's support doubled as a chest of drawers, the primary storage for clothing.

When the motor home was actually used for sleeping, Abe and Don were assigned the bottom bunks due to their bad knees. They slept with their heads toward the front of the bus, placing their feet into the enclosed area formed by the chest of drawers, vehicle walls, and beds. In fact, the four men rarely slept in the motor home. They preferred the comfort of motels, and used their beds in the bus only when napping while the Road Lynx was underway or when a remote situation compelled the use of the bus for sleeping overnight.

The Road Lynx featured user-friendly bathroom facilities, including a large shower. By restricting the travel group to only men, privacy was not a factor.

The four guys used the bus kitchen sparingly, reflecting their preference for dining in restaurants rather than cooking and cleaning. When the kitchen was used, it was normally Don who used it to make coffee, warm leftovers or heat convenience food in the microwave oven. Don stocked the refrigerator with sandwich material, snack vegetables, dips, soft drinks, iced tea and desserts. The foursome preferred paper plates and cups for easy disposal as opposed to washing dishes, although each man had a personalized diner-style coffee mug on board.

The Road Lynx was big enough to attract attention by itself, but behind the bus was a twenty-four-foot long, eight-foot tall auto racing trailer with a front right side door and power lift rear ramp. The same recreational vehicle dealer in Springfield that modified the Road Lynx had painted the trailer to match the bus. Together, the two units formed a rig totaling fifty-nine feet in length, one foot less than the maximum vehicle length allowed by the most restrictive state laws and regulations. The rig could travel in any state of the United States or any province of Canada.

Walt parked the big rig in the north parking lot at Ozark View, signaling his arrival with a short blast from the Road Lynx's horn, the same horn that is standard equipment on many tractor-trailer rigs. The rig consumed all of the lot's middle parking spaces, and it drew attention.

Within a few minutes, Don arrived with his inferno-red PT Cruiser laden with snack foods, beverages and paper goods. Don, Walt and Roy moved most of the supplies directly from the PT Cruiser to storage in the bus. Roy placed a box with extra paper goods in the trailer (or "garage," as the friends called it).

Before they left the next day, the PT Cruiser, Abe's motor scooter, four Ozark View high back rocking chairs, four aluminum-framed folding lawn chairs, a card table, one charcoal grill, three full golf bags and one large tool chest would go into the garage. On previous trips the foursome had made little use of the grill or tool chest, but all agreed these items should always be carried with them. The Stella, PT Cruiser, golf bags and chairs were well-used on each trip.

Each man except Abe carried his clothing and personal items directly from closets or drawers in his house to the Road Lynx where each had assigned space. Walt, Don, and Roy helped Abe carry and store his things. Abe's laptop and Roy's CPAP for his sleep apnea would be the last essential items loaded on board Friday morning. Permanently stored on the bus were four eighteen-inch duffle bags, one each red, yellow, blue and green. These bags were used to carry clothing and personal items into and out of hotels.

At dinner Thursday evening, the four friends sat by themselves, but visited with numerous residents who wanted to hear about their upcoming adventure. Ruth and Cyn had flown to Florida on Wednesday, and it seemed to the four guys that Ann had gone with them. From time to time though, one of them would be struck by the reality that Ann was eighty miles away at Neosho, and would not be returning with Ruth and Cyn. They missed their lady friends.

Before retiring for the night, Abe and Don spent the maximum time allowed in a hot tub. Although their activity had been paced throughout the day, they both were sore, and neither wanted to "load up" on their medicines for fear of oversleeping and being groggy for the start of the trip.

Early Friday morning the last items from each cottage went onto the bus, and each cottage was locked before the four travelers walked to the dining room for the breakfast buffet. All four men carried loaded platters from the breakfast buffet. "Our trays look like we don't anticipate eating for the next two weeks," Don observed.

Abe lifted a fork full of colorful scrambled eggs and stated, "These eggs, what they call 'Southwest Style,' taste like they've just been scooped from an iron skillet over a campfire. I can even taste a little mesquite smoke in 'em. I've looked around outside a couple of times for a campfire, but have yet to find it. These eggs are one of my favorite things about this place."

Don offered, "If you miss them too much during our travel, we'll find a park where we can build a campfire, and I'll burn some eggs and peppers for you. Seriously, the selection of eggs here is great, and they all seem freshly prepared when served on the buffet. That's not an easy thing to do."

Don looked to his right and saw Emma Smith, the Ozark View Food Service Manager, approaching their table carrying two brown bags with handles. "Emma, we were just complimenting your breakfast buffet."

"I'm complimented by the way you've loaded those platters. Are you going somewhere you won't be able to eat?"

"We won't be able to eat like we do here," Abe praised. "Whatcha got in the bags? Southwest Style Eggs?"

"Sorry, no eggs. But you'll enjoy a fresh pecan pie, a banana cream pie, two 'little' sandwiches made of whole loaves of French bread with every kind of lunch meat and cheese we have in the kitchen, plus two bags of snacking vegetables, and a generous supply of cookies."

"You want to get rid of us, don't you," Walt kidded.

"If we run out of food, can we drop by here and pick up a couple of more bags?" Roy asked.

Emma smiled. "Hey, we want you to have a good trip. And it's easy for me to fix these bags for you because you're really going to help my kitchen budget by being gone for three weeks. You know the Ozark View policy, you pay for the dining room whether you use it or not."

Abe had quit eating his eggs. "Even so, Emma, it's nice of you to pack us a travel package. I'll miss your pies, cookies, sandwiches, entrées and eggs. Are you sure you can't pack us some eggs?"

"I can't, because the eggs would spoil, you would die, your heirs would sue Ozark View, and I would lose my job."

Abe's mouth wrinkled. "You're safe from my heirs. If I were to die at your hand, there would be no lawsuit."

Abe's comment stopped the conversation. Emma, Walt, Don, and Roy stared at Abe, each trying to think of an appropriate quip. Finally, Walt, the consummate insurance agent, broke the silence. "Emma's right. It's amazing how many spoiled food claims I handled for the food service operators my company insured."

Roy returned the conversation to the earlier cheerful level. "Emma, I'll carry out food from this place any day. Especially, I'll carry out your pies and cookies. Thanks."

"You're welcome. Guys, have a wonderful trip. I need to get back to work and check the line."

As Emma was speaking, three other residents of Ozark View approached the table, the first of many. For the next thirty minutes, the four travelers ate their hearty breakfasts while actively visiting with their friends and neighbors.

When they walked from the dining hall, the foursome found thirty or so residents standing in the parking lot and under nearby walkways. The guys would get a big send-off.

Don checked the trailer doors and the hitch before boarding. Roy boarded and looked through the bus to see that everything was properly stowed. Abe boarded, immediately sat at the table and opened his laptop computer. Walt took the driver's seat and started the engine, closing the door as soon as Don boarded. With the others settled, Walt shifted to drive, gave one long blast on the horn, released the brake, and started forward. The crowd cheered and waved. The foursome waved back, although only Walt's wave was seen because of the tinted windows and glaring sun. As the bus moved, Abe noticed a rental truck parked in front of Ann's cottage. Someone new was moving in. Abe set his jaw and felt tears in the corners of his eyes.

# CHAPTER 7

"As soon as you're on I-44, we'll talk about our route," Abe advised Walt, who had chosen to skip the Branson traffic and head north toward Springfield via a route locally known as "the back way."

"Good. You're the trip planner and navigator. Besides, I want to practice handling this rig before we get into a long conversation."

"Where are we going today, Abe?" Don asked.

"Vandalia, Illinois. Do you remember that little flat course you played a little over a year ago?"

"Yeah, I remember that Roy almost holed out on a 170-yard approach shot on the 13th hole."

"I expect to do it again," Roy forecasted.

"I have a five dollar bill I'll bet against that," Don offered.

"We'll have to set the rules on that bet. How do we define "almost holed out an approach shot?" Roy asked.

"If I remember right, your ball was within a foot of the hole last time. Let's say the approach shot has to be at least 100 yards, and come close enough for a gimme putt. I think I'm very generous with that definition." Don made this offer as he placed a hot cup of coffee in front of Roy.

"I think you're generous with your five dollars, and I accept that bet." Roy grinned as he took a first careful sip from his thick diner mug, which bore a large red "R."

Don and Roy's bet would be the first of many placed over the next three weeks. Even though numerous Federal Reserve notes would pass back and forth during the trip, the net result would be little gain or loss for any of the three golfers.

Their seats in the bus, the conversation, and their respective roles were already consistent with those of previous trips. Walt would drive. Don would do what little cooking would be done, but would also be sure the beverage supply, snacks, and other goods were ready and available. Roy would do general housekeeping and maintenance. Abe planned. Walt, Don, and Roy had tacitly agreed to let Abe make the plans, set the pace, and determine routes of travel. The four men respectively accepted one another's contributions and limitations. They were friends.

Branson is forty-five miles south of Springfield in southwest Missouri, normally a forty-five minute trip in a passenger car. But from southwest of Branson in a thirty-five foot motor home pulling a twenty-four foot garage over the "back way," the trip took a little more than an hour.

On the north side of Springfield, Walt steered his big rig onto Interstate 44, a route angling from Wichita Falls, Texas to St. Louis, Missouri, roughly paralleling famous Route 66 through Missouri. Walt took a good five miles to set his pace before he asked Abe about the route they would follow.

Abe was ready, and everyone listened. "I've booked golf for y'all at Vandalia, Illinois; Columbus, Ohio; and at two courses around Stamford, Connecticut. Stamford is as far northeast as we'll go. Then we'll go down to Bethpage, on Long Island. Roy, that's in New York." Abe grinned. Roy had little sense of geography outside the oil patch states in which he had worked as a landman.

Roy returned Abe's grin, sipped his coffee, and listened as Abe continued." I have you scheduled on two courses at Bethpage, which has five courses. You'll play the Black course, where the U.S. Open was played in 2002, and then the Green course which is 10 percent shorter with the same par. You might recover your golf egos on Green after playin' the Black course first." Abe smiled again, but the three golfers understood his meaning. Bethpage's Black course would be a challenge to their game.

"After Bethpage, we'll go down to Washington, actually to Maryland. I have a hotel for us, and tickets to the Greater Washington Professional Golf Classic. I don't have any golfing scheduled for y'all, but you may want a break by then, assuming rain doesn't give you an earlier unscheduled break." The three nodded in response, and Abe continued. "From Washington, we'll play tourist, make a couple of stops in Virginia, and drive through the Smoky Mountains to Asheville, North Carolina. I've scheduled y'all a golf outing in Asheville, along with a tour of the Biltmore Estate. I've tentatively planned golf in Knoxville, Tennessee. After that, we boogie on home through Nashville and Little Rock. At Little Rock, we'll turn north for a short drive to Branson. By that time, we'll all be ready to get out of this bus for a while."

Don responded first. "That's a heavy schedule, Abe. I don't know if my knees will allow that much golf, but it sounds like a fine trip."

"Just keep your five dollar bills handy, Don. You're going to need 'em," Roy jabbed.

"Do you have five bucks with you, Roy?" Don responded.

"I don't need cash. You're going to provide."

Walt had not participated in the conversation as he paid attention to traffic, which was finally beginning to thin slightly as they moved away from Springfield. "I think it's a great plan. I look forward to Bethpage Black. After I play it, I'll probably look forward to Bethpage Green. I assume I stay on Interstate 44 until St. Louis, then follow Interstate 70, Abe?"

"Right. We'll look at a map over lunch." He jumped as he added, "Oh, there's something else. I haven't scheduled golf for you guys between Columbus and Stamford. We'll mostly be rollin', but could get off the bus to visit the Pro Football Hall of Fame in Canton, Ohio, or take a quick look at downtown Pittsburgh and its famous three rivers."

"I want to do both," Roy answered.

"I don't think we can, and make the rest of our schedule. Canton and Pittsburgh are on alternate routes. Our key dates are set by the Washington tournament and the appointments I have with financial people and lawyers in New York."

Walt and Don chose the Hall of Fame.

Roy nodded his approval, and Abe acknowledged the vote, "Okay, after Canton we'll drive as far as we can that day, and will stop somewhere in the eastern half of Pennsylvania. We need to make Stamford the next day at least an hour before your tee time. I hope weather doesn't ruin the schedule.

Over his shoulder Walt offered, "I checked out the national weather report on television last night. It didn't show rain in our travel area for the next several days."

Don stated, "Abe's appointments in New York are the most important thing. We can be flexible on everything else."

Abe looked through the big windshield up the road, and thoughtfully replied, "Maybe so, maybe not, Don. But we must be flexible."

• • •

As the Road Lynx passed an exit onto I-55 leading to points in Central and Northern Illinois, Walt announced from the front passenger seat, "Guys, I grew up about a hundred miles north of here. My folks' farm was south and west of Peoria."

Roy asked from the driver's seat, "So why didn't you stay on the farm? You look like a farm boy grown old."

"My older brothers wanted to farm, but I didn't. I wanted to be a math teacher and football coach so I went to Illinois State University, not far from home. I double majored in math and physical education, and got a job near Peoria teaching math and coaching.

"So, your college math major explains your uncanny ability with numbers?" Roy questioned.

"No, I was born with inherent math ability. That ability probably drove me to study and teach math."

Don interrupted, "Let me guess. You lost your love for teaching when after a couple of years of small pay checks, you decided it would be impossible to raise a family on teacher's pay?"

"That, and a friend of mine in the insurance business was looking for someone to run a little agency he and a couple of other agents were buying in Springfield, Missouri. They taught me the business, and I did very well. I eventually bought out all of the original investors, who, by the way, did very well with their investment."

Abe asked, "Your two sons took over your agency when you retired, didn't they?"

"Yes, and they have now bought me out. All I have to worry about are my private investments and traveling with you guys."

Don asked, "Your wife taught school for most of your marriage, didn't she?"

"Yes, Pat taught for over thirty years, mostly in Springfield, where she retired. But, five years after she retired, we learned she had cancer. She was gone within five months of the diagnosis. Soon after I lost her, I sold the house we had lived in so long in Springfield, and moved to Ozark View."

Roy encouraged, "Your story has a happy ending. You met us!"

"That's a nice thought, but I hope the story hasn't ended yet."

Don asked about Roy's wife, "Mae taught, too, didn't she, Roy?"

"Yes. She taught in Pampa, Denver, Oklahoma City and Wichita. We lived a few other places for short periods, too short for her to get jobs everywhere we lived."

"Had she retired before her car wreck?" Walt asked, referring to the automobile accident that had taken Mae Cole's life.

"No. She loved teaching, and wanted to teach until she could no longer do so. I guess she did."

Abe changed the direction of the conversation." Don, did you have any restaurants in this part of the country?"

"I had restaurants in suburbs of St. Louis and Chicago, which caused me to drive through Illinois frequently. When Gin traveled with me, we would golf at one or two of the courses in these small cities and towns. After playing our home course in West St. Louis County, the flat courses here were a treat."

"Tell me again. How long were you and Gin married, Don?" Roy asked.

"Twenty-six years. The aneurysm she died from ended a very happy marriage. But it might have been a blessing for her. She didn't have to endure my business demands any more. She also missed dealing with our problem boy when he went off the deep end."

Roy glanced around from the driver's seat at the tall thin graying Italian stereotype. "Was Gin Italian, too?"

"No, she was a pleasant mix of Northern European stock: French, Dutch, Scandinavian, and English. Maybe the English is the source of her name, Virginia. Or, it could just be American, like she always said it was."

"I've only seen one of your kids. He looked Italian." Abe then asked, "What do the rest look like?"

"A mix, representing the people of Europe."

Roy interrupted the conversation with, "Walt, my boy, your break has been long enough, I got us through St. Louis, and I'm going to turn off at the next exit for a driver change and leg stretch."

• • •

Within fifteen minutes of exiting Interstate 70, Walt had parked the Road Lynx at the Vandalia Public Golf Course, Don had paid for three green fees and two golf carts, Roy had loaded the carts, and the four had driven to the first tee. Abe rode with Don, enjoying the sunshine and cool breeze. After nine holes, Don drove Abe to the Road Lynx where Roy carried a high back rocker and stool from the garage so that Abe could nap in the shade of a sycamore tree while his buddies played nine more holes. The four friends knew how to recreate.

During dinner at a steak restaurant chosen by Don, Abe sat quietly as the three golfers described their round, including Roy's approach at the thirteenth hole which had landed wide of the green in a sand trap. Halfway through their steaks, Abe announced, "I have plans beyond this trip, and you three are involved. That is, you're involved if you want to be."

Don, Roy and Walt stopped eating, and looked at Abe. None of the three spoke, but simply waited for Abe to continue. He said, "I've asked my lawyers and financial people to restructure my assets, to simplify them and to put almost all of them in a trust fund. That trust fund will be used to help people who have been hurt by scoundrels of corporate finance, like Ann was. I don't yet know how much will finally go into the trust, because I'm gonna have to pay taxes on some overseas income. In the tax man's parlance, it's called taxing repatriated earnings. Anyway, all I'm uncertain about is the amount of money that finally goes into the trust. It will be somewhere between two hundred twenty-five and two hundred fifty million dollars. After I die, I want you three guys to be trustees. In fact, I want to name you trustees from the start, along with me. Whaddya think?"

All three of Abe's friends sat absolutely still and said nothing for a full thirty seconds. Finally, Roy stammered, "Good grief, Abe, where, what did, or how did you get that much money?" He struggled to speak his swirling thoughts.

"That's not important. I'll just say that my import/export business was profitable, and I managed to hang onto and invest the profits in such a way that my little bundle kept growing. All you guys really need to know is that my plans are real, the money is real, and the need is real."

"How do we determine who we give money to, or should that be to whom we give the money?" Walt asked.

"I've got people working on that. If y'all will be trustees, I want you to help me answer questions like that."

Don was thoughtful." Do we need to meet with your contacts in New York, Abe?"

"Not this trip. Right now, I have to make all of the decisions, about moving assets to fund the trust. If I have your permission to name you as trustees, I'll set it up. You get involved after the trust is formed."

"Abe, all of us are old." Walt paused before he added, "Maybe not as old as you, but old. Don't you want some younger people as trustees?"

"Later," Abe responded." But I want y'all to help me find the right people. I'm impressed by some of your kids."

"Not all of them?" The foursome knew Don was referring to his forty-nine-year-old "problem child."

"Definitely not all of them," Abe replied straight-faced." And there are some sharp younger people I don't know well at Ozark View that might be good candidates. Some of them are barely over sixty years old."

Roy questioned, "So, we just say 'yes' and wait?"

"Yes."

Walt's voice broke as he spoke, "I think it's great, Abe. I want to be present when you tell Ann."

"I hope she'll accept," Abe answered." She turned me down when I first offered help. Maybe she'll accept if she knows the trust is for a lot of people in her situation."

Roy spoke. "Even if Ann doesn't accept help, it's a wonderful thing you're doing, Abe."

"Absolutely!" Don agreed. "And thank you for including us."

"Y'all are my friends. You're my family, now."

Walt thought of the conversation earlier that morning with Emma in the Ozark View dining room. "Uh, Abe do you have any family that would object to what you're doing with your money, or about the three of us being trustees?"

"Except for you guys and Ruth, Cyn and Ann, I have no family. That's what I meant this morning when I told Emma that she wouldn't be sued by my family." Abe shifted his eyes among his three friends as he added, "But, if Emma does poison me, y'all can sue Ozark View."

# CHAPTER 8

Abe peered at the road and buildings ahead. "We should see the hotel on our right any time now, and when we pass it we should be exitin' to the right. I don't like comin' to this pretty area and stayin' right on Interstate 95 in Stamford, but I didn't think you would want to drive this rig through small streets, Walt. There it is. Take this exit comin' up."

Walt switched on the bus's right turn signal. "I like this hotel just fine, especially its proximity to the expressway."

Five minutes later, Walt had the Road Lynk parked in a lot reserved for RVs. The parking was shared by three hotels clustered near the expressway exit, and was a full city block from the foursome's hotel. The first order of business was to unload Don's PT Cruiser and Abe's Stella. Walt and Roy then transferred golf bags to the PT Cruiser while Abe put a few items in the "top box" on his scooter.

The group drove to the hotel's main entrance, checked into the hotel and soon exited through the door they had just entered. Walt, Don, and Roy left for an approaching tee time at the Rocky Shore Golf Course, thirty minutes away. Abe planned to explore. The golfers were to call Abe when they finished playing. They would return to the hotel, move into their rooms, and then look for a good seaside restaurant.

Abe sat on his shiny-black scooter under the high roof of the hotel's portico looking intently at a map of Stamford. He mentally charted a route to his destination, started the Stella, and rode into Stamford traffic. He was soon away from the hubbub of the I-95 corridor, and found a small road heading north between homes that had to be 150 years old. Abe followed the road as it wound around small hills and more antique homes. He noticed the sporadic small business buildings in the neighborhoods, most of which were once neighborhood grocery stores, but were now converted to other uses, not all of them commercial.

As the Stella climbed a road following the slope of a hill, Abe saw a curve ahead that had a slight pullout. Abe slowed and pulled over, glad that he was on a scooter. The space would not accommodate a car of any size. He noticed the asphalt on the turnout had recently been repaired, and then saw what looked to be a new stone wall, with a bench against it. He had not seen the wall in the photo he had found when he hacked the Glistening Spring website from the computer in the Branson Internet café, but that photo was at least a year old. The wall was three feet high and definitely looked new. He was glad the wall was no taller. A rugged tree that he had seen in the photo stood at the end of the wall.

Abe stopped his scooter close to the wall, got off and pretended to look in his pockets. He then opened the scooter's top box, as if looking for something. However, he concentrated his attention on a spot beyond and below the wall, across a small stream: the 12th green of Glistening Spring Golf Club. Abe could clearly see a foursome on the green. He looked at the golfers, the green layout, and the stream. He then looked up, down, and across the road before remounting his scooter, and resuming his climb up the winding roadway. Abe assessed the pullout to be a very quiet spot. As he rode away, he wondered how many people he had killed on golf courses. He had lost count.

• • •

For a time in his career, Abe had considered a golf course to be a dangerous location to ply his trade, because a rifle shot would always be noticed in the solitude. However, after Abe began using his "weapon" a green near the boundary of a golf course became a perfect spot for an assassination. Abe had retired from the killing business and had not used the weapon for at least eight years. He was glad he had quit, but felt compelled to temporarily forsake retirement in order to avenge the wrongs done by the Mid-North scoundrels.

In the mid-1950s, Abe and a brilliant business acquaintance, a German physicist, used technology similar to that of a laser to develop a light stream that could cut human tissue at a distance of 250 feet in ideal atmospheric conditions. Soon after building their first research model, the physicist was killed in an automobile crash, leaving Abe as sole possessor of the weapon. At the time, the United States and Russia were well into the nuclear arms race. Considering the arms race and the maxim that a secret is only a secret as long as it is known only to one person, Abe determined to tell no one about his new weapon, especially the United States government. He chose to keep the knowledge to himself, and expected someone else to develop at any time, without his help, a similar weapon over the following years. No one had. Or, at least no one had as far as Abe knew, but it would be difficult to know if someone else were covertly using such a weapon.

Abe's weapon was effective for several reasons. The light stream was invisible, perfectly clear. The cutting point on the stream could be adjusted to slice an inner length of tissue without injuring the victim's skin. The unit required only ordinary daylight for power and was extremely compact. When "fired," the weapon made no noise whatsoever. Abe initially built two working models. One he housed in a set of 1950 Army-issue forward observer field glasses, and the other he housed in a pair of dark black plastic eyeglass frames popular in the 50s and 60s. Abe had used his weapon to cut arteries, heart tissue, brain tissue, intestines, appendixes, and knee cartilage. Victims had apparently died from heart attacks, aneurisms, intestinal distress, strokes, and, where appropriate, bad falls. Because the result appeared to be the result of a natural ailment or an accident, Abe could work well within the weapon's range where he could mingle with a crowd. Abe particularly remembered one hated dictator whose knee cartilage he had cut as the obese tyrant stepped from the top step of a massive granite staircase. The man's knee had collapsed, and he had tumbled downward the equivalent of two floors, one bruising crunch at a time. By the time he stopped bouncing and rolling, the tyrant was no longer capable of tyranny. Abe always smiled when he remembered that particular fall.

Assassination had been Abe's second form of income for most of his life, and his first form, the import/export business, had been a perfect cover for the second. He could move freely about the world, seeking new deals, enhancing old business—and killing people. Had an astute international detective been collecting the right data, he might have noticed that often when Abe visited a country, someone of note died there. But Abe's assassinations were subtle, so much so that Abe required payment be made for his services even if the party of concern simply "quit living." Abe did not accept all business offered. He chose to only practice his skills on people he considered to be harmful, feeling that he should only exterminate "mean guys." He ignored the fact that a few of the "mean guys" were "mean women." With the abundance of mean people in the world, Abe had always had plenty of business.

• • •

At the crest of the hill near Glistening Springs, the road ran flat between substantial fences surrounding huge homes. Abe turned his bike, and unhurriedly rode down the route he had ascended. He rode leisurely, but not so slowly as to attract attention. He tried to observe everything. He confirmed that the spot on the curve overlooking the twelfth green would be the perfect spot for him the next morning.

In the old downtown, Abe stopped for a cup of strong black coffee and a large cinnamon roll. Abe's breathing was heavy while he ate the sweet roll. He hoped he could complete his mission while he was able. After finishing his mid-afternoon snack, Abe headed to the hotel where he napped before the golfers returned and chose a restaurant for dinner.

• • •

The selected seaside restaurant was really a bayside restaurant, and the bay looked like a muddy lake bed when Don parked in the restaurant's lot. Boats tethered to rings on tall poles sat on the mud flats, and nothing moved. The tide was fully out, but would soon reverse and again flood the bay.

Inside the restaurant, Abe raised his attention from his menu and spoke. "I played Rocky Shore a couple of times when I came here on business, but never scored well. I kept usin' woods when I should have been usin' irons. Did y'all find the sea breeze challenging?"

Don answered, "Walt and I did, but Roy used his experience from playing all those years in the constant winds of western Oklahoma and Kansas."

"Did you use a wood even once today, Roy?" Don asked.

"Three times, when the wind was at my back."

Walt turned to Roy. "Is that how you drove to the green on number seven?"

"Naw, that's my standard distance. I normally have to hold back." Roy grinned.

"That ball flew forever. I was impressed." Walt recounted. "Then it rolled up a slope, and stopped below and four feet short of the hole."

"From there I two-putted," Roy confessed with a grin directed toward Abe. "I got a lot of sympathy from my playing companions, though."

Abe offered a crumpled smile, and suggested, "The wind must have died."

The waiter interrupted the men's conversation when he placed a basket of bread on their table, and offered recommendations for fish and other marine life harvested off the Atlantic Coast. He left with orders for big meals.

Walt restarted their conversation as he dipped focaccia bread into the plate of oil and herbs." Roy, have you heard the results of your treadmill test?"

"No, and my only telephone is my cell phone in my pocket. That's the number the doctor's office should call with the results. The phone has been charged and in my pocket all along, and I haven't heard anything."

Don spoke, "I can imagine a scene next month in your doctor's office. A nurse says, 'Doctor Jones, I just found the results for the treadmill test Roy Cole took six weeks ago. I think I know why he died yesterday. ' The doctor replies, 'Oh, well there is no need to bother with it now.' You wonder if anybody is paying attention, don't you?"

Roy agreed, "Yeah, if you fall off the medical production line, nobody will notice."

Walt changed the subject. "Speaking of production line, Abe what's our schedule for tomorrow? We were so busy looking at New York and the surrounding area as we passed through, we didn't talk much about what we're doing here. Rocky Shore was a challenge. Do you have an easy course for us next?"

"Yeah, Chestnut Hills. You'll like it. It's a sweet little course that will make you enjoy being outside as much as you enjoy playing golf. You'll have to hit the ball straight. All the fairways are tight and lined with trees."

"What time do we tee off?" Don asked.

"Eight-fifty."

"I noticed you had the Glistening Spring Golf Club website on your laptop screen yesterday. Were you thinking we might play there?" Walt asked.

"Oh, well, I thought there might be a possibility that travelin' golfers such as you with memberships at the prestigious Table Rock Golf Club might be able to play at Glistening Spring. I played there many years ago as the guest of a business associate. It's a pretty and challengin' course. But Glistening Spring has few reciprocal arrangements.

In the parlance of the hillbilly comedians in the Branson music shows, them folks at Glistenin' Spring is just plain uppity."

Abe was not being honest with his friends. Glistening Spring had a completely different interest to Abe. On his computer the day before, he had confirmed that Ed Harm's foursome had its normal 10:10 Tuesday tee time.

Don held his hand under focaccia dripping with oil as he moved it toward his mouth. "The place you booked us sounds nice. I could care less about the uppity spots. But our schedule is taking a toll on my knees. I may have to skip tomorrow. What are you doing Abe?"

Abe just couldn't tell his friends that he was planning to murder a scoundrel. He thought quickly, hoping to encourage Don to either play golf or not leave his room the next morning. "I'm gonna sleep in. I might ride around on my bike a little. I enjoyed exploring today, and might do a little more. I just don't know."

Don unknowingly relieved Abe's tension. "I'm going to the hot tub as soon as we return to the hotel this evening. I hope that helps enough that I can play tomorrow. The trees in this part of the country are gorgeous. I would like to play that tree-lined course."

Roy suggested, "Why don't you come with Walt and me even if you're hurting. After you tee off in front of the clubhouse, you can pick up, and not play. The scenery is probably worth the green fee. If you want, you can just pitch and putt, or whatever."

Walt grinned slightly as he said, "Good idea, Roy. There's no need to ruin a nice outing by playing golf, anyway."

Don agreed. "I like the idea, too. But I am still going to the hot tub when we get back to the hotel."

If Abe had been a praying man, he would have said a prayer of thanks. He could stick to his plan. He might sleep in a little late, though. His appointment was not until 12:30, just after noon.

# CHAPTER 9

Abe did not sleep late, although he slept well through the night. He was downstairs in time for the hotel's breakfast buffet. He lamented the buffet did not have Emma's Southwest Style Eggs, but he made do with a heaping supply of crisp bacon, three over-easy fried eggs, a generous helping of home-style fried potatoes, four pieces of thick toast dripping in butter, a selection of melon slices, a cinnamon roll, two twelve ounce glasses of orange juice, and dark coffee. A waiter helped Abe carry his big breakfast.

Before going to the buffet line, Abe had found his three buddies at a round table in the far corner of the restaurant. He was happy to see Don wearing one of his favorite golf shirts, and to learn Don planned to play golf, or at least ride with the others. Don's decision to play golf eliminated a possible problem for Abe, and increased his appetite.

As his waiter placed each item of Abe's breakfast in front of him, his friends' faces glowed with smiles, but none of them spoke. Abe noticed their faces and said, "A man should eat a good breakfast every day. There is absolutely no tellin' what he might have to do during the day."

"Riding a motor scooter and looking at the scenery is a heavy load," Roy suggested. "You should fortify yourself."

"If I thought I might live a long time if I controlled my intake, I would probably eat cereal for breakfast," Abe confessed." But from what I see ahead, I might as well eat what I want."

"Kind of an extended last meal scenario, huh?" Walt asked.

"That's accurate," Abe replied.

Don held his knife and fork still as the stared at Abe's plate. "I want to see what you eat for your very last meal. Based on this breakfast, you'll need three waiters to carry it to your table."

"My last meal will probably be a clear liquid served through a tube by an ugly nurse, nothin' like this stuff." Abe crunched a thick strip of bacon.

Don asked, "Do we all know what we would want for a last meal?"

Walt had an answer, but deferred to his friend, "You first, Don. You've probably thought about it."

"I have thought about it. My choice is the lasagna that one of my restaurants served in St. Louis. The chef was pure Italian, and his cooking style was pure Italian. Any lasagna would not do. It would have to be made by that chef."

"Is he still alive?" Abe asked.

"Yes, I think. He's about twenty years younger than me, but I've lost contact with him."

"What would you have with that lasagna?" Roy asked.

"I don't care what, if anything. I would take a double helping of that lasagna rather than side dishes. How about you, Roy?"

"If we are going to be specific, I want a Texican Sampler Platter as done by a little Tex-Mex restaurant in Pampa, Texas. Uh, Pampa is in the Texas Panhandle for you guys that don't know your important geography."

"When was the last time you ate there, Roy?" Walt asked.

"The last time was about two years ago. I visited a cousin in Amarillo, and we drove fifty miles to Pampa just to eat at that little restaurant. I got the platter and was not disappointed."

Walt divulged his selection. "I'd drive fifty miles for a good chicken fried steak, but I don't have to. There are a couple of places in Branson that fix it as well as anybody. I'd want mashed potatoes, gravy, green beans flavored with bacon, and a couple of fluffy rolls to go with it."

"Do you take that meal through your mouth, or do they inject it directly to your clogged veins?" Don kidded, and then turned to Abe.

"Okay, Abe, you inspired the question. What would your last meal be?"

"A thick medium-well steak with fried potatoes and a huge green salad with lots of fresh tomatoes."

Walt observed, "Did you notice that we've all thought about what we would like for our last meal?"

Don slightly disagreed, "I don't know if I've thought about it in terms of a last meal, but I definitely know what my favorite meals are, and which one is numero uno. I have a long list of favorites."

"We're blessed, aren't we," Walt concluded.

Everyone nodded, and Abe changed subjects." Y'all don't have to sit here and watch me eat. You have a tee time soon."

Roy, who was known for letting time get away from him, looked at his watch." You're right. I need to go to the head before we take off, I'll meet you guys in the lobby. Abe I've paid for the rooms. Turn in your key whenever you leave. We'll meet you at the motor home after golf."

Abe watched the three golfers leave, and thought about his target for the day. *I wonder what Edward Harm had for his last meal this morning.* He then thought about Harm having breakfast in his mansion, probably served by his house staff while Abe's friend Ann ate a breakfast she had fixed for herself in the kitchen of her daughter's home. Abe crunched hard through another bacon strip.

● ● ●

Back in his room, Abe took one more look at a photo of Edward Harm. He did not want to make a big mistake and kill the wrong person. He chuckled and said to himself." I hope he doesn't play golf with an identical twin." Harm was distinctive in that he was tall and extremely thin, had gray hair, a narrow face, and a black tiny split pencil mustache that looked in Abe's photos to have been drawn by a kid using an ink marker. Harm's ears were tall and pointed, and the tan of his face showed on the left side of his chin a one-inch horizontal white line, probably a scar. Satisfied, Abe placed the photo and other information about Harm in his coat pocket. He again checked the tee times for the morning at Glistening Spring. There were no changes. Abe would keep his appointment.

Abe left the hotel, and carried his small duffle bag on his scooter to the motor home. He unpacked his bag, and then exited the bus carrying a folded sweater wrapped around a pair of Army green field glasses. He placed the sweater and glasses in the top box of his scooter. He knew the glasses were in working order. He had tested them on a squirrel in the woods near Ozark View before he and his friends began their trip.

Abe looked at his map of the Stamford area, and decided first to ride along the coast, second to find a cinnamon roll like the one he had enjoyed the day before, and third to keep his appointment. Abe wanted to put several miles on his scooter before his appointment. Across from the hotel, he spent three dollars to fill the scooter's fuel tank before he headed south toward the Stamford Harbor and Long Island Sound. He rode to Greenwich Point Park where he enjoyed the waves pounding on the rocky shore as he used his pocketknife to shred the contents of his Edward Harm file, depositing the shreds in two smelly trash cans. He roamed through Stamford, and finally found a donut shop near downtown Stamford where he relaxed his hands while sipping strong coffee and eating his second cinnamon roll of the day.

His appointment approached. Abe slipped away from the donut shop on his Stella, and found the road he had scouted the day before. He drove up the road, not stopping at the turnout, and not looking at the golf course. He again turned at the top of the hill and idled down the twisting road, this time stopping at the pullout. He wanted his scooter to be headed downhill.

Abe sauntered to the wall and looked over the town, especially the golf course. He could see four golfers had hit from the 12th tee, and were in their carts. Glancing at his watch, Abe estimated this foursome was directly preceding Harm's group. Abe moved to the scooter, opened the top box, and pulled his green field glasses from the folds of his sweater.  It was time to work.

Abe slowly shuffled back to the wall, trying to act as if he had nothing to do, and that inspecting the view from the pullout was merely a lark. Abe first nonchalantly looked into the distance toward Long Island Sound, then across town, next at the Glistening Spring clubhouse, and finally at the green below him. One ball was on the green. Another landed as he watched. He looked up the fairway. Ooh! Abe's timing was closer than he had wished. The foursome approaching the green was Ed Harm's group. Harm was in a cart. The first ball on the green appeared to be Harm's.

Two more of the foursome had to hit approach shots. Abe made himself look away as they did so. He aimed his field glasses toward the harbor area, keeping his glasses far enough from his eyes so that in the corner of his vision, he could see the green near him. He watched the other two balls land and roll closer to the hole than Harm's. Harm would putt first. Abe grinned slightly. Harm would be putting for a birdie that he would not make.

Abe mentally checked his process, and made sure his weapon's disguised safety was in the "off" position. He watched as long-legged Ed Harm pulled a putter from his bag and strolled onto the green toward his ball. Abe was surprised at the speed with which Harm stepped behind his ball, assessed the putt, and moved to address the ball. Abe focused his field glasses on the side of Harm's head, and fixed the distance. When Abe slipped a purposely long fingernail into a barely noticeable cut in the tattered housing of the field glasses, Ed Harm crumpled onto his putter, which forced him to roll to his left toward the hole, where he fell hard onto the soft short grass between his ball and the hole. Ed Harm was dead before he landed.

Abe put his glasses beside him below the wall, and continued to look at the green. He tilted his head slightly, hoping to make any observer think he was curious and surprised about something he had just seen.

Nobody on the green noticed Abe. Harm's playing partners had been watching Harm's ball as he addressed it, and were dumbfounded when they saw Harm fall. They heard no noise, nor saw any injury. One of the golfers hustled to his cart to get his cell phone that he was not supposed to have with him. He dialed 911. Harm's other playing partners tried to find a pulse, or discern breathing. They couldn't. One took a cart to tell approaching golfers of their problem on the green. The golfer with the forbidden cell phone drove to the clubhouse to inform the club staff of the emergency and the pending arrival of the ambulance. The third stood on the green with nothing to do but look at the body of Ed Harm lying dead still on perfectly manicured grass.

While Harm's golf partners dealt with their emergency, Abe moved to his bike, put away his glasses, mounted his scooter, and meandered downhill. On the way to his motor home, Abe met an ambulance running with lights and siren.

Abe went directly to the bus. He used the power lift to open the back ramp of the traveling garage, and drove his scooter inside. He raised the ramp, and went into the motor home. He found a pitcher of tea in the refrigerator, poured himself a glass, added lemon, took a long swig, and retrieved a file to study before his friends returned from their golf outing.

The golfers arrived soon after one-thirty. Abe had advised them well, they loved playing Chestnut Hills and had scored well by taking short controlled shots rather than trying to overpower the course. Don had restricted his activity to approach shots and putts. He had pain, but not like the night before.

While Walt maneuvered the Road Lynx out of the parking lot, Don brewed a pot of strong coffee, and soon began making sandwiches to order. Abe admitted that he had been a bad boy that morning by eating two cinnamon rolls. He wanted only half of a sandwich.

As they ate, Roy told Abe that in the Chestnut Hills clubhouse the threesome had heard a man had died on the Glistening Spring course "around noon." Jokes about the man's death were flying fast. For example, "Before calling 911, the dead man's playing partners consulted the club rulebook to determine whether they should putt out before calling, or if they should drag the guy off the green and let the people behind play through." Another: "The club pro had to decide whether to let the ambulance on the course or whether to haul the body to the main gate on a greenkeeper's cart. The jokes got bad fast."

Abe asked, "Did anybody at Chestnut Hills know the man?"

Roy shook his head. "Apparently not. Nobody in the clubhouse mentioned a name. They sort of assumed they wouldn't like him if he was playing at Glistening Spring, and kept telling jokes."

Abe slowly shook his head. "People can be cruel."

# CHAPTER 10

"Morning, Roy! Did you sleep well?" Walt startled nearby diners in the small breakfast room of the motel in Bethpage, Long Island, New York, as Roy approached the table already claimed by Walt and Don.

"Like a log. Abe was still puttering around the room and on his computer checking investments or something when I went to bed. Within minutes, I was asleep. When I woke up this morning Abe was moving about the room, trying to loosen his joints. I didn't hear anything in between."

Don offered, "I was beat when I hit the sack last night. I slept for about five hours, but woke up aching all over. I took some of my special circumstance pills, the ones I'm not supposed to take often because of side effects. I went back to sleep and didn't wake until six-thirty. I feel rested and have little pain."

"You'll have to give us four strokes, if you're playing without pain," Walt demanded as they began the banter and betting on the day's golf.

Don countered, "On Bethpage Black, you should give Roy and me a stroke per hole, except for the par threes. This is a long course, suited for your game, Walt."

"Can't say I've ever found a course suited to my game," Roy muttered.

Walt challenged his golfing buddy." Hey, that shore side course we played Monday was exactly your game. Straight long iron shots, roll on or short approach, one putt. That's your game."

"Then I should definitely get a stroke each hole on Bethpage Black."

"Y'all are goin' to the grave negotiatin' your golf bets," Abe warned when he approached the table unnoticed. "How's the buffet?"

"Good, the biscuits are commercial, but good," Don responded.

"Do they have pancakes on the line, or do I have to order 'em?"

"I didn't see them on the line. What's your deal with pancakes all of a sudden?" Don said.

"I just got a cravin' sometime in the wee hours of the morning."

Roy nodded to a movement behind Abe, "Well, here comes our waitress. You may express your cravings to her."

Abe did so by ordering the "Mountain Platter" of butter pecan pancakes. He then sat as his friends ate their buffet breakfasts. "There was a blip in the financial news this mornin' about that guy that died yesterday at Glistening Spring. He was one of the Mid-North scoundrels. His name was Harm. He was the Chairman of the Board who brought down the company. Good riddance, I say." When he received only minimal response from his three friends, Abe asked, "Are y'all happy with your rooms?"

"Yes, you're a good travel agent, Abe," Walt complimented." We were talking about how well we slept. How about you?"

"I didn't get to bed very early, and when I finally did I didn't sleep well. I was thinkin' about an email I got from my financial advisor. My financial folks and lawyers have agreed on a trust structure, and a process to put it together. The step-by-step process is important to avoid wastin' money on unnecessary taxes. Sometimes I think these guys really earn what I pay 'em. Sometimes I think they just invent pseudo obstacles to overcome so they can justify what they charge me."

"Are they close to having the trust ready?" Walt asked.

"Yeah, but it won't be a trust. It will be trusts, plural. We'll have one domestic trust and one foreign trust. That way we won't pay a bunch of money on repatriatin' earnings until such time as the money is needed. The finance guy says that some of the best investments are going to be outside of the United States over the next few years so there's no need to bring money into the country, pay taxes on earnings, and then send the reduced amount back out of the country to invest in Singapore or some other place. By signin' on as trustees, you guys may be gettin' into more than you want to deal with in your retirement."

Walt wiped his mouth with a big red napkin, "I think the trust's purpose is worth any inconvenience to me. I'm still pleased you're including us."

Abe nodded. "I'm glad you're willin' to help. The death of the Mid-North conspirator yesterday brought Ann to mind again. I really want to help people like her. And, she's probably better off than a lot of people. Can you imagine getting' your savings wiped out if you don't have a family to fall back on? Hell, what would happen to an old goat like me?"

Roy grinned. "You're leaving yourself open to harsh speculation on our part."

"I know you're kiddin', but every outcome that I can think of would be miserable," Abe countered.

The waitress brought a platter with pancakes overlapping in an elliptical four-inch mound. Walt asked, "Abe, are you going into Manhattan today to work with your advisors, or are you going to spend the day here eating that pile of pancakes?"

Abe poured syrup on the mountain, and began eating from the right side of his plate. "This won't take long 'cuz I'm not gonna eat all of 'em. And, I have to boogie. A car, maybe a limo, is pickin' me up in thirty minutes. I still have some things to look over before I take off. Pass that coffee pot, will you Roy?"

Roy passed the pot and commented, "Our tee time isn't until eleven. We can finish your platter for you."

"Do you want three or four of these now while they're hot?"

"No. I was joking."

Don spoke seriously, "Back to your trust matter. Will you get your business finished today or will you have to go back to Manhattan tomorrow?"

"I'll have to go back. I guess the financial people and lawyers could FedEx stuff to me. But, since I'm here, I'd rather take care of everything in person. I have a long 'do list.'" Abe thought of his non-financial purpose for being in Manhattan, but did not mention it.

Walt expressed a concern he had discussed with Don earlier, "How are you holding up, Abe? It sounds like you have two full days ahead, and you haven't exactly been napping for the last few."

Abe purposely kept his eyes on his pancakes. Walt's question bothered him. What did Walt or the others know about his activities yesterday? Abe had stayed upstairs after Roy had left in order to check news reports concerning the death of Edward Harm. "What do you mean? All I did yesterday was ride around lookin' at the ocean, trees and town, and then ride down here on the bus. Ridin' is not heavy work. I ate two cinnamon rolls yesterday, but that's not heavy work, either." Abe waited for a bad surprise or question.

It didn't come. Roy spoke. "I think I know what Walt is concerned about. I haven't seen you nap like you normally do."

"I haven't and you haven't. I don't want to nap when we're travelin' in such interestin' country. I'll nap when I get home. Besides, I expect to take a permanent nap before too much longer."

Don used the opportunity. "Where do you think you'll take that nap, Abe?"

"Right where you lay me. Don't start on the Jesus stuff again. I like you, but you worry more about eternity than I do. I don't even know if there is an eternity. The stars keep formin' and dyin'. Maybe I'm just a fadin' star that nobody as good as your Jesus would want around 'em all the time, like forever. You guys are lucky that you've only known me for a few years, and won't have to be with me much longer."

"When the time is right, when you change your mind and want to talk, let me know." Don relented.

"Okay. Right now, I gotta go get something real finished for after I die. I'll call it layin' up treasure on earth for those that are still around and need it after I'm gone." With that Abe pressed down on the table to help himself rise from the chair. "Tip the waitress for me, will ya? I forgot to add anything to the check I signed." He shuffled off.

None of the remaining three said anything until Abe exited the dining room. Don spoke first. "Doesn't want to hear about it, does he?"

Walt shook his head. "He doesn't want to think about it, either."

Roy offered two positive thoughts." You said the right thing when you made yourself available when Abe does want to talk about it, Don. Let's pray right now for our friend. I'll pray first. You guys can add anything you want."

# CHAPTER 11

The driver of a black Lincoln Town Car was waiting when Abe appeared at the hotel door. He opened the right rear door for Abe to slide into the car. He closed the door, got behind the wheel, and soon drove into stalled traffic on the Long Island Expressway. To an experienced Long Island driver, traffic might have been moving at a normal pace. Abe thought he could have moved faster on his Stella. Just as he was beginning to wonder if the creeping traffic would hamper his schedule, the traffic began to move again, to his relief.

Abe felt pressed by his plans for the day. Fortunately, all three of his appointments were in the financial district of lower Manhattan. During the morning, he would meet with his attorneys. That should take a couple of hours. In the afternoon, he would meet with his financial manager. Between the meeting with the attorneys and the meeting with the financial manager, he had an appointment with a scoundrel, Fred Fogg. Fogg did not know Abe had a meeting with him, and if everything went right, Fogg would never know.

One issue had concerned Abe from the beginning of his plan. What if Fred Fogg changed his schedule because of the Ed Harm's death? That could really muddle Abe's schedule for the scoundrels. Oh well, he always had reasons to come to New York. Make a plan, but be flexible.

The Lincoln stopped in front of a towering building supported by columns and arches. The driver had apparently called ahead, and Abe's door was opened by a young man so neatly groomed he would have looked like a mannequin had he stood still. "Good morning Mr. Brown, welcome to New York. I'm Stuart Range of Nelson, Hushback, and Quinton."

"Good morning, Stuart. Call me Abe if your firm allows such informality." Abe grabbed the assist handle to help exit the car.

Range reached to help, but didn't quite know what to do. Abe would have gotten onto his feet just fine if his right foot had not slipped on the edge of a slick granite curb. Abe went down, grabbing Range and pulling him down with him. The driver and two passers-by were prompt with help. The mannequin was lifted first, then Abe.

Abe quipped, "If I get any stiffer, I'll have to be moved around in the back of one of those pickup trucks with a hydraulic lift on the corner of the bed. I prefer the Town Car."

Stuart apologized, and began wiping anything that appeared foreign from Abe's clothing. Abe stopped him, assured both Range and the driver that he was okay, and that he was ready to go inside.

The trip to the waiting conference room was uneventful, if one is in the habit of riding elevators for long periods of time. Abe quietly suggested, "Stuart, let's not mention that we fell on the curb." Stuart was relieved. Abe had a new friend.

Abe's meeting was with Tom Queen, who had helped Abe make a lot of money in the import/export business, plus one associate and three assistants, including Stuart. After brief introductions, Abe looked around the room and said, "I see expensive billin' meters runnin' so let's get to the business. Besides, I may die anytime." The smiles about the billing meters turned solemn when Abe suggested he might soon die.

Tom Queen and his associate, an expert in trusts, led the meeting. Queen and his staff had blended guidance from the trust attorney with their knowledge of Abe's investments, and had devised two trust agreements. Abe's ability to speed read and comprehend the agreement surprised the young assistants, but not Tom Queen. He and Abe kept the meeting moving until they concluded it at eleven-thirty. Changes would be made to the draft agreements, preferably before the meeting with the financial people that afternoon. Any changes in the financial plans would require preparation of new drafts, which Abe would review the next day as well as executing certain facilitating documents.

As the meeting concluded, one of the younger attorneys commented on the irony of working on a trust to benefit victims of corporate greed on the day after one of the greediest of corporate raiders had suddenly died while playing golf. Abe replied only, "Stranger things have happened."

Abe again refused an invitation to lunch in Nelson, Hushback, and Quinton's dining room, saying he had a short lunch meeting with an old acquaintance. Stuart Range escorted Abe to the street level, asking repeatedly if he could order a limo or a cab to take Abe wherever he needed to go.

"It's just a few blocks, and in this city I like to walk, or shuffle as I do now. Besides, you know I'm not good at gettin' out of cars." Range laughed and relented. Abe was relieved that Stuart did not insist on walking with him. It was important that Abe be by himself.

Around the corner from Nelson, Hushback, and Quinton's building, Abe pulled a pair of black-framed glasses from his inside coat pocket. He then began playing the role of tourist, looking upward at towering buildings, shuffling slowly, reading signs, and staring at people.

Abe wandered onto Pine Street, still looking upward almost as much as he looked ahead. He had a little extra time, so he explored the bar and grill to which Fred Fogg reportedly dashed at precisely twelve-forty each day. It was nothing special, just a meeting place. Abe speculated as to why Fogg and his group met each day in this bar. What did they discuss? Was someone passing information that should not be passed?

Abe was back on the street at 12:34, standing in bright sunlight, looking at the tall buildings, but with quick glances monitoring the door across the street, the door through which Fogg would soon dash. He lowered his sight to look directly at the door, reached to the left upper corner of the glasses, and turned off the safety. Moving an indiscernible lever on the top of the right earpiece on his glasses, he set the distance to his target, a spot three feet off the curb. He then moved his left hand near the left earpiece, placing his forefinger on the top of the temple and his thumb on the bottom.

Abe was near the curb, which made him nervous because cars, particularly taxis, were passing his spot at speeds much greater than Abe considered safe. The revolving door across the street began to move, and Abe poised. Fred Fogg dashed from the door, checking traffic to his right. He saw a small break and stepped quickly into the street. Just before his left foot hit the street with his second step, Abe squeezed his earpiece. Fogg's knee collapsed, and Fogg fell under a speeding cab. Abe heard the sickening thuds, and saw blood squeezed from New York's latest traffic victim. By the time the cab stopped, Fogg had also been crushed by a trailing cab. It was a messy sight. Abe looked, covered his mouth as if he might vomit, and shuffled toward the closest street corner.

Around the corner, Abe lowered his hand from his mouth, removed his glasses, and shuffled further down the street in the direction of his next appointment. Into three curbside trash cans, Abe dropped shredded pieces of the file he had carried in his pocket. Two scoundrels down, one to go. But was there a fourth? He had more work to do.

# CHAPTER 12

Abe exited the limousine much better than he had that morning. He moved slowly, clearly intent on taking the shortest course to his room. He was thinking of the medicine from his Houston doctor, the pills he took when he was in severe pain. Abe's plan was to order a hamburger from room service, take a hot shower followed by the Houston pill, and go to bed for the night. If he didn't see Roy before he went to bed, he would leave a note for him. Abe did not want to go to dinner, he did not want a report on the day's golf, and he certainly did not want to tell anybody about his day. He would see his buddies in the morning at breakfast.

From a table in the lobby lounge Roy spotted Abe, and called to his tired friend. Abe looked, and started to wave, but changed his mind as pain shot through his arm and shoulder. Instead, he smiled meekly, turned and shuffled to the table where only Roy and Walt sat. "Where's Don? Still on the course?"

Roy grinned, "No, he's with the concierge, determining where we're going to eat dinner."

"Make your reservation for three. I'm beggin' off. I'm hurtin', and all I want are my Houston pills and a good night's sleep. I'll order a bite from room service."

Walt showed concern for his friend's condition. "Abe, I think today did you in. I hope tomorrow will be an easier day for you."

"The day didn't do me in. I did. I scheduled too much, and tried to do everything on the schedule, plus some. I'm worn out and I hurt."

"What can we do for you?" Walt asked.

"Nothin', except excuse me and let me go to bed."

"We'll see you tomorrow. What time do you think you will be awake and moving?" Roy asked.

"I'll see you around eight-thirty at breakfast if you're up and around by then. Y'all have a tee time right after noon, I think."

"Right. We'll see you tomorrow, Abe. Get some rest." Walt admonished.

"Oh, how did y'all do on Bethpage Black?"

Roy answered. "We all hit the ball well, hit it straight, and hit it many times. That's a long course."

Abe rocked his head slightly up and down showing understanding but said nothing, and shuffled toward the elevators.

Walt spoke the obvious. "The guy's exhausted. He really overdid himself today. At least he had a car to and from town, and didn't have to ride his Stella."

Roy smiled slightly at the thought of Abe riding his Stella from central Long Island to the financial district in Manhattan. "Yeah, and he didn't have any parking issues, either."

"Think about it. He's eighty-six years old. He is trying to simplify his two hundred fifty million dollar estate so much that you and I can manage it, he's dealing with top financial and legal people in New York, he has arthritis and cardiac problems, and he's tired at the end of the day. I know young men in excellent health that would be tired after the day he's had."

"And we don't know what else he might have done today in his spare time."

"As if he had a lot of spare time."

• • •

"Gentlemen, I hope you like lamb." It was Don, returned from the concierge's desk. "You two are awfully serious. What's going on?"

"You first," Walt said. "Why do you hope we like lamb?"

"That's what you're eating tonight. I thought I remembered a good restaurant in this area that specializes in lamb. The concierge confirmed my memory of it, and we have reservations at seven o'clock. I even have a map to guide us. Now, why so serious?"

"Did you see Abe?" Walt asked.

"No. Is something wrong? Talk to me."

"Nothing is really wrong. It's just that Abe is exhausted. He dragged his old body through here while you were with the concierge. He's going directly to bed, and will not be joining us for dinner."

"He had a big day, huh."

"Yeah," Roy responded. "Rearranging a two hundred fifty million estate can be taxing."

Walt clarified, "Tiring would be a better word, Roy. Abe is trying to avoid taxes. Rearranging his estate and minimizing taxes is a tiring effort."

Don expressed his concern. "I hope he finished the process today, and doesn't have to go to Manhattan tomorrow."

"He has to go. He'll meet us for breakfast at eight-thirty."

Don suggested what the other two had already thought, but not expressed. "Do you think one of us should go with him tomorrow?"

"I've thought of that, too," Roy said. "But he's not in shape to answer such a question tonight. Let's ask him at breakfast tomorrow."

Don volunteered. "I can go. I took enough shots today to satisfy me for several days. Did you tell him how we scored?"

"Roy did, but only vaguely," Walt replied.

Don nodded his head as he looked at Roy. "Speaking vaguely is a good idea when discussing today's golf roun . . ." Don stopped talking when Walt jumped from his chair and moved toward the television set over the bar.

"Turn the TV volume higher please," Walt asked the bartender.

The television was tuned to a popular business news channel, and on the screen was a headline, "Ex-CFO of Mid-North Killed."

Don and Roy saw the headline and joined Walt closer to the bar just as a reporter speaking from a narrow street in New York began her story. "The former Chief Financial Officer of Middle North Public Service Company was hit and fatally injured today by a taxi as he crossed this street, Pine Street, in Lower Manhattan around noon. Witnesses said that Fred Fogg fell as he dashed into the path of an oncoming cab, which was unable to avoid hitting Fogg. Fogg suffered multiple injuries from which he died in a New York Fire Department ambulance in route to Downtown Hospital. The death comes almost exactly twenty-four hours after former Mid-North President Edward Harm died of an aneurysm while golfing in Stamford, Connecticut. Both Fogg and Harm were targets of ongoing investigations of fraud allegations at Mid-North, which crumpled into bankruptcy in the middle of 2003 only weeks after reporting record first quarter earnings. Fogg resigned soon before the company filed for bankruptcy protection. A spokesperson for the Securities and Exchange Commission told me the investigation will continue in spite of the deaths. So far, other authorities have not commented. This is Sylvia Storm, reporting from the financial district, New York." The program cut to a story about cattle breeding in Wyoming.

Walt thanked the bartender, who asked, "Did you know the guy who was killed?"

"No, but I knew a little about him and how much he hurt some people."

"Oh yeah, he hurt a lot of people!" The statement came from a middle-aged man at the bar. "My wife's family lost a big chunk of their net worth because those jerks took down Mid-North. Good riddance to Fogg and Harm. I hope whoever else was involved dies soon, too. But, harshly with great pain would be better. Fogg and Harm were lucky. They died quickly. They deserved a slow painful death."

Walt did not want to encourage conversation with the man at the bar. He said only, "Yes, one of our friends got hurt by them, too," and followed Roy and Don to their table.

Don spoke with pauses, "It's an amazing coincidence.... that we were in Stamford yesterday.... and in New York today."

"It's more amazing that at the time of the death, our friend, Abe, was touring, or conducting business in the area," Roy added.

Walt spoke barely above a whisper, "Unlike our friend at the bar, I'm glad they died of natural causes, or at least a normal accident. Abe is a man of action, he hated those guys, and he was in the vicinity."

"I wonder if anybody besides the four of us, Abe included, knows that." Roy questioned.

"I wonder if someone can just wish someone dead so much that it happens." Walt added.

Don shook his head. "No to both of those questions, and we're jumping beyond reason to even think there is a connection between our presence, especially Abe's presence, and the two deaths."

Roy affirmed Don's appraisal. "You're right, and I'm getting hungry. What time do we leave for dinner?"

Walt and Don smiled at Roy. They had privately discussed how quickly their friend Roy could move a conversation away from an unpleasant subject. In this case, they welcomed the switch.

"Right now," Don answered.

# CHAPTER 13

Abe slipped from his bed. He felt better. His joints were stiff, but they were not radiating pain like they had the night before. Roy was still asleep, but he had not gone to bed at seven o'clock the night before as Abe had.

Very quietly Abe shuffled to the door, opened it enough to reach the *New York Times* hanging in a clear plastic bag on the door lever. He closed the door and shuffled into the bathroom. He carefully closed the bathroom door and reached for the lighted switch with which he turned on a bank of lights over the sink. He did not flip the other switches.

Abe touched the counter to be sure it was dry before he spread the first section of his paper, placing the rest of the paper on the toilet. The banner headline related to another bombing in Iraq, but a secondary headline announced, "Second Mid-North Executive Dies." Abe read through the story, looking for any hint of anything other than coincidence. He found nothing. Witnesses reported Fogg was several feet away from anybody when he fell, and that he clearly was not pushed nor tripped by anyone. The story used the magazine quote Abe had read earlier indicating Fogg liked to take chances. This time Fogg lost his bet with traffic. None of his three ex-wives would comment about his death, nor would Gus Whitby, the third executive known to be involved in the Mid-North collapse. Abe noticed, "known to be" and wondered if another name might soon surface.

Satisfied Fogg was dead, Abe gently refolded the first section, and found the business section. He spent more time in this section than in the rest of the newspaper, just as he had for all of his business life. He turned off the light, slipped out of the bathroom, placed the paper on the desk, and gathered his things for his morning bathroom routine.

Thirty minutes later, Abe exited the bathroom and found Roy reading the article about the two former Mid-North executives. Roy told him of the television news report the previous evening, and the comment made by the man at the bar. Roy carefully did not raise the matter of their little group's proximity to the death events.

Abe raised that issue, "If I'd known those scoundrels were gonna die in public while we were so close, I would have bought ringside seats. I hope whoever else is involved gets dead, but I would like 'em to be shot." Abe's comments ended the conversation as far as Roy was concerned. Abe had said all he wanted, too.

While Roy used the bathroom, Abe employed his computer for more news items, and for more research. He was a little nervous about making the inquiries he did on the Internet, but he continued. He felt that he had an excuse should anyone be able to trace his inquiries and develop a suspicious link to the scoundrels' deaths. Abe found two articles containing speculations that at least one silent investor was involved with the three known Mid-North culprits. Abe hoped the two deaths would cause authorities to conduct a deeper investigation, and soon identify any additional conspirators.

• • •

At breakfast, Abe again surprised his friends. After ordering two poached eggs and a bowl of oatmeal, he pulled a folded piece of white paper from his pocket, and handed it to Don who was sitting to Abe's left. He spooned his oatmeal. "Write your full name, address and Social Security number on that paper, Don. Then pass it to Walt and Roy. I need the information for the finance people and the lawyers." Don pulled out a pen and began to write.

Roy reported Abe's reaction to the morning headline. "When Abe read about the scoundrels' deaths in the paper today, he said he would have bought ringside seats if he had known they were going to die while we were nearby."

Walt frowned, "It would be sad for people to be so happy about your death. How would you like to look down and see people dancing around your coffin, saying 'good riddance!' or something similar?"

Roy embellished the thought. "Former stockholders of Mid-North might send cheerleaders to Harm's and Fogg's funerals."

Don asked his friends, "Do you think the third scoundrel is preparing to meet his Maker?"

Abe spoke without the playful tones used by the others, "I hope the third scoundrel is sweatin' blood, but I doubt it. He's probably very happy that his two buddies can't testify against him. These deaths may limit the government's ability to convict any of the Mid-North jerks, which would be a shame."

Roy asked to all at the table, "Didn't the paper indicate there is only one more man who is under investigation? I thought conspiracies like Mid-North's normally involved a cast of a dozen or so."

Don answered, "Only one other person was identified in the paper this morning or by that article that Abe showed us the day Ann moved away. Abe?"

"I don't know that there are any others." Abe only spoke a fact, and did not mention his gut feeling that at least one more person was involved, maybe as the ringleader.

Walt raised his voice, "I want to change the subject. Abe, when you arrived exhausted at the hotel yesterday, your three buddies became concerned about you. We want one of us to accompany you today. I think Don's knees are screaming that it should be him. I don't think he would impair your business, certainly not if you coach him before the meetings. What do you think?"

"Well, I've done this sort of thing by myself for all of my life, but by the time I got back to the hotel yesterday I was doubtful I could finish what I need to do. I thank you for your suggestion, and would like Don to accompany me. I just admitted being old, though."

"None of us can do what we once did, Abe," Roy consoled.

"Can you two play the Green course without me?" Don asked with a straight face.

Walt answered. "It'll be tough. But I'm also concerned about you, my friend. Those knees of yours are not as young as they once were."

Roy added, "After you 'conquered' the Black course yesterday, Green wouldn't be a challenge for you today, Don."

"If I 'conquered' every course like I 'conquered' Black yesterday, I wouldn't still be playing golf. Man, I hit that ball a lot yesterday. In addition to my knees, my shoulders and back are sore this morning."

Abe turned the conversation back to business. "Well, Don, I'd like for you to go with me. I'm wearin' a business suit just because that's what's done here, but you can feel free to wear a golf shirt if you want. We are the client." Abe smiled. "I like that! We are the client." He emphasized "We."

Don shook his head. "I can change. There's no need for me to be distractive even if we are the client. I'm finished with breakfast; I'll go change now. What time do we leave?"

"Nine o'clock. There'll be a limo out front."

"I'll meet you in the lobby," Don affirmed as he stood. He turned to Roy and Walt and encouraged, "Hit the ball straight today guys. And relax. You won't have the pressure of beating me."

# CHAPTER 14

Just before nine o'clock the same limo and driver that had taken Abe to Manhattan the day before pulled from the hotel driveway carrying Abe and Don. The two men were quiet as they each surveyed local buildings and landscaping. Don especially enjoyed the beautiful flower beds which lined the drives and sidewalks of nearby buildings.

Abe spoke first as the limousine pulled onto the entrance ramp for the Long Island Expressway. "You are now about to enjoy sittin' with a few thousand people in a very long parking lot."

Don smiled, and tried to look around bushes that limited his view.

As the limo gained speed and slid into the traffic flow, Abe expressed his surprise, and suggested, "Well traffic is movin' pretty fast. I'd better tell you who we'll meet with and what we'll talk about. Like I said earlier, most of this has to do with movin' my investments so that the trusts are easily manageable. I'm bein' careful to not allow these people to lock us into somethin' that would require routine extra work on their part, which would increase the cost of managin' the trusts."

"Do you think they would do that?"

"Yes, although they may be most sincere in their suggestions and methods. Sometimes these people feel that nothin' will survive if they're not involved constantly. They may not think of their recommendations as income assurance, but I see some of them as bein' just that."

"Might you be overly suspicious?"

"I'm always suspicious when money is at issue, and very suspicious when a large amount of money is involved. The odor of money draws flies and rats, much like garbage does. The smell of big money draws smarter rats."

"Have you been working with these people long?"

"Some of 'em. I should tell you about 'em, starting with Tom Queen."

"Who is he?"

"He's a Senior Partner of Nelson, Hushback, and Quinton, a large law firm that handles a significant amount of international business. He wasn't a Senior Partner when I first met him. He was a young attorney who replaced another young attorney who had been assigned to my business, but whom I didn't trust as to skill or integrity. Together Tom and I made a lot of money. Too bad for him, he had to share a big chunk of his with the firm. Partly because of my business he eventually became a Senior Partner. What he learned from handlin' my business helped him be effective for some really big corporations, and then he really made money. He also worked his ass off, and he always treated me as if I were his only client. He's one person I trust. Too bad he's also gettin' older, and may soon retire. He has lately limited his client list, and is turnin' more work to junior attorneys."

"Is there anybody else on your account?"

"According to the billings, the whole dang staff is on my account, but only one or two of the junior guys have done much for me. I met a new guy yesterday who is sharp, but young and inexperienced. His name is Range, Stuart Range."

"How about the financial people?"

For the next thirty minutes, Abe briefed Don on people with whom they would meet, and what he expected from each. Abe told him to expect a warm welcome. "These guys are very anxious to meet you, Walt and Roy because they're lookin' for their future income. If you asked 'em, they would say their interest was building client relationship rather than securing future income. But they wouldn't give a flip about relationship if income wasn't associated with the relationship. I apologize for my pragmatic attitude, but I learned a long time ago to think in terms of hard currency."

"Nobody will expect decisions from me today, will they?"

"Except as to what you want for lunch in the dining room at Nelson, Hushback, and Quinton, no. Yesterday, I made all the decisions about movin' money, openin' and closin' accounts, and key issues in the trust agreements. But I've left a lot of flexibility in selection of beneficiaries until Walt, Roy and you have a chance to consider everything. The lawyers don't like the beneficiary matter to be so open, and may raise the issue today. They may ask you for your ideas. Go ahead and give 'em your thoughts, but you and I should agree now to leave the flexibility in the original agreements. The agreements can be amended later by a super-majority of the trustees. Super-majority is defined in the agreements as seventy-percent of the trustees, which means that unanimity will be required to make a change if there are only three trustees; all but one must agree if there are four or five trustees, and five must agree if there are six or seven trustees. I hope the trust never has more than seven trustees."

"Should I feel free to ask questions, or should I wait until the trusts are executed?"

"Feel free to ask anything about the trusts, or the investment program after the trusts are created. But I prefer you not ask questions about any of my business or the assets that I'm going to put in the trusts."

"Got it."

"One issue will be when to execute all the documents. You, Walt, Roy and I will have plenty of reading and discussing to do once we have the almost-final drafts. We'll email the attorneys any changes, and they can prepare the final documents for us to sign. We'll have to fit document signin' into our busy travel schedule. Maybe the lawyers can meet us in North Carolina or Tennessee. They can come to us wherever we are. I don't want to come back to New York just to sign papers."

The two lapsed into silence as they viewed the Manhattan skyline. In another fifteen minutes they were in the midst of the financial district, and soon stopped in front of the building sitting on columns and arches. Again, Stuart Range opened the limo door. This time, though, Abe did not slip on the curb, and the three men were soon between the columns, headed for an elevator.

Don was warmly welcomed, and the meeting proceeded roughly as Abe had predicted. During discussion of trust issues, the attorneys and financial managers tended to direct their conversation to Don to be sure that he understood the issues. When Tom Queen asked Don for his thoughts concerning the selection of trust beneficiaries, as Abe had predicted he would, Don demurred, saying only that flexibility was essential. Don was silent during discussion of the transfers of Abe's assets, except to agree that the execution of the trust agreements and movement of assets to the trust should be subject to a schedule of transactions required to first transfer assets to the place at which or from which they would be transferred to the trusts. Throughout the meeting, Don was impressed by Abe's financial and legal acumen, as well as the professionalism demonstrated by the people in the room.

During one of the financial presentations, Don noticed that Tom Queen was not listening to the discussion, but was looking intently at Abe. To Don, Queen's face exuded contemplation and amazement.

In the dining room, Don chose chicken cordon bleu, with rice pilaf, asparagus, and a Caesar salad. It was excellent, as was the wine selected by Queen.

As salads were served, Don overheard one of the younger financial people ask Abe, "Mr. Brown, are you aware that two former executives of Mid-North Public Service have died unexpectedly within the last two days?"

Abe responded, "Yes, I read about it this mornin'. It reminded me that life is short, and that we should be nice to each other."

When Tom Queen and Stuart Range escorted Don and Abe from the building to the waiting limousine, Stuart carried a heavy leather briefcase full of draft documents that had been prepared by the law firm's administrative staff while Abe, Don and the others enjoyed lunch. Queen stepped slowly, walking with Abe several paces behind Don and Stuart as Abe shuffled across the building lobby. It was then that Queen spoke softly into his old friend's ear, "Abe, the fourth and, as far as I know, only other man in the Mid-North scandal was Gilbert Glass, the California financier. He officially resides in San Diego, but spends summers at a second home on Lake Tahoe. He's in and out of both places, of course, traveling all over the world. I think the whole Mid-North scam was Glass's plan. He is a scoundrel, deluxe."

Abe nodded, "I knew there must be somebody smarter. Thank you, Tom."

"You're welcome. Are you planning to retire again before long?"

"I'll either retire or die soon. I hope to finish my work before I do either."

"You've been a good friend, Abe. I will always appreciate you for what you have done for me, and for what you've done for oppressed people all over the world."

"I continue to appreciate you, Tom. Good-bye."

Abe's "good-bye" came as the two reached the lobby's revolving door. Queen slowed the door, allowed Abe to precede him, and from the next compartment controlled the speed of the door to accommodate Abe's slow shuffle. Just outside, they shook hands. Tom said, "Good-bye my friend."

Abe nodded, said nothing more, and shuffled to the door of the limousine. He shook hands with Stuart Range, and stated firmly, "We'll be talkin'. Thanks for your good work, Stuart." As he turned from Stuart to the open door of the limousine, he thought, *That guy is awfully smart to look so much like a mannequin.* Abe was grinning as he sat beside Don.

When the car pulled from the curb, Abe looked out the back window and offered a short wave to his old friend and his new friend. He then turned to Don, who was smiling at him. "What's with the smile, Don? Did you enjoy our meetin'? How was the chicken cordon bleu?"

"My smile relates to your big grin. I'm dying to know what's making you smile so broadly. As to your other questions, I felt like a rookie on the bench at my first major league game, but I enjoyed the meeting. The cordon bleu was excellent, as good as any served at my restaurants. Now, 'fess up. Why the big grin?"

"I was thinkin' about how smart Stuart is, but how much he looks like a mannequin. It's incongruous." Abe did not tell Don that he was also grinning because Tom Queen had identified the fourth scoundrel.

"Range is stiff, isn't he? He seems intent on being perfect. Poor guy, he should back off a little. Setting a high standard is one thing. Seeking perfection is seeking failure."

"But he's smart. I asked Tom to assign him to the trust matters. Tom agreed."

"Good. He should outlive all of us."

"We'll feel younger working with a young guy." Abe pressed the intercom switch to address the driver. "We have time. I want to do a little tourin'. How about going over to Broadway and head up to mid-town? Let's go through Times Square, by the Library, around Rockefeller Center, skirt Central Park, then over to Park Avenue and back down through Little Italy and Chinatown to this area. We'll cross the Brooklyn Bridge and go toward the old Navy Yard. Then, we can turn around and head out to our hotel."

The driver acknowledged Abe's instructions, and turned his attention to his right mirror. To change his course he would have to promptly move across traffic for a right turn.

Don pointed upward toward the air space once occupied by the World Trade Center Towers. "Abe, it's amazing how many people worked in the World Trade Center, more than the population of a pleasant-sized city."

"I'm astonished by how people stack themselves on top of one another on this island. I like my space too much to live and work like these folks do. But this prob'ly will be my last time in New York. I want to see a few sites."

"Once we're traveling east on Long Island, we can look at those documents in that case Stuart carried out for us."

"Don, I like your strong work ethic, but let's wait until Walt and Roy can go over the business with us."

"To be successful in the restaurant business, one must work. Old habits die hard. And, this trust business is fascinating to me."

"I'm glad you're so interested, and plenty smart enough to follow what went on today. I'm thankful you came with me."

"You're most welcome. Like I said, I'm fascinated by all of this. Uhh, you don't seem so tired today, Abe."

"No, the agenda was not as full, and I think it helped that you were with me. I was whipped yesterday. This old body just doesn't handle intense business activity like it once did." As he said this, Abe turned to his side window to look at a familiar building. When he turned back to Don he added. "We should take our time to review those papers, and to figure out how we'll run the trusts. I'd rather go slow and be sure everybody understands everything. When we're ready, we'll fax any additional changes to Tom and let him know he can send a couple of people with the final documents to North Carolina or Tennessee, or wherever we are when we're ready. We can sign those papers anywhere."

Don looked directly at his friend. Abe, we're taking a tour of New York because you think you won't be back, and you're busting your tail to get the trusts formed and running as soon as possible. I know we should all be prepared to die at any time, especially at our ages. You seem to be making good preparations on some fronts, but do you have your soul prepared?"

"If you're asking me if I've accepted your Jesus and not told you, the answer is no. I've read that your Jesus wants us to be good, and that he told people he helped to 'Go and sin no more. ' I'm too bad for your Jesus to have anything to do with me, and I ain't sure I'm done sinnin'."

"God's grace offered through Jesus Christ is greater than the greatest of sins, or even the greatest accumulation of sin. That's what's fantastic about it!"

"Don, I love you like a brother. That is, I think I do. I'm using an expression. I never had a brother, and can only guess what that expression means. What I mean is that I like you as well as I've liked anybody in my life. I appreciate your long-term concern for me, and I really think I understand why you have that concern. But I've done some bad things in my life, things so bad I don't want you or any of my other friends to ever know about them. I've also read the Bible. On one business trip I speed-read the Bible from cover to cover. I know that Jesus tells those he helps to go and sin no more. I don't want to promise that yet. I might have to sin again. I'll let you know if and when I'm ready. You don't have to keep askin' me."

"I would love for you to know the peace and joy that comes with believing in Jesus Christ. But I'll back off and give you space."

"Thanks. Let's just enjoy our tour."

For the next three hours the two friends enjoyed their tour and chatted. From time to time, Abe thought about the third and fourth scoundrels. The fourth might be a problem for Abe, but he would soon deal with the third.

• • •

That evening, at an excellent seafood restaurant chosen by Don, the four friends reported on their respective day's activities. Abe sat quietly as Don told Roy and Walt about his and Abe's day. Don occasionally asked Abe for clarification of a point from their meeting, but he primarily talked and answered Walt and Roy's questions. Walt and Roy happily reported they played Bethpage's Green course much better than they had played the Black course the day before. The two did not say so, but while they played they had agreed that they were more relaxed because they knew Don was with Abe in Manhattan. Over dessert, the group discussed alternate routes to Washington, chose a longer route with brief stops in Philadelphia, Amish Country and Gettysburg for pure tourism purposes, and agreed to an early start. They would make numerous rest stops so that they could read and discuss the trust documents along with their ideas for policies and procedures of the trust. The trip was becoming a working vacation for Walt, Roy and Don. For Abe, the excursion had been conceived as a working trip.

# CHAPTER 15

On each of their trips, Don, Walt and Roy rotated the assignment of "Treasurer for the Day," abbreviated in conversation as "TFD" or "Treasurer." The TFD would pay all charges for a particular day, and at the end of the trip the four men would settle their accounts. Occasionally during each trip, Abe would announce that a particular charge, normally for a very nice meal, was on him. The TFD for that day would pay the bill as he normally would, but would note on the receipt that Abe would be responsible for the charge when the group settled accounts. For the past three trips, Abe had scheduled the TFD in advance of travel, and had made all reservations in the name of the man who would pay the bill. For the current trip, Abe was especially grateful for the TFD process. His would have no credit card charges in the vicinity of the scoundrels' deaths.

Roy was the TFD for May fourteenth, and was last on the bus after paying the hotel charges in Bethpage. By the time he boarded, Walt and Abe had plotted a route across Long Island that Walt felt he could most comfortably navigate with the Road Lynx and trailer. They chose a southern course, which eventually led them around the south edge of Brooklyn and across the Verrazano Narrows Bridge. They crossed Staten Island, entered New Jersey and met the New Jersey Turnpike at Linden. There, Walt turned the bus south toward Philadelphia and Washington.

• • •

Saying he wanted to "look up some stuff," at Hightstown, New Jersey, Abe directed Walt to a public library. While his three friends sat in the bus reading documents, munching on sweet rolls and sipping Don's coffee, Abe used the library's Internet access under the same ID he had used at the Branson Internet cafe. Thus, Abe began his file on Mr. Gilbert Glass, the fourth scoundrel.

Abe already knew something of Glass, a famous shady character in the financial world. Glass had been involved in the savings and loan disasters of the 1980s, but had escaped prosecution. In the 1990s he often benefited from early positions in computer tech companies whose stock prices were subsequently hyped to ridiculous levels before collapsing. Glass always managed to sell out before each collapse, and Abe felt that Glass was the source of most of the hype. Knowledgeable investors knew not to invest in any business involving Gilbert Glass.

Abe's research soon reminded him that Glass had founded several charitable organizations with large tax-deductible contributions. One of Abe's financial advisors had once told him that Glass filled the well-paid officer positions and board positions in each charity with his family, or more precisely, former family members. Apparently Glass used the charities to provide for his wives and children lost in his long trail of marriages. Glass's matrimonial history could only be called successful if measured by number of marriages.

As Abe surfed the Internet in search of more information, he confirmed that Glass had one kind of consistency in his life. For twenty years, he had maintained a principle residence at La Jolla, California, and for most of that time he had owned a second home on the northwest shore of Lake Tahoe. Each year Glass helped fund the North Lake Tahoe Fourth of July celebration, and remained in residence at Tahoe until after the Trans Tahoe Regatta on the second weekend following the Fourth. Abe decided that this scoundrel would require a special trip, one he did not want to make, but would.

Abe next turned his attention to the third scoundrel, the one he would soon meet. He confirmed that Gus Whitby had twenty-four clubhouse tickets for the Greater Washington Professional Golf Classic, which was held annually at the Basswood Country Club where Whitby was a member. Obviously, Whitby would be entertaining guests. Likely he would be at the tournament throughout the final two days of play. Abe examined the course layout on the tournament's website even though he had so often seen the television broadcasts of the annual tournament that he felt like he already knew the course. He guessed that Whitby would not wander the course, but would situation himself at one of the greens or tees near the clubhouse. Abe looked over the course map, narrowing the probable locations to grandstands behind the ninth, fifteenth or eighteenth greens. He felt he should look for Whitby near one of these greens, perhaps in a grandstand. Abe did not like to work in such a crowded public place, especially one with television cameras. But he had done it before, and he could do it again. He logged off the computer, and left the library.

When Abe returned to the bus, he found his three friends discussing the trust documents, and asking questions that none of them could answer. Roy in particular wanted definitions of legal terms, a throwback to his oil and gas leasing days. Abe and Don started joking they should have brought Tom or Stuart with them from New York. Walt had begun listing questions and issues. The distinction between each classification somewhat blurred so that his list was only a point-by-point list of items for further discussion or research.

Don served Abe a cinnamon roll and a cup of coffee while Walt moved to the driver's seat and started the bus. The group was soon rolling toward Philadelphia, their next planned stop.

• • •

With Abe's guidance, Walt found the Independence Center's new motor coach parking area and soon had the bus and trailer parked in two spaces. The group forsook the shuttle, which would have taken them to the Independence Center, and instead walked to a small busy restaurant known by Don to be famous for Philly cheese steak sandwiches. All skipped dessert after Walt mentioned that during the afternoon they would pass through Amish country, where they would likely find tasty fruit pies.

Stuffed, the four men walked through Independence Historical Park to the visitor's center. When they found the next available tour of Independence Hall would be forty minutes later, they wandered through more of the park before joining their numbered tour group in the brick courtyard of Independence Hall. Even as they waited they were overtaken by thoughts of two hundred years before. Inside the building, the men grew somber and appreciative of the courage of the signers of the Declaration of Independence, the financial supporters of the revolution, and the members of the Continental Congress. They were impressed that the price paid was dear for almost half of the fifty-six men who for freedom pledged their lives and fortunes. At least nine had died directly as a result of the war. At least fifteen were bankrupted either by giving their wealth to finance the war, or through confiscation and destruction by the British or looters. Abe mentally compared these patriots with the four scoundrels with whom he was dealing. *Yep, the scoundrels should be struck down!*

● ● ●

The stop for pie at the Amish community of Bird-In-Hand followed a drive of many miles through beautiful farmland featuring huge white barns, big white houses and small black buggies. The berry and apple pies were delicious, and were passed around the table for tasting. Roy ordered an extra slice each of apple and blueberry pies which he shared with his three friends. The coffee was good, but not as good as Don's.

Before the bus departed Bird-In-Hand, Don re-supplied the refrigerator with a selection of lunchmeats and cheese from an Amish market.

He also bought a large supply of beef jerky, summer sausage, assorted breads, crackers, and locally produced chips. Food, especially snack food, was a high priority to the Road Lynx's occupants.

• • •

The stops in Hightstown, Philadelphia, and Bird-In-Hand had each taken longer than planned, and had reduced the time available for Gettysburg. The four men decided to forego a visit to the battlefield's museum and to only make a quick self-guided tour of the battlefield. In the battlefield they stopped four times for closer looks at the terrain or to read informative markers, but such stops were limited by lack of time and by lack of available parking for their long rig.

Even with an abbreviated battlefield tour, it was after nine o'clock in the evening when the friends arrived at their hotel in Rockville, Maryland. The men had left their hotel on Long Island at seven o'clock that morning. The four old travelers were tired.

# CHAPTER 16

At 8:00 A.M., the group met in the hotel dining room for breakfast. Don and Walt arrived first, and selected a table near a window through which they could see a misty morning. They were drinking coffee and reading different sections of the *Washington Post* when Abe and Roy approached the table.

"So, how are you two feeling today?" Don asked.

"Refreshed," Roy answered." I was dragging last night when we checked in."

"I was draggin', too," added Abe. "And, this morning my bones did not want to get out of bed. 'Refreshed' doesn't fit my condition this morning. 'Awake' is the most active word I can use to describe how I feel. I may wear out early today, and come back here."

Don, who was TFD, counseled, "The car service you asked me to hire will pick us up and drop us off whenever we ask, and we don't have to travel as a group. To return to the hotel, we only have to appear at their pick-up point on the Basswood Country Club grounds."

Roy cautioned his friends, "That'll work fine for Abe or any of us if we leave the tournament before the last few players have finished. But, if we wait until play is over for the day, there'll be a crowd at that pick-up point."

Walt agreed with Roy's assessment, and stated his inclination, "I want to watch the pros make good golf shots. I don't have to see every one of those shots, and don't care to stay until play is finished. I can read the paper tomorrow to learn who is leading, not that I care much."

All agreed to an early departure, knowing Abe might leave even earlier than the others. Abe knew the length of his day would mostly be determined by when or whether he found the third scoundrel.

A pretty lady in her forties drove the car that arrived at 9:50, twenty minutes late. She apologized for her tardiness, saying traffic was horrible, even worse than usual for the expressways and suburban roads north of Washington, D.C. She was obviously a golfer, talked continuously, and gave her four passengers a complete rundown of tournament play and resulting scores through the first two rounds. She briefed the men on the procedure for returning to their hotel, and suggested that to avoid the lines at the pick-up point, they should leave early. Her assessment of traffic had been accurate. Seventy-five minutes were required to travel less than fifteen miles to the Basswood Country Club.

Near the drop point, the four received their official programs, rented folding seats, and purchased matching wide-brimmed straw hats bearing the logo "Greater Washington Classic 2004." Abe regretted that the brim on the straw hat was not quite as broad as the brim on the hat he left in a closet on the bus, but he was pleased his straw hat looked exactly like hundreds of others on the course. He wanted to blend in.

At breakfast, the four had developed a plan of action for the tournament. Walt, Don and Roy, who wanted to stretch their legs after so many hours in the bus the day before, would walk the course from the first tee to the last hole, stopping to watch whatever action they might encounter as they walked. Their past experience told them that they would see a good mix of tee shots, long fairway shots, approach shots, and putts. Abe would stay close to the tees and greens surrounding the clubhouse. The three would look for Abe after their walk, but if they did not meet earlier, the four would meet at a refreshment tent behind the ninth green at two o'clock.

Abe looked at his program and saw that over the next hour several of the world's top golfers were scheduled to tee off on the first hole. Abe wandered that direction, thinking that his quarry might also want to see the favorites. The crowd around the first tee was tightly packed. If Gus Whitby was in that crowd it was extremely unlikely that Abe would see him at a sufficient distance for Abe to do what he was there to do. Abe wandered on.

Sunshine appeared as Abe approached the ninth green. The sunlight felt good for a while, but it caused the water from the overnight rain to vaporize from the grass, adding to the weight of the already muggy air. Abe decide to restrict his physical effort, and to wait in one place. He found a spot near a sandy bunker just below the ninth green. From where he unfolded his chair he could watch bunker shots, chip shots, and putts, as well as people in and around the crowded grandstand behind the green. The crowd continued to grow, but it was nothing close to the mass of humanity at the first tee. Abe could survey the crowd at will.

After forty-five minutes, Abe needed to use the restroom. Although the grandstand had filled, and the standing group had grown, Gus Whitby had not appeared. Abe stood, folded his chair, and headed to a nearby bank of port-a-potties. After he had relieved himself, Abe took advantage of the privacy to pull from his left rear pocket a photograph of Whitby. It had never happened, but Abe had always been concerned about mistakenly killing a look-a-like. He was wary of carrying a picture of his intended victim, but he was more concerned to be accurate when he identified his target. He stared at the photo for two full minutes before he returned it to the pocket of his trousers.

Abe wandered past the clubhouse and past the eighteenth green where golfers who had teed off early that morning were finishing their play. These guys were not contenders, as demonstrated by the slack crowd at eighteen.

Abe bought a ten-dollar hot dog in a refreshment tent, and added free mustard from a squeeze jar at a tall table. He had intended to carry the hot dog with him, but chose to linger in the tent when he saw a golf cart labeled SECURITY stop just outside. An old acquaintance wearing a golf shirt also marked SECURITY stepped from the cart and walked into the tent. Abe was thankful to be wearing his dark glasses and broad-brimmed hat, and he promptly turned to the closed circuit television screen overhead toward the back of the tent. Abe kept one hand holding his hot dog near his face as he pretended to watch the tournament on the screen. But in his peripheral vision, Abe concentrated on Sid Self, a man who was once such a nuisance to him. Abe began to regret his decision to kill Whitby at the golf tournament. It was too public, and one old acquaintance could expose him. Abe sighed when Self took two cold drinks and returned to the cart without glancing toward the few people in the tent.

Abe rebuked himself. He was out of condition. These little incidents had been part of more than one assassination. Maybe his personal fortitude had slipped. He had a job to do, and second-guessing himself would not help. He left the refreshment tent smiling broadly.

Abe found a shady spot against the crowd control rope that would serve his purpose. It was thirty yards forward and to the right of the fifteenth green. He could see people sitting in the grandstand, standing around the green, and sitting or standing against a rope on the opposite side of the fairway. Abe realized that those people could also see him, and when he looked at the television cameras behind the grandstand, Abe knew he would also be seen by millions of television viewers watching golfers approach the fifteenth green. *Oh well, just do the job. This is why I suggested we buy the broadest brimmed hats available.*

"Nice shady spot here, Mister Brown!" Don's greeting startled Abe.

Abe stopped panning the grandstand, and let his field glasses drop on their strap to his chest. "Yes, and we can see a lot of action here. We can see the tee shots which should land about there," pointing to a spot on the fairway as he talked. "We get a close-up view of the approach shots, and we can see the puttin'. The shade is a bonus."

Roy was standing next to Walt behind Don." We can also see the leader board, and we can be on TV. Should we take off our hats so the folks watching back home can see us and be envious?"

"The folks back home are sitting in air conditioning as the television crew quickly moves them to action on different holes. They are seeing more golf, and they are cool. It's hot and humid here in real life," Walt complained.

Don looked over his shoulder, "Grumbling are you, Walt?"

"Only a little. Everybody in this part of the country gripes about the heat and humidity."

Abe looked at his three friends. "You three are all wet. Did y'all run around the course?"

Don had opened a folding chair beside Abe. "No, we strolled and we stopped frequently."

Walt returned the conversation to the golf tournament as a ball landed almost right in front of Abe, about four feet from the rope. "Oooh. Look where that ball landed. We have a perfect seat to watch a makeable chip shot."

As Walt spoke, Abe's heart jumped. Gus Whitby had joined the group of people standing under the leader board next to the grandstand. To cover his next act, Abe asked, "What did they just change on the leader board?' Abe raised his old Army field glasses to look at Whitby, and was preparing to hit Whitby immediately when he noticed strange activity to Whitby's right, Abe's left. He turned his attention to see a man on the ground. Tournament marshals were moving quickly. One was using his radio. Another grabbed an emergency first aid kit, and rushed to the fallen man. A spectator stepped from the crowd, spoke to the marshals, and began checking for a pulse or other indication that the man was alive. The spectator apparently found no such sign and began CPR.

"This is a good day for a heart attack," Roy appraised. "Hot, humid, no wind. Standing and walking works the heart pretty hard."

"I'm surprised people aren't dropping all over the place," Walt added.

"Yeah, me too," Abe agreed, but he thought, *This is not a good day for two heart attacks within minutes and a few feet of one another.* Abe grew nervous, and silently questioned himself, *Did I do that?* He mentally inventoried his every movement over the past few minutes to assure himself that he had not accidentally hit the wrong man. Then Abe thought, *Did somebody else kill that guy? Has someone developed a weapon like mine?*

Roy broke Abe's contemplation. "Wow! That ambulance cart got here fast." He was referring to an elongated golf cart bearing a stretcher, two emergency technicians, and their equipment, which had arrived near the fallen man. In a matter of minutes, the technicians made their appraisal, loaded the man onto the stretcher then onto the cart, and were on their way. Although the cart had flashing lights, it had only a squeaky horn to help clear its way though the crowd.

While the emergency team was working, a television camera panned the crowd, only briefly showing the emergency technicians working with the fallen man. The play-by-play announcer dolefully reported, "Play is halted at the fifteenth green as marshals and technicians attend to a medical emergency in the crowd."

The announcer's partner, or "analyst," had played on the pro tour for eleven years with moderate success. He complimented the tournament staff's prompt response to the emergency, and discoursed on the human issues of a golf tournament and the enormous task of dealing with large crowds. On direction from his producer's voice in his headset, the analyst concluded his comments with, "Now, let's go to the sixteenth green and Red Simmons." A few minutes later when television attention returned to the fifteenth green, the analyst again praised tournament officials and stated, "Play was stopped only twelve minutes for the medical emergency."

The announcer added, "Well, we certainly hope the man being assisted recovers soon. Now, Hal Greengate is preparing to chip to the green. His tee shot landed in excellent position in front of and to the right of the green." The camera focused on Greengate and his ball right in front of Abe, Roy, Don and Walt.

The commentator added, "I hope the delay has not affected Greengate. He's recorded an excellent round so far, and is now on the leader board, moving up. He excels with his wedge. This shot is for an eagle."

Greengate's shot rolled to a stop two feet from the hole. He would get a birdie. Television attention switched to Greengate's playing partner whose second shot had bounced off the front of the grandstand and was lying on the back edge of the green.

Abe looked again to the spot where Gus Whitby had been standing. Whitby was gone. Abe would have to wait. Abe considered the impact of the apparent heart attack near the grandstand, and finally resolved that the fifteenth green could stand two medical emergencies in one day. He should wait for Whitby to return.

• • •

On his new wide-screen television in his apartment overlooking New York's Central Park, Tom Queen watched the Greater Washington Professional Golf Classic. He rarely watched televised golf, and was today watching the crowd as much as the golfers, searching for his old client and three new clients. Queen was further interested because he knew Abe might be looking for Gus Whitby at the tournament. His heart quickened when he saw his friend Abe Brown casually sitting in shade near the fifteenth green while a medical emergency halted tournament play. Queen caught a brief glimpse of an EMT giving CPR to a hatless black man. Queen knew Gus Whitby to be English; white-skinned—not black! Was Abe out of practice? Had he made a mistake?

• • •

At the Ozark View Retirement Center, four men and two women cheered when they saw their friends sitting behind Hal Greengate's chip shot. More Ozark View residents would have seen them had it not been nap time.

• • •

The oppressive heat continued, and Abe felt himself losing strength and resolve. He would have to do his job tomorrow. Abe and Walt returned to the hotel where they had a light snack then napped in their respective rooms. The four friends later had dinner in the hotel's main dining room, and called it an early evening.

Roy summarized their situation, "Traveling can be very tiring if you are old."

# CHAPTER 17

When Abe woke, he was hurting. He knew he would hurt all day, or at least until he had finished his work that day. He did not want to take his powerful medicine from his Houston doctor until he had done the job, hopefully by noon. He did not, though, expect to be so lucky.

Abe sighed when he looked out the hotels room's window. A light rain was falling. That could spoil his plans. Or, it might give him time to recover. He turned on the television, using the mute button to avoid waking Roy who was still asleep, masked with his CPAP device.

Abe used the remote control to work through the menu, which seemed to feature pay-to-view movies rather than television. He could not find a channel with scrolling news, particularly local weather news.

Abe forsook the television, and powered on his laptop on the cluttered desktop. Within minutes he had located the web page for the Greater Washington Professional Golf Classic, reading that play would be delayed due to rain, with the first golfers scheduled to tee off at noon. The announcement stated that officials were continuing to monitor weather conditions and forecasts, and that ticketed fans should check the web site again before traveling to Basswood. The announcement also suggested that fans should dress appropriately for rainy weather. *Obviously,* thought Abe.

In the lower left corner of the web page, Abe noticed a statement about the man he had seen collapse on the course the day before. The article identified the man, stated he had died instantly, praised the prompt response of tournament marshals and emergency technicians, and expressed condolences to the man's family. Abe surmised the article had been written by one of the tournament's public relations people using a fill-in-the-blanks form for such a situation, and wondered just how many words were unique for yesterday's event. *I hope the PR people need their form today, too.*

At breakfast, the four friends concurred with Abe's recommendation to keep their scheduled car pick-up even if rain continued. By doing so, they would avoid the rush of the crowd arriving en masse around noon if play resumed. Only a few people would go early. There would likely be plenty of room to wait in the restaurant tents. Besides, each of the four friends had expansive golf umbrellas, which would keep them dry as long as the light rain continued to fall straight down.

Abe had another reason for his suggestion that he did not share with his friends. He was betting that Gus Whitby would also be at the course that morning, and would be an easier target in a smaller crowd. If Abe could hit Whitby somewhere other than around a green, he would avoid national television coverage of Whitby's death event.

When their car arrived on schedule, the four old men stood waiting under the hotel's portico. They wore the wide brim hats purchased the day before, and carried golf umbrellas, light rain jackets, and tote bags. They were ready for an adventure, even if it proved to be nothing more than walking in the rain at a pretty place.

At Basswood, the crowd was smaller than even Abe had thought it might be. Apparently, most people believed the rain would continue throughout the day, delaying the tournament until Monday. The small crowd pleased Abe, provided his target arrived.

For a few minutes, the four stood near the limousine drop point, watching sparse arrivals of other hearty golf fans. Abe thought he should stay close to this spot, and maybe get his man soon after he stepped from his car. But when he watched a Town Car skirt the drop point, and ascended the inclined driveway to the Basswood clubhouse, Abe shook his head and silently rebuked himself. *What was I thinking? Whitby is a member here. He and his guests have clubhouse privileges, and Whitby's car will go directly to the clubhouse. He's probably sittin' in the dining room right now with his guests. Make another plan, Abe.*

Abe surveyed the tents and buildings. People were lingering under canopies and porches watching the rain. Abe looked up the hill toward the clubhouse. His angle was poor, but he could partially see the veranda which yesterday he had noticed ran at least two hundred feet across the clubhouse, facing the course. A person standing on that veranda could look over 80 percent of the course. The porch itself was a good eight feet above a driveway that ran between the clubhouse and the first and tenth tees. There were no nearby trees. Abe opened his tournament map. He picked a rain shelter on the course from which he could watch for Whitby on the veranda. He wanted some luck, preferably good luck. *Now, how to get to the little rain shed?*

• • •

"You must stay on the paved pathways, and if we get any lightning, you must immediately get under a shelter," cautioned the marshal standing on the walkway to the course.

"We will. We want exercise and fresh air, even in the rain," Abe responded.

The marshal stepped aside and let them pass. "Yes, those tents are going to get stuffy when the crowd grows. But not many people are coming out in this rain. This crowd is nothing like the one we had yesterday."

The four old men looked like a short, slow moving train as they walked single file around the ninth hole and followed the cart path downward toward the confluence of tees and greens near the ninth tee. Abe saw that they were too late. The shelter he had picked was full. They kept moving as Abe, who was the engine on the little train, looked around.

Abe's perseverance was soon rewarded. Just ahead was a long covered bridge crossing a creek flowing from a one-acre pond, which provided a water hazard for two holes. As the men wandered onto the bridge, the rain grew harder and heavier. The bridge made a good shelter. Abe looked around, careful to not look first at the clubhouse veranda, which was clearly in view across the pond.

Roy was first to mention the veranda. "Hey Abe, you should have ordered clubhouse tickets. We could be sitting on that veranda sipping coffee, and discussing why in the world people are wandering around the course in the rain."

"How many of those people on that porch do you think are watching us?" Don asked as he turned to look at the veranda.

"A self-conscious person would say 'all of 'em are,'" Walt surmised. "I learned when I was selling insurance that most people are timid."

"I'll bet those aren't timid people on that porch," Abe countered as he pulled his field glasses from the old case hanging on his chest. Abe shuddered slightly as he thought about the lack of sunlight. He would have to do the job on one shot. The little battery in his weapon would be slow to recharge in the dark, rainy weather. He relaxed a little when he remembered that only once in his career had it taken more than one shot to kill a man. Then he thought, *I'm getting' ahead of myself. First, I have to find Whitby.*

Don had his glasses up before Abe. "I see why people aren't standing near the edge of the porch. There's a yellow rope close to the first line of tables, and people are graciously not blocking the view of people at the tables. Nice crowd."

Abe stated an excuse to pan the crowd with his glasses. "I wonder if there are any famous people up there, maybe the President, Vice-President, senators, movie stars, or whoever." He scanned the first row of tables. He did not immediately see Whitby. However, at least one person at each table was seated with his back to the course. Of those, one man's head looked like it could be Whitby's, but Abe thought it best not to kill a "maybe." At a table on the far right, Abe spotted two senators. He called his friends' attention to the senators as he scanned the second row of tables.

Abe suddenly realized that if Whitby were on the veranda, he likely would be sitting with his back to Abe. Any good host would give his guests the preferred seats with a view of the course.

Abe looked again at the "maybe" head. The head turned, and Abe got a profile view. It was Whitby, no doubt. Abe looked at other people at the table for eight, with every seat full. There would be a crowd, but no television. Abe adjusted his weapon for distance then looked away. He slightly lowered his glasses, and from the corners of his eyes surveyed his traveling partners. They were busy looking at the celebrities at the table with the senators.

Whitby was not a good target as long as he remained seated. Abe could cause brain damage, but not easily. He would rather cut a major artery, or pierce the heart muscle. Maybe Whitby would again expose a side of his neck. Wait. A lady stood at Whitby's table. Whitby also stood, and remained standing as the lady slipped between chairs to leave the table. Whitby's back was exposed to the golf course as Abe pressed his fingernail into the curved slot on the side of the field glasses. Gus Whitby grabbed his chest, slumped, and toppled backward over the yellow rope onto the wet tile near the veranda's edge.

There were no marshals or medical emergency personnel on the veranda, only dining staff. It would be fully three minutes before emergency medical technicians were alerted in their ambulance across the parking lot from the clubhouse. The four physicians who emerged from surrounding tables gamely administered CPR, but observers could tell they knew it was hopeless. Gus Whitby was dead.

"What's going on?" Don pointed to the point of commotion on the porch.

Walt swung his glasses from the end table to the action more at the center of the Veranda. "Dunno. I was looking at the senators. Did you see what happened?"

Roy lifted his glasses to his face." I wasn't watching the porch. I was watching the ducks on the pond."

"Yeah, I was lookin' at a duck on the pond, too," Abe added.

"It looks like someone's on the ground." Roy reported.

"Do you think he or she tripped on that yellow rope?" Walt asked.

Don answered, "I think it's a he, and he fell across the rope. He took it all down, including most of its stanchions."

The four watched the action on the porch, alternately raising and lowering their field glasses. After several minutes, Abe saw two uniformed people rush onto the veranda. He announced, "Here come the EMTs again."

Don put down his glasses, and addressed Walt. "What are the odds of two medical emergencies at a golf tournament, Walt?"

Walt continued to look through his glasses. "I don't know how the rain might modify the results, but you could expect several people to crash to the ground with anything ranging from heart attacks to heat exhaustion on a hot humid day like yesterday. That's especially so in a crowd like this that has a lot of older people in it."

"The rain has stopped." Abe's weather comment distracted attention from the porch.

"Good, maybe we'll see some golf today." Roy's attention was now fully diverted from the porch.

Don suggested, "If we finish crossing this bridge, we can walk to a place from where we can see the golfers putt on number two and tee off on number three. I noticed the spot yesterday when we walked. I think the cart trail runs almost there, and there's a shelter with a restroom nearby."

"Lead on, Mister Don" Roy invited. Don stepped off with his three buddies following in single file with umbrellas opened. Trees continued to drip water. As they approached their destination, they heard a siren as an ambulance carried the motionless body of Gus Whitby from the Basswood grounds to a nearby hospital, from where his remains would be transferred to a funeral home.

By noon, the greens were declared playable, and the first competitors teed off. Golfers were soon putting on the second green and teeing off on the third hole. Few spectators bothered to walk through the wet grounds to these early holes. The four old guys from Branson spent the next two hours watching non-contenders play through. Then they followed the leaders through the balance of the course. Even on later holes, the crowd was less than half of what it had been the day before. Abe was glad that he and Gus Whitby had arrived early.

Don noticed that Abe was more talkative than he had been for a week or more, and was pleased that his old friend seemed to again be himself. When Don and Walt went to a concession stand for refreshments for the four, Don quietly mentioned to Walt his observation concerning Abe. Walt agreed, "It's as if someone flicked a switch on Abe's body, changing it from quiet operation to normal operation. I wonder what triggered the change."

"I don't know, and can't even guess. There's a lot we don't know about Abe. Maybe something in his background causes these mood changes."

"Whatever the reason, I'm glad the Abe we know is back."

"Yeah, me too. Will you carry Roy's drink? I'll get Abe's."

# CHAPTER 18

When he awoke at five-thirty on Monday morning, Abe chose to not leave his bed. He rolled over and stared at the room's dark drapes around which slipped bands of greenish glow from the hotel's perimeter lighting. Abe thought about his recent three assassinations. He was slightly sorry that he had killed three men who did not expect to die at such early ages. But he was happy that those three men would not be able to again hurt so many people as they had when they crashed Mid-North. He was certain if they had not "gotten dead" they would have repeated their scheme, injuring more people. Abe thought, *Scoundrels like that just can't quit.* He next considered, *Am I one of those scoundrels who can't quit? I did for a while, but I came out of retirement. Should somebody kill me? I've hurt a bunch of people, but not innocent victims. I wonder if Don's Jesus cares how many people I've killed, even if they were all rotten bad people? What would Jesus do if I were to do as Don has asked, and suddenly declare I want to accept his forgiveness? Don and I would probably get a bad surprise. No, I'm a scoundrel, too. Too bad for God, I'm sure.*

Abe's left knee ached more than his right knee. He rolled from his right side to his left so that the left knee would be against the mattress. *If there really is a hell, I'll be seein' Whitby, Harm, and Fogg there along with a lot of others I've killed. I'll be smilin' though, 'because I sent 'em there early, ahead of me.*

Abe continued to lie still. A tear rolled from each eye, the one from the right eye dripping from the bridge of his nose. *I didn't want to come out of retirement. I don't want to go get the fourth scoundrel. I don't have a good feeling about it, even though I trust Tom Queen's information. I feel danger to me and to my friends. Is there any way I could do the job without using my friends? No, there isn't. I have to have them to get around. I also need them for cover. I hate to use them. They would never agree with what I'm doing. But Gilbert Glass needs to be killed even more than the other three Mid-North scoundrels. Glass was the ringleader. Besides, who knows how many people Glass has hurt in his other shady deals. Of the four, Glass is the one I want to hit more than the rest. I'm so tired.*

Abe slipped into troubled sleep.

• • •

"Where's Abe?" Walt asked Roy as Roy approached the table Don had chosen near the buffet.

"He's still asleep. When I got out of bed at seven o'clock, he was stirring as if he might wake up. But he didn't, and when I finished in the bathroom, he was sound asleep."

Don listened to Roy, and nodded his head. "I'm not surprised. I'm amazed he stayed at that golf tournament all day yesterday. I was ready to leave long before he was."

"Yeah, I dozed off before our car got off the Basswood grounds," Walt responded. "That was a long wait for a car after the tournament ended."

"Abe seemed to enjoy the tournament yesterday more than I've seen him enjoy anything for a while," Don added.

Roy was still standing, ready to move to the buffet. "This trip must be taking a toll on Abe's old body."

Don agreed. "We'll let Abe sleep. Today was planned as a down day, or a tournament day if either the Saturday or Sunday play had been rained out. We can linger around here this morning. This afternoon, we'll go into Washington to see the sights. If Abe's still tired, he won't want to go with us. Roy, have you ever seen the original Declaration of Independence, the White House or the Capitol Building?"

"Only in photos. I'm anxious to see them. But right now, I'm anxious to get to the buffet." He walked off.

Walt and Don returned their attention to their plates, and were soon rejoined by Roy. As they ate, they discussed the tournament, and the players they had seen over the previous two days. They stopped cold when a conversation from a nearby table drifted into their hearing." Did you read that the guy that collapsed at Basswood yesterday was one of the jerks that ruined Mid-North?"

"I hope he died," was the immediate response at the other table.

"He did. He was dead on arrival at the hospital; had a heart attack."

"Where will he be buried? I want to desecrate his grave."

"You'll have to get in line."

"All three of the jerks involved with Mid-North have died within the last week."

"Too bad they didn't die a couple of years ago."

"Well, at least they won't be pulling any more Mid-North's."

"Somebody else will."

Roy held his fork loaded with egg about two inches above his plate. He had moved nothing on his body while listening to the conversation at the nearby table. He spoke just above a whisper. "Don, you saw the guy fall, didn't you. You called our attention to the porch when we were on the bridge."

"I did and I didn't. I was looking at a table a little to the left of the dead man's table. Through my glasses, I saw people start looking and moving to my right. That's when I swung my glasses to look at the center of the commotion and asked you guys what you had seen. You said you were looking at ducks on the pond, Roy."

Roy put his fork down. "I was. How about you, Walt?"

"I was looking at the group at the far end of the porch. Abe said he was looking at a duck, like Roy was."

Roy whistled lightly. "Abe will be disappointed to know he came so close to seeing a scoundrel die, but missed it."

Walt agreed, "That's like looking away just as a golfer's tournament-winning putt drops into the hole on the eighteenth green. Abe will be very upset."

Don shook his head. "I think he'll be satisfied to know another Mid-North scoundrel is dead. How many scoundrels were there supposed to be?"

"Three I think," Walt answered.

"So they're all dead. Does it give you an eerie feeling to know that we were in the vicinity when they died?" Roy asked.

Don answered, "If they had been shot, I would suspect one of you guys, or Abe. But two died of natural causes, and the third ran in front of a speeding taxi."

"Divine providence?" Walt asked.

Don thought, and responded. "I guess it could be. God struck down some dishonest people in the Bible era. He normally doesn't work that way now, as far as I know. But he could."

Roy lifted his forkful of egg, and took it directly to his mouth. As soon as he did, he wished he had waited. He wanted to ask a question. Finally, he cleared his mouth. "Do you think Abe will want to go to Washington with us?"

Don shook his head. "No, I noticed last night at dinner he was really getting weak. He overdid himself yesterday. But he certainly enjoyed the tournament once play finally started."

Walt concurred, "He was in rare form. He joked more than I've seen him joke for some time and he moved about better. I think he took an extra pain pill at the refreshment tent by the second and third holes right after we got off the bridge."

Roy added, "He took another one right after lunch. He might have covered his fatigue with the pain pills, and couldn't tell what he was doing to his ol' body."

"I'm glad he can rest today. I like the thought of light activity this morning for me as well," Don said, as Roy's cell phone began playing "Stars and Stripes Forever."

Roy interrupted the song by answering his phone. "Hello, this is Roy."

"Roy, this is Abe. Are y'all havin' breakfast?"

"Yes. We're taking our time and enjoying the buffet. How're you feeling this morning?"

"Lousy." I didn't take a pain pill when I first woke up this morning. Now I can hardly move. I've ordered room service, and I've taken my normal morning pills. As soon as I eat, I'm gonna take one of my Houston specials to knock myself out, and go back to bed. Y'all go on into Washington or whatever you plan to do without me. Check on me before y'all go to dinner if y'all come back before you eat. I'll either see you this evening or tomorrow morning."

"Okay. We'll call you when we get back from Washington, before we go to dinner."

"You be sure and visit the National Archives. Those documents give witness to how smart, brave, and God-fearin' our nation's founders were. Every citizen oughtta see those documents, and be thankful for those guys."

"Will do. Call on my cell if you need anything."

"Okay, and don't be concerned about wakin' me if you need to come back to the room. Once I take my special pill, a bomb wouldn't wake me."

"Good. Sleep well, and I hope you feel better this evening."

"Thanks. There's someone at the door. Room service or the maid, I guess. Anyway, 'bye."

Roy relayed Abe's comments to Walt and Don, and asked, "Do you guys ever wonder about Abe's 'Houston doctor,' the one who gives him those special pills? You don't suppose those pills come from some doctor somewhere who is not restrained by the U.S. Food and Drug Administration rules."

"That could be. Abe says he's been all over the world. Who knows what pharmacies or doctors he has used in the past." Don speculated. After a pause, he redirected the conversation to current activities. "Do you guys want to go into Washington as soon as we finish here? I'll get my car."

"Let's go."

# CHAPTER 19

"Good! I'm glad he's dead! I hope he went straight to hell. Whitby was the guy that pooped off all of Mid-North's money on stupid stuff. It's kinda nice that we were so close when he died and got to see him stretched out on that wet veranda."

Roy smiled. He was packed, ready to leave, and was sipping coffee while he waited on Abe. "We thought you would be pleased," Roy said, referring to Don, Walt and himself. "We learned about it just before I talked to you yesterday morning. You sounded miserable when we talked, so I didn't tell you then."

"I was miserable when I talked to you. I only stayed awake long enough to eat. Then I took my pill and went to bed. Today, I feel good again, especially good considerin' your news about Whitby." Abe changed subjects. "Did y'all go into Washington yesterday?"

"Yes, and I loved it. It was my first time in Washington. I want to come back."

"Did you go to the National Archives?"

Roy nodded his head slightly as he answered, "Yes. I got chills as I looked at the Declaration of Independence."

"Think about the difference between the founders of this country and the three Mid-North scoundrels. Some of those guys that signed the Declaration of Independence sacrificed everything for their fellow countrymen. The three Mid-North scoundrels did their best to take everything from the people that trusted them."

"I don't think there will be any memorials or historical markers for the three scoundrels, do you?"

"And there shouldn't be." Abe zipped his duffle bag. "There, I'm packed. Are you ready?"

"Yes, let me get your bag. Why don't you carry that newspaper with us? Don and Walt are already on the bus. Walt paid the hotel bills earlier." He looked around the room for the third time, and followed Abe into the hall.

• • •

Once everyone was settled on the bus, Abe pulled a map from his briefcase. "Okay, guys, let's talk about the plan for the next few days. First, we're goin' down to Mount Vernon to see General Washington's place on the Potomac, then on to Charlottesville to see Monticello, and the University of Virginia, one of the first universities in our nation. We'll stop there for the night. I wanna buy a little mobility scooter there. I can't drive my Stella onto golf courses, or into stores. People just don't understand. Anyway, I think I could go more places with y'all if I have one of those little scooters people can drive inside or outside."

All chorused agreement, and Don asked, "Do you know what you want?"

"Yes, I think. I've been lookin' at ads in those old folk's magazines that lay around Ozark View. I've also questioned a few Ozark View residents who have scooters. I'm not particular. In Charlottesville, we'll find a good medical supply business. It'll have enough selection that I can get something to meet my needs. When I die, I'll leave it to somebody at Ozark View."

"Now, that's planning," Roy commented.

Abe smiled as did Walt and Don. "After Charlottesville, we'll go west a few miles to the Blue Ridge Parkway, and meander south on it. It's one of the prettiest drives in America."

"I've heard about it for years," Roy said.

"We can also stop at the picnic areas, and relax while we go through the trust documents and discuss how to manage the trust." Abe was back to business.

"How far south are we going on the Blue Ridge?" Walt asked.

"Eventually, to Asheville, North Carolina. But tomorrow around noon, we'll stop at Roanoke. Y'all have a tee time there."

"You do look after us, Abe." Roy was ready to get back on a golf course as a player rather than as a spectator.

"Somebody has to." Abe smiled. "I'm plannin' on two more days on the parkway before we get to Asheville. We want to relax. Because of that tournament and all that business in New York, we've pressed ourselves pretty hard. We are retired, you know."

"Can we finish going over the trust business in time to get our comments to the lawyers and meet them in Asheville?" Don asked.

"You do have a capacity for work, Mister Stone. We might, but we might not. We can always meet the lawyers in Nashville, or someplace else on the way home. Are you concerned I might die before I sign the agreements?"

"That thought occurred to me yesterday when you felt too bad to get out of bed," Don acknowledged.

Abe nodded his head in agreement. "A legitimate concern, but I don't want to rush the process too much. I intend to stick around a few more months. I want to make the Alaska trip."

"Good," Walt exclaimed.

Abe smiled, "I'm glad you agree with me, Walt, as opposed to being happy I might be dead, like I'm glad the three scoundrels are dead." He broadened his smile, "But, back to this trip, I haven't planned a hotel for the next night. We'll stay on the bus in the park with the bears."

"I hope we don't scare 'em," Walt joked.

"We'll compensate for it in Asheville. We have reservations for three nights at a really fine resort with two beautiful eighteen-hole courses. Y'all will enjoy those. And, we have to plan at least half of one day to tour the Biltmore Estate."

Don was thoughtful. He asked, "Abe, haven't we added a couple of days to the trip? That extra time at Asheville and in the park will push our return to Branson almost to June if we also stop in Knoxville, Nashville, and Little Rock.

"I've got a plan. We'll not stop and golf in Knoxville like we planned, but will drive directly from Asheville to Nashville. I think we can have the lawyers meet us in Nashville in the afternoon. We'll sign all the documents, have a nice dinner, and let them get to know you three. From Nashville, we'll take a more direct route to Branson, crossing the Ohio and the Mississippi rivers at Cairo, Illinois, and then drive straight across southern Missouri to Branson. We should be home on, aah, the twenty-fifth. If we get too tired, we can stop somewhere for another night on the road. I think we'll get home in time for y'all to unpack, and leave to see your families over Memorial Day."

The three agreed with Abe. Don got on his phone to change a few reservations.

•  •  •

The men enjoyed their visits to Mount Vernon, Monticello, and the University of Virginia. In Charlottesville, they found a medical equipment dealer with a selection of eight scooters. Based on its compact size and long-range battery, Abe chose a blue three-wheel mini scooter, and rode it from the showroom. He promptly dubbed it his "blue scooter" to differentiate it from his black Stella.

At dinner that evening the four tourists discussed the difficult time period during which George Washington and Thomas Jefferson led a new ragtag nation. They understood why the famous gentlemen were so happy to finally retire from public life and return to their beautiful homes. Don, who had noticed during the day that Roy spent a long time looking over the Potomac River from the lawn at Mount Vernon, chided Roy that he was dreaming of running his fishing boat on the Potomac River.

Abe again chose dinner to surprise the group. "I've really enjoyed this trip, and with the bus and such helpful travelin' companions, have fared much better in terms of health and fatigue than I thought I would. I wanna plan another trip!"

Walt responded first. "Where to, and when? I'm game."

Don added. "Me too, but remember we have the Alaskan cruise in late July."

Roy followed. "I'm in, Abe. But when you told us you wanted to buy a little scooter, you sounded as if you expected to die within the next month or so. I guess you're thinking we'll travel soon, huh?"

"Yes to all of you. Our current plan for our Alaskan cruise is to fly to Seattle, cruise roundtrip, and fly home. We could drive the bus to Seattle, cruise, and drive home to Branson. We would take different routes to and from Seattle."

"Can you handle such a long trip, Abe?" Don asked. "You're talking something over four thousand miles. If you add miles for diverse routes and sightseeing, it could easily be a five-thousand-mile trip."

"I don't know. I might die along the way somewhere. Y'all could just pack me in ice and take me home. Or, y'all could just leave my ol' body along the road."

Walt spoke. "Any of us could die in route. I talked to Ruth today. She told me last week one of the new guys at Ozark View went to sleep in his recliner on his patio and didn't wake up. I didn't recognize the name. She described him, but it didn't ring a bell. She said he was only sixty-seven years old."

"Gotta be ready anytime." Don used the opportunity to convey to Abe that he shouldn't let himself die without accepting Christ.

Abe ignored Don's message. "Well, I've got some more things I want to do before I die. I want to see some of those beautiful canyons in Utah. I've seen the Grand Canyon, but not the ones in Utah. Also, I want to spend some time at Lake Tahoe, one of my favorite places."

"I would like to see Yosemite and Sequoia National Parks," Roy chimed in.

Don showed a little support for Abe's idea, but still had questions. "I'm looking forward to Alaska, and would be happy to see more of the West. But Walt, the bulk of the driving falls on you. How do you feel about that much driving?"

"You guys had better hope I don't die on the West Coast," Walt said with a little grin across his face.

Don volleyed, "If you die on the West Coast, we'll have to hire a driver to get us home. Maybe your replacement wouldn't eat as much as you."

Roy pulled a notebook from his pocket. Let's make a list of what we each want to see. Abe, I assume you want to do trip planning. Right?"

"I can do that while you guys play golf in Asheville."

"How many weeks are we talking about for this trip?" Roy asked. "There's a lot of open space across the western part of the United States."

Abe's eyes slipped into a stare as he looked toward Roy. "I don't know. We're booked for a July twenty-fourth cruise. We'll have to get to Seattle by then. But we can take our time comin' home, and wander all over if we want to. What's the earliest that you three can go?"

Around the table, each man related plans. When the group determined Don's return from visiting family in Minnesota would be the critical date, Don asked, "Give me a couple of days to deal with mail and laundry before we leave."

"I shall try to accommodate your domestic requirements as I plan, Sir Don," Abe promised. Abe did not mention that the trek across the West would be another working trip for him.

# CHAPTER 20

"Mister Brown, I have to agree with you. This drive is one of the prettiest in the country." The comment came from Roy, as he stepped down from the bus at a turnout on the Blue Ridge Parkway a few miles south of Blowing Rock, North Carolina.

"I'm glad you agree, Roy," Abe responded. "Would you help me get my Stella out? I think I'll drive up and down the road a bit. It's not exactly exercise, but at least I can feel the wind blow by me."

"Glad to," Roy answered as he headed to the side door of the garage. Abe shuffled after him.

Roy opened the door and pulled a ramp into position. Abe followed him into the trailer. By the time Abe was inside, Roy had unbuckled the straps that held the Stella upright where it sat in blocks in front of Don's PT Cruiser. The Stella was parked facing the side door, though it fit into the blocks and straps from either direction.

"You are a marvelous designer and handyman, Roy," Abe complimented. "This rig you made to stow the Stella works perfectly. Do you want to ride the bike out, or should I?"

By Abe's position and body language, Roy knew Abe wanted to maneuver his bike from the garage. "You do it. I'm not gung-ho about riding down that ramp. You seem to get a thrill out of it."

"The word 'thrill' may overstate the feeling, but I'm anxious to ride the bike. I like the bus, but I feel as if I'm seein' this beautiful world pass by from ninety feet away. I want to feel like I'm in this place. Bikin' a little will help do that."

"Do you want your blue scooter, too?"

"No, thanks. I'll use it when we stop later down the road at a trail shown on the map as having handicap access. You're going with Walt to the waterfall down this trail here, right?"

"Yeah, the map says it's a two-mile hike. I hope the trail isn't straight down going away and straight up to return."

"You may be huffin' and puffin' when you return." Abe pushed the Stella's starter. He eased the machine forward and soon had the sleek motor scooter out of the garage. He stopped near the bus's door.

"Do you need something, Abe?" Don asked.

"Yeah, my field glasses, and my big hat."

"I'll get them for you. You aren't going to wear your helmet?"

"No, people seem to be drivin' slowly and safely on this road, and it's smooth. I don't plan to fall off the bike."

"The Park Service doesn't want you cracking the pavement with your head. But I agree. If there is a safe place to ride a scooter without a helmet, this should be it." Don's concurrence came as he disappeared into the bus after waiting for Walt to exit.

"Walt, how long do you think it will take you and Roy to complete the trip to the waterfall?"

"I guess forty-five minutes each way, plus time to enjoy the view and to stop and rest if we have to climb much. We'll plan to be back to the bus in two hours."

"Gotcha. I'm gonna motor back the way we came. I saw a couple of overlooks that we couldn't stop at. I think Don's gonna walk back that way while I ride."

"I am." Don returned with Abe's hat and field glasses. "I took the glasses out of their case. I assume you don't need it."

"Thanks, no, I don't want the case. I wanna hang the glasses on my neck." Abe slipped the binoculars strap over his head, donned his big hat, turned his bike and headed north.

"Good idea, Roy." Don motioned to the two rocking chairs that Roy had brought from the garage and set beside the bus. "When Abe and I get back, we'll probably want a nap. See ya later." Don began striding north, watching Abe ride off ahead of him.

Abe loved the cool wind brushing past him, and he marveled at the blue haze, which gave the Blue Ridge its name. He rode several miles north, stopping twice before he turned and headed back toward the bus. He pulled off twice more to look at the vistas and rode slowly, well under twenty miles per hour.

Abe was thinking how much he would enjoy a nap when he rounded a curve that he knew to be about a mile from the bus. Just ahead, he recognized the backside of Don walking full stride on the shoulder of the roadway. Abe also noticed a white sedan very slowly completing a U-turn not far behind Don. The car's driver suddenly stopped the car as it overtook Don. A passenger jumped from the right side of the car, pointed an object at Don and said something Abe could not hear. Abe pulled off the road and stopped against and behind a huge hickory tree. Through his field glasses, Abe confirmed the passenger, a dirty young man with scraggly blond hair, was pointing a pistol at Don.

Don first raised his hands, but on apparent instructions from his assailant reached into his front left pocket, extracting his combination money clip and credit card holder. He passed it to the robber, who kept his gun trained on Don.

Abe released the safety on his field glasses, and focused the distance to the robber's head. His friend Don was in trouble, but maybe not mortal trouble, and Abe questioned what to do. *Should I kill the punk to be sure he doesn't hurt Don?* Abe had never before used his weapon in direct defense of himself or friends.

Abe waited. He would feel awful if the man shot Don, but Abe had reasons to not kill the assailant. The first was Abe didn't think robbery was offensive enough to merit the death penalty, and the second was Abe did not want to tell his friends and the local police about his weapon. He might be able to avoid disclosing his weapon, but he was not sure. Also, even if they did not mention it to the police, his friends would notice the similarity of the robber's death with the recent deaths of three scoundrels while Abe was nearby. Abe determined to only chance exposure if obviously necessary to save Don from physical harm.

Abe watched as the robber again said something to Don, who responded by slipping his cell phone from its belt holder, and passing it to his assailant. Abe adjusted the range on his weapon and held his fingernail over the slot. But Abe was shaking. He had difficulty keeping his weapon focused on the thug's head.

The thief motioned with his gun toward a large boulder away from the road and slightly to the robber's right. Don turned slowly and began walking to the rock. Abe debated whether to trigger a shot of hot light into the robber's head. No, the dirty assailant was only generally pointing the gun in Don's direction. He did not appear to be aiming for a certain shot. Abe decided if the thug took better aim as Don walked toward the rock, Abe would kill him before he could shoot Don.

As Don approached the rock, the thief began backing toward the car. It looked to be now or never, and Abe expected the robber to raise his gun. He didn't, but jumped into the car as Don passed the rock. The car sped off.

Abe focused his glasses on the back of the car. He memorized the license tag, verbally repeating the numbers and letters until he had dialed on his cell phone the nationwide number for the local highway patrol. He repeated the license number twice more as he waited for the North Carolina Highway Patrol to answer. Abe grinned when he saw a mile marker just ahead across the road.

The patrol dispatcher efficiently took Abe's summary of the robbery, the mile marker, a description of the car, the car's license number, and a description of the robber. She immediately broadcasted the information to highway patrol officers and other police departments in western North Carolina. She asked Abe a few more questions, took his phone number, and told him he would soon be contacted by an officer.

Abe glided his Stella toward the big rock. He stopped short of his target, raced the engine a couple of times, and called, "Don, you can come out now. Your robber has fled to the south."

Don stepped from the woods fifty feet north of the rock. "Did you see it?"

"Yep, and the highway patrol now has all of the information they need for a prompt arrest." As he said this, Abe glanced frequently down the road to the south. "I'm assumin' the thugs aren't gonna come back this way. I got pretty concerned when you turned and started walkin' to the rock. I thought you were about to get shot in the back. I didn't know what to do." Abe was speaking a half-truth.

"I'm glad you did what you did. If you had charged down the road like Don Quixote on a Stella, we might both be dead."

"I was impressed with how calm you were, Don."

"Well, there are two reasons. One, I've been robbed before. For a while in one of my restaurants, robbers took more from the business than I did. I closed that location."

"Good idea."

"The other reason is that getting killed by a robber is a much better way to die, or transcend to heaven, than dying of some painful disease. When the thug pointed the gun at me, I thought I was about to meet my Maker and was perfectly happy to do so."

Abe wondered if Don would have been disappointed had Abe used his weapon, causing the thug to die at Don's feet. He kept this thought to himself, and suggested, "Let's go down to the bus. I hope the robber jerks didn't decide to stop there. I don't think Walt and Roy are back yet, but I'd hate to find the bus or PT Cruiser missing." Abe moved forward on the long seat, and Don squeezed himself between Abe and the top box. Don was glad the ride would be short.

Don raised his voice to speak into Abe's left ear as the scooter's motor gained speed. "Abe, you're shaking!"

Abe turned his head so that his words would carry over his left shoulder. "Yeah. I was plenty scared for you, and I didn't know what to do. I think the stickup rattled me more than it did you."

"Thank you Abe. I don't know what other actions you considered, but you did exactly the right thing."

• • •

A park ranger overtook them as they arrived at the bus. "Is one of you Abe Brown?"

"I am," Abe acknowledged.

"And, I suppose you're the robbery victim?" He asked, looking at Don.

"Yes. I'm Don Stone. The robber took my money clip, a credit card and a cell phone."

"Well, you'll be happy to know that with the help of a local sheriff's deputy who happened to be nearby, two of our rangers stopped your assailants as they left the parkway at the next exit. Our rangers have your money, credit card and cell phone. They asked me to verify the name on the credit card."

"Donald Stone."

"I'll call 'em, then we'll have to fill out a form. This is a federal crime, you know."

Don raised his head slightly. "Oh yes; the robbery occurred on national park land. It's a federal crime."

As the ranger talked to his counterparts at the park exit, Don boarded the Road Lynx, and started a pot of coffee. He smiled appreciatively as he thought about how much Abe was shaking when they rode back to the bus. Maybe Abe shouldn't have any coffee.

Twenty-five minutes later the form was complete, the ranger, Abe and Don had consumed six mugs of coffee, and Abe was no longer shaking. The ranger took a call from the arresting officers who wanted to bring the suspects and the recovered property to the picnic area so that Don could identify his assailants, and his property.

Abe interrupted before Don could agree. "We shouldn't let these thugs know that we're four old men travelin' in this Road Lynx. If they get released on bail, they may come after us. The guy that robbed Don looked pretty casual with that gun. Why don't we meet your officers somewhere?"

"I can take you to them at the park exit."

"Good ideas from both of you. Let's go," Don agreed.

The ranger informed them, "There will be no bail. Your assailants escaped last week from an Ohio jail where they were being held for armed robbery and murder. They have a list of other charges pending against them in three states. It's a good idea for them to know as little about you as possible."

Abe started shaking again. *I shoulda killed 'em,* he thought. *Those thugs coulda killed Don just for sport. God, thank you that they didn't kill Don while I did nothin' to stop 'em.*

Abe realized he had just said a prayer of thankfulness. Later, he would think more about his prayer, and would shake more.

# CHAPTER 21

"Don, you did a heck of a job on those Southwest Style Eggs. Did you get the recipe from Emma?" Abe pointed to his empty plate.

"No, I've known for a long time how to chop spicy ingredients for scrambled eggs. The distinct ingredient is the wood smoke that circles over the skillet sitting on an open fire. I'm glad you liked them. I did, too."

"Carbon and cholesterol are probably good for you, Abe." Roy chided.

"I noticed you cleaned your plate, Roy," Abe countered.

"Yeah, I love both carbon and cholesterol. Let me have your plates, gentlemen. I shall properly dispose of them so that some hungry bear doesn't wander into our camp and ask to share our breakfast."

Walt handed Roy his empty plate. "I might have heard a bear last night. Something was scratching at metal. I guess it could have been a big raccoon."

Don looked at Roy as he gathered plates, "We can't call this a camp. We slept in comfortable beds in a big house on wheels, and I cooked most of the breakfast in a small kitchen. The closest thing to camping is cooking the eggs outside over a fire, and eating at a concrete table in a campground on the Blue Ridge."

"My idea of 'roughin' it," Abe quietly stated.

"Did everybody sleep okay in our humble abode?" Don asked.

Abe groaned, "No, I kept thinkin' of that thug pointin' that gun at you, especially at your back when you walked to the rock. Several times during the night I awoke suddenly and shook. I was plenty scared for you, my friend."

"Thanks, Abe. I appreciate your concern. Maybe we should start our business discussion, and forget about the heist. Walt, you said you have an idea we should discuss first?"

"Let me go get my laptop. I worked last night after you three went to bed so early. Don, will you make more coffee?"

"On the way." Don slid off the end of the concrete bench, and headed to the bus. "Uh, we are going to hold our meeting in this beautiful outdoor conference room, aren't we?"

All agreed, and everyone moved to the bus to get documents, notepaper, computers and more coffee. Soon the four reassembled around the hard table.

Walt began the meeting. "I'm bothered that our discussions of managing the trust have been scattered over a variety of subjects. Each session we begin discussion with one aspect, such as how to pick beneficiaries, but somehow switch to a different aspect almost without knowing we've changed topics."

Walt's three friends were listening, but made no comments. They were awaiting Walt's suggestions.

Walt turned his laptop on the table so that all four of the men could see the screen. "I did an outline of the topics we need to discuss. I suggest we follow my outline, and reach concrete conclusions on each item before moving to the next. Do you guys agree?"

They did.

"Good. Now the first item is to very clearly define the purpose and scope of the trust. We're going to get in trouble if we don't define that better than the trust documents do as they are now written...."

Roy spoke. "We can't be everything to everybody. We should be very specific in what we will or will not do to help someone. For example, we should help Ann whose pension source was eradicated by the

Mid-North bust, but I don't think we need to give money to that guy at Ozark View from Shreveport who used to be in the oil business and happened to lose some of his investment money in Mid-North stock."

"So you're saying we limit our assistance to people whose retirement funding has been destroyed." Don was looking over his reading glasses as he questioned Roy.

"Yes. Retirement funding that is directly related to employment. Defined pension plans, retirement stock purchase plans, 401K plans, that sort of thing."

Abe nodded, "I agree. That's my original idea, stated better than I've ever said it. I 'specially want to look after the faithful employee who saved consistently, didn't make a lot of money, and counted on his or her retirement plan for gettin' by in retirement. When rich scoundrels steal from good steady honest people, the scoundrels should be shot and the honest people should be helped."

Don put down his coffee mug. "I agree. Walt, you're an old insurance guy. Can you word that for us to fit the names of retirement and employee savings plans?"

"Yes, I think one of the agreements has an addendum listing those plans. I'll work from that. Abe's lawyers and financial people may have already done most of the job."

Item by item the four guys worked through Walt's outline. It was effective. Perhaps because they had spent earlier sessions randomly discussing key issues, they reached conclusions quickly. There were only two items for which they needed further counsel, and Don used his cell phone as he sat at the picnic table to pass the questions to Tom Queen. Queen promised to call soon with answers.

By the time they finished, the four soon-to-be trustees of the Abe Brown Retirement Assistance Trust had agreed on most issues, but acknowledged they needed additional experience and conversation to fully resolve others. Of mild concern was that the Abe Brown Retirement Assistance Trust acronym would likely be ABRAT, or "A Brat," as Roy enunciated it.

The four agreed the trust would benefit retirees and spouses whose retirement plan benefits get eliminated or seriously diminished by corporate theft or mismanagement occurring after retirement or within the ten years before. Benefits would not be paid to anyone having other sources of income or sufficient assets to maintain a "comfortable standard of living," to be later defined. Benefits would end upon death of retiree and spouse, and would not be paid to other heirs, devisees, or other successors. ABRAT benefits would be adjusted or ceased should any private or government guarantor assume responsibility for a defunct retirement plan and begin making payments to retirees.

As to how to use the money in the trust, the four soon-to-be-trustees agreed to maintain the principal, and to pay out only the earnings on that principal. They decided the Trust's total annual benefits should approximate the amount of expected annual earnings of the trust, with a goal that for any five-year period all earnings would be paid out and the original principal amount maintained for future earnings.

The foursome had earlier discussed many ways to determine a standard benefit, and how much to vary from that standard. Based on the results of research by Walt, the four agreed the standard benefit for an individual beneficiary would be a flat monthly amount equal to the monthly average cost of housing in the United States, as last reported by the U.S. Census Bureau. With approval of the trustees, the standard benefit could be adjusted up or down based on a beneficiary's need and other circumstances. The four guys recognized that this last provision might provide more flexibility than they wanted, and could force trustees to review all cases. Roy summarized the little group's quandary and hope. "We'll have to learn from experience, and be flexible."

The four guys had just begun to discuss a policy for finding and selecting beneficiaries when the park ranger Abe and Don had dealt with the day before drove into their camp space. His boss was with him. She was a petite, pretty redhead, not much over the age of Walt's, Don's, or Roy's grandchildren.

The rangers told Don and Abe that a federal judge in Statesville had ordered Don's assailants held without bail, and that the thugs were in jail with extra security. The ranger and his supervisor had come to take additional statements from Don and Abe, and they enjoyed Don's coffee and sweet rolls while they did so. As the rangers drove away, Don noticed that Abe was shaking again.

When the four returned to the matter of finding and selecting beneficiaries, Don's suggestion prevailed. "We should be flexible but formal, or we will soon find ourselves sued by anybody that can make a discrimination claim. We won't initially advertise, but will contact administrators in bankruptcy or default situations to determine who has been hurt by a failed retirement plan. We can then invite those harmed by each plan's failure to apply for benefits. We should also consider anyone who happens to learn of the trust and applies for benefits. Experience will eventually guide us on this matter, too."

None of the four soon-to-be trustees wanted the expense of a big staff to administer the trust. They decided to hire an administrator and small staff based in Branson to help the trustees manage the overall trust and selection of beneficiaries. They would hire a benefit management service to actually pay benefits, and would continue the relationship with the same financial management service and legal counsel that Abe had used to manage his business affairs. All hoped that Tom Queen would not retire soon, and that Stuart Range could learn fast.

The four decided other matters on Walt's list as they shared coffee and sweet rolls in their serene, picnic-area conference room. The men agreed to hold as many meetings as possible outdoors in pretty places.

Before boarding the bus and heading to Asheville, Abe thanked his three friends." Gentlemen, I've known for years that I was gonna die and leave behind a bunch of money. I've formed many plans as to what to do with that money, but none of them gave me confidence the money would prove worth the work to accumulate it, or that I could count on whoever would look after the money after I die. Now I feel good. The money will help good people who've been hurt by scoundrels. The trust will be managed by three friends I trust and by successors chosen by those three. Y'all mean more to me than anybody I've ever known except for one wonderful lady who died before we could be married. I've lived a lonely life, but tried to do some good. Some people would say I've done more harm than good, but I'm sure I tried to do more good. Now the fortune I accumulated will be of real value, and I have a family of friends. I feel good. Thanks."

It was an awkward moment for Abe's three friends. They had never before had to deal with such a matter of Abe's heart. They had dealt with his joking, ranting, crankiness, and no-nonsense business manner, but they had never been close to crying with their friend. Finally, Walt said it. "We love you like a brother, Abe."

Everybody hugged and picked up something to carry onto the bus or garage.

As Roy loaded chairs into the garage, his cell phone rang. *I hope its Doctor Jones with positive treadmill results,* thought Roy. But the caller wasn't Doctor Jones.

"Hi, Roy. This is Ruth. Is this a good time to talk?"

"Hi, Ruth. Yes. We just finished a business meeting conducted at a picnic table beside the beautiful Blue Ridge Parkway."

"Business meeting, huh? I guess that means you were playing partner gin rummy, poker or some other game like that. Who won?"

Roy suddenly remembered that Ruth, Cyn and the others at Ozark View knew nothing about Abe's trust. He realized he should leave such disclosure to Abe. "Abe asked Don, Walt and me to discuss some of his business matters. What's going on there?"

"Another death and another victim of Mid-North. Hans Gustafson had a stroke and died within an hour. He and his wife lived just west of the Central Building. Did you know him?"

"Yes, I knew him. He and another fellow on that end of the bluff liked to pitch horseshoes. They would do it for hours, except in the summer."

"That's him. I talked to his sweet wife this morning. He had returned to their cottage early yesterday morning from the horseshoe pit, not feeling well. She said he sat down at the dining table to drink a glass of water, and a few minute later was unconscious on the floor." She pulled the emergency cord. Help came fast, but it was too late. Gret, that's his wife, said she knew he wasn't going to make it when she first saw him on the floor. She only hopes he heard her tell him she loved him. She'll be lost without him. Gret said she had always thought that she would die first. She's had a long list of ailments for years. He had none."

"At our age, we gotta be ready to go. How old was Hans?"

"Seventy-seven. Gret is younger, in her late sixties."

"When is the funeral?"

"Next Tuesday, in a small town northwest of Kansas City, where they lived most of their lives before coming here. They have family and friends there. We're going to have a chapel prayer service here with Gret tonight before she leaves tomorrow."

"Is Gret going to stay at Ozark View?"

"She said she is planning to."

"Who is the new victim of Mid-North?"

"I should have said victims, plural. Kurt and Samantha West. He worked for Mid-North in the upper Midwest. They didn't have all of their saving in Mid-North, but enough that they are in financial trouble and are considering leaving Ozark View."

"I get sick every time I hear of someone getting hurt by the Mid-North scoundrels. Tell Kurt and Sam to hold on. We know of something that will likely help them. But I don't want to talk about it until we're home. By the way, did you know that the three guys who brought down Mid-North have all recently died?"

"Yes, Kurt told me that as well as when and where they died. It's spooky that they all died while you four guys were nearby."

"Yeah, we're a little spooked, too. I'm glad they all died of natural causes with witnesses."

"I hear one of them died at that golf tournament you were at, the one Abe invited me to attend."

"You missed a hot, humid, rainy event. Two spectators died. One really near to us."

"We saw it on TV. You four looked good in your matching hats. You'll see when you get back. Cyn recorded it."

"Any other news? The other guys are ready to go, and they're looking at me."

"No, but the weather has been beautiful. We've been playing lots of games on our patios. I love to be outside in weather like this. Oh, one more thing. We miss you guys and your banter. When are you planning to be home?"

"We should roll in on the twenty-fifth or twenty-sixth. We're going to stay at Asheville a couple of days, then stop for a day in Nashville, then get on home."

"Is Walt surviving so much driving?"

"Yes, but Don and I have been relieving him more than normal."

"How's Abe? Is his heart any worse, or his arthritis?"

"Abe's doing very well. He exhausted himself one day when he went alone into Manhattan to do some business. Don went with him the next day in case Abe had any problems, but he didn't. Abe also survived one very long day at the golf tournament by staying in bed the next day. After that, he's been in top spirits. He got a little rattled on the Blue Ridge yesterday, but I'll let him tell you about that when we get home. Oh, he bought a little scooter to help him get around."

"I thought he took his Stella with him."

"I mean he bought one of those scooters designed for folks with handicaps to help 'em get around in stores and other places."

"What color is it?"

"Only a lady would ask that question. Bright blue. He calls it his blue scooter to differentiate it from his Stella. And, Ruth, the other guys are waiting on me. I gotta go. We'll see you next week."

"'Bye, Roy. Be careful."

"Will do. Thanks for the news."

"You're welcome. Good-bye."

When Roy boarded the bus, he announced, "That call was from Ruth. She gave us added incentive to get the trust up and running. Kurt and Samantha West were also hurt by the Mid-North collapse. They're considering moving from Ozark View."

Abe started to ask Roy a question, but Roy continued with his announcements." Oh, and y'all know Hans Gustafson, that guy who was always pitching horseshoes? He suddenly died of a stroke. The funeral is Tuesday near Kansas City." Roy barely paused. "Ruth says that we have missed some great weather, and that she misses us."

Finally, Abe was able to ask, "Did you tell Ruth about the trust?"

"No, and it was a shock to me to realize that we haven't told anyone at Ozark View about the trust. Or, at least, I haven't. Have any of you?"

When he saw only negative responses, Roy added, "Abe, I think this is your baby to announce. The trust is your idea and you're funding it. You should announce it as soon as we get back."

"I'd like y'all to announce the thing. It would embarrass me to announce that I've funded the trust. I need your help, fellas."

Don spoke. "Okay let's not tell anyone at Ozark View about the trust until we have an announcement ready, which should be before we arrive home. We'll have another meeting at a picnic table to decide how to handle it. Roy, while you were on the phone, the rest of us decided to stop at the next town in order to email Tom Queen the few changes we have for the agreements. We'll also ask him to bring a couple of his people and the key financial people along with their golf clubs and the final trust documents to Asheville in time to play golf day after tomorrow. We'll sign the documents, play golf and have several meals together so that everybody can get to know each other. Then the next day, we'll head home at full speed. Rather than stopping in Nashville, we'll stop at one of the pretty lakes in Tennessee or Kentucky, sleep in the bus, and get an early start so that we can get home early afternoon on the twenty-fifth. Do you agree with that plan?"

"Yes, except it's uncivil to go through the pretty state of Tennessee as fast as we will. We should plan to come back to enjoy Tennessee by itself. In fact, I think I made this speech when we last roared through Tennessee on the way home from Florida."

Walt shifted the bus from park to drive, and moved onto the Blue Ridge Parkway.

# CHAPTER 22

"Abe, you had a good idea to get everybody together to execute the documents and to get acquainted." Tom Queen addressed his old friend as the two of them sat at a round table near the edge of a screened veranda on the second floor of the Mirror Mountain Resort at Asheville, North Carolina. Their view easily included four holes on both of the resort's two manicured golf courses. With the aid of Abe's field glasses, the two men could also see portions of three additional holes on each course. Their view was otherwise blocked by the north and south wings of the hotel and by huge pine and hickory trees among which the course had been built.

"I agree, but it wasn't my idea. It was Don's. I noticed our golfin' buddies have been switchin' cart mates. That's another good idea."

"I wonder who suggested that."

"Any of them might have. Don, Roy, and Walt are really good about sharin' their ideas, and discussin' 'em freely. That's one reason I wanted 'em to be trustees. Besides, I trust 'em to always try to do the right thing."

Tom smiled, "The essence of the word 'trustee.'"

Abe lifted his field glasses to watch a ball land far down one of the fairways, right in its center. "Tom, how does Stuart have time to perfect that golf swing and work for you, too."

"It helps that he's single. His world is mostly law and golf. He is meticulous in both."

"Don worries that Stuart is seekin' failure because his only goal seems to be perfection."

"I understand. We've dealt with that issue more than once. He has literally exhausted himself on projects by striving for perfection, not just excellence. I've counseled him, and he has shown signs of relaxing. Experience will help him accept appropriate standards."

"Stuart's probably a low handicapper who's not happy with his golf game."

"Exactly. He carries a six handicap, but is not satisfied with it."

"I think Stuart just influenced Roy's drive. After Stuart hit such a long pretty shot, Roy tried to mash his drive. He sliced it into the next fairway." Abe put down his field glasses as he spoke.

"I get nervous when you aim your field glasses toward our friends, Abe."

"Don't worry. The safety is on. My fingers are not close to the trigger. It's good cover for me to use these glasses for somethin' other than my special work."

"When the television coverage of the Greater Washington Tournament showed that black man lying on the green and you sitting nearby looking through your field glasses, I became very concerned. I knew Gus Whitby was white. I've never known you to make a mistake, but I thought you had."

"For a second, I thought I might have. But I mentally retraced my actions for a minute or so, and confirmed I hadn't hit the wrong guy. It was hot and humid there. A lot of people were at risk of fallin' over dead."

"What were you looking at?"

"Whitby."

"You're kidding! Might two people have fallen onto the green?"

"It almost happened. But I was distracted when the other guy fell first. By the time I regained my composure, Whitby had disappeared."

"So, you got him the next day on the clubhouse veranda?"

"You know I don't like to talk about these things. Let's change the subject."

"I'm just impressed, that's all. You took out three scoundrels in five days."

"If I'd had time, I would've spread 'em out, but I'm runnin' out of time. I hope the fourth scoundrel is sweatin' blood right now. And, thanks for tellin' me about him."

Tom squirmed. He was slightly uncomfortable discussing his old friend's success in killing the scoundrels, but Abe's thank you for identifying the fourth scoundrel clearly involved Queen in Abe's activity. The implication made Tom very uncomfortable, but he responded to Abe's statement. "Glass probably thinks he's home free because the key witnesses to his Mid-North crimes are dead. And, you're welcome for the information."

"I knew there had to be somebody smarter and more contemptible."

"He's contemptible, all right." Tom paused. "Last night at dinner, I overheard Walt tell Stuart you four are planning a trip out west."

"If I live long enough to do it."

"Good luck. The goal is worthy. Should I counsel you like Stuart that you don't have to achieve perfection?"

"I don't think of it as perfection. I just think of it as doin' the job completely. Doing the job perfectly would require more time than I have. Not only do I have little time, but I'm much slower. Between my arthritis and heart problems everything requires extra effort. Over the last week or so, I've been sorry I refused the heart treatments my doctors wanted to do. Somehow, I've kept going though. It's a good thing I learned perseverance during my career."

"I think you were born with it. Like Stuart."

Abe now squirmed, but not much. Squirming hurt. "I want to change the subject again. Which one of my three buddies brings the most to the table for the trust work?"

"Overall, Don. Walt and Roy bring a good deal to the table, too. Your trust will be in good hands. But I wish you would pick a few young people to be trustees alongside Don, Walt and Roy." Queen motioned to the golf course. "A couple of those guys out there on the course that I brought along with Stuart would do a great job."

"I like what I've done. I'll let my three friends pick other trustees. They can get the benefit of Stuart and the financial people by payin' your exorbitant fees."

"I'm pleased our fee schedule has grown to its present level, partly because of you. You know you get our lowest fees, don't you? We charge everyone else more."

"No, I don't know that. But it's nice to hear." Abe lifted his glasses to watch Walt putt on a green fairly far away.

"Abe, what are you going to do with your special equipment when you die?"

"Do you want it?"

"No. What will you do with it?"

"I've identified several options. One is to have it buried with me. I don't like that idea very well. Another is to dismantle and destroy the equipment once I think I'm through with it. But I won't know for sure when I'm through with it. I can only guess. One idea I've had is to pass it to one or all of the trustees." Abe looked at Tom. "You're the only person besides me that knows about my special equipment. What do you think?"

"I'd like it destroyed or buried, but available in case our society needs it."

"You've just stated my quandary."

The two men sat in silence. Each took another sip of iced tea. Both were thoughtful. Abe broke the silence. "I've always been concerned that some enemy of our country would develop a similar weapon and have an advantage over us. In that case, I would want my weapon available for our defense. I've tried to watch for signs that somebody has the weapon, but so far have found none."

Tom nodded. "When the guy fell on the green at the Greater Washington Classic, I first thought you had made a mistake, but then I wondered if someone else had just used a weapon similar to yours."

"Kind of a 'two shooters' story, huh?"

"Yes."

"I had a similar thought once I knew I hadn't accidentally hit the guy."

"So, what are you going to do? What's the default if you do nothing?"

"I don't know what I'm going to do, but I have a plan should I happen to die before I take care of the matter."

"Who will execute that plan if you're dead?"

"Don."

"Does he know?"

"No."

"You had better tell him."

"Yeah. I've been puttin' it off."

"When are you going out west?"

"July. I'll tie it together with a cruise we have scheduled for late July."

Tom sat, smirked, smiled, chuckled, and began to shake as he laughed. Finally, he said, "That's delicate. Tie a kill together with a cruise. Very casual."

"I've always liked a good cover. Let's change the subject."

# CHAPTER 23

From the woods of northwest Kentucky, an elevated two-lane highway leads across river bottomland to a towering structural steel bridge spanning one and one-tenth mile over the Ohio River to the east side of a narrow peninsula, the southernmost part of Illinois. About one mile south of the west end of the Ohio River bridge, even closer to the southern tip of the Illinois peninsula, an equally high bridge spans slightly less than one mile over the Mississippi River to flat farmland in southeast Missouri. East of the Mississippi bridge and south of the Ohio Bridge, the rivers converge, becoming the mighty Mississippi to flow south toward Memphis, New Orleans and the Gulf of Mexico. Travelers crossing these two rivers are in Illinois only a few minutes unless they choose to drive a mile north on the peninsula for a stop in the little city of Cairo.

Walt Wilson's eyes were fixed on approaching traffic on the twenty-foot width of roadway on the Ohio River bridge as he steered his eight and one-half-foot wide, fifty-nine-foot long rig toward the Illinois side of the river. When he met a truck, bus or motor home, only three feet of passing space was available. Walt was very uncomfortable. He flinched each time the Road Lynx's left mirror came within inches of the mirror of an oncoming, equally wide vehicle. In his peripheral vision he glimpsed the spectacular view from the tall bridge, but he dared not take his focus off the roadway and approaching traffic.

As the Road Lynx got to the midpoint of the bridge, Walt's traveling companions paid no attention to the roadway and traffic. They were each against a window looking at the swirling flow of the flooded Ohio River far below. There was no barge traffic. The water was moving much too fast for safe navigation. It was springtime, flood time.

When the Road Lynx reached the Illinois peninsula, Walt turned right, heading into Cairo. His palms were sweating, as was his forehead. "That was scary. Before I do it again, I want a break. I'm treating myself to a big ice cream cone, maybe a sundae, or a freeze."

"I'll buy," Roy offered. He was very thankful that Walt, not he, had driven over the big bridge.

Walt found a dairy store with a large gravel parking lot. He pulled the motor home to the back of the lot, and parked in the shade of a huge sycamore tree. Walt, Roy and Don walked to one of three service windows through which all of the cold treats offered by the little roadside retailer were served. The men returned to the bus with three varieties of freezes for themselves and a large banana milk shake for Abe.

Walt, showing no interest in leaving soon, plopped down on a bench seat at the dining table. The group sat at the table and in side chairs discussing events of the past two days. Nobody mentioned to Walt that he had one more long and narrow bridge to drive across.

Roy spouted, "I can't believe we blew across Tennessee like we did. That little three hour excursion into the Great Smoky Mountains National Park at Gatlinburg was like a short lick on a double dip chocolate ice cream cone. After that, we only stopped once for fuel and to stretch our legs. Then, we pulled into that pretty campground at Kentucky Lake, and barely got out of the bus. Meantime, we're planning a motor home voyage across the great western deserts. Something isn't right. We're retired. We should slow down."

Walt offered a positive spin to Roy's thought. "Maybe you should just think of this as recreating quickly. We are retired and old, and we have a lot to do fast."

Abe apologized, "Roy, I appreciate your indulgence. This fast track stuff is my doing. I'm the guy who complicated our eastern trip with all of the business matters, and I'm the guy who has asked that we go by bus to Lake Tahoe, one of my favorite spots. After I'm gone, y'all can meander all over the country in the motor home. Remember though, y'all will have your duties as trustees of ABRAT."

Don held his blue plastic spoon above his toffee crunch freeze. "Roy, I agree we didn't do justice to Tennessee or Kentucky, but I think the business portion of our trip is worth the price. I'm enthusiastic about the trust, and I'm glad we took time to get acquainted with the guys from New York. Let's come back soon to explore Tennessee, Kentucky, and the adjacent states. We can stay at Gatlinburg and Pigeon Forge for a while. I would be happy to park by one of the pretty streams or lakes for a week. Walt may soon weary of driving, though."

Walt stopped digging in his chocolate toffee freeze and assured the group. "I like to drive, even though I don't like to creep across bridges like the one we just crossed. Roy's right. After the cruise, our travel should include longer breaks at nice places."

Roy spoke for the group. "We appreciate you, Walt. I'm glad you were driving on that big bridge. I hope you don't want to pass the wheel to me before the next one."

"Naw, there's no need for two of us to have the experience. You can drive on the flat land in southeastern Missouri."

Don diverted everyone's attention from driving the bus. "Gentlemen, I know I'm the abnormal work ethic guy, but are there any other tasks to accomplish before we get back to Branson? We've signed the agreements. We are now trustees. We have an announcement ready. We have suggestions from the New York finance people concerning payment services, and we've identified a work item: to check local Missouri banks which might offer such services. We've established a recruitment policy, benefit policy, contract policy, and employment policy. We know which personnel agency we will contact in Springfield. Stuart Range is taking care of legal filings with the State of Missouri. Walt is going to arrange insurance. Is there anything else?"

Roy added, "We know which administrative service companies we want to contact in Branson. Walt and I will do that."

"We haven't talked about an office," Abe almost whispered.

Walt had an idea. "I know of several small offices in a modest-but-decent building between Ozark View and downtown Branson. For a reasonable monthly rental we could have adequate space for the small staff we're planning. Renting an office soon would give us an address, a place for files, a place to meet and a place to work. We would also have the feature of 'going to the office' to work with trust matters. That will help us turn off thoughts about the trust when we're home."

Don expressed concern. "An office will lead to telephone service, Internet service, utilities, office equipment, et cetera, et cetera. Next thing you know, we'll need a company car."

Roy grinned. "A car won't be necessary. We have unlimited access to a PT Cruiser and a Stella."

Abe supported the office idea. "We should be willin' to pay for a little overhead. This is a multi-million dollar operation. I agree we don't want lavish overhead, but we need functional overhead so we can better manage the trust."

Don acquiesced, "Okay. Roy, you're an old landman and real estate agent, and, Walt, you know the market for offices in the area. Will you two add 'find an office' to your list of work?"

"You could have just said that I'm retired from land and real estate work without using the word, 'old.' But I'll put finding an office on my list." Roy looked at Walt, who nodded his agreement.

Abe asked, "Is there anything else? Walt's been nursin' that freeze, but is gettin' close to the bottom. He may soon work up the guts to drive across another bridge. Is there anything else we need to talk about?"

Don had one more item. "We should discuss coordinating communication with the finance and legal people in New York, as well as anybody we deal with locally. But we can do that after Walt gets across the Mississippi and we're traveling westbound in the flat lands of Southeast Missouri."

Abe asked, "Anything else?"

There were no new items. Walt had finished his freeze several minutes before. He reluctantly moved to the driver's seat.

# CHAPTER 24

Ann Walker stepped from her grandson's Dakota pickup truck into the waiting arms of Ruth Birch. Ruth, larger than Ann, enveloped Ann with her hug and refused to let go. Cyn, Walt, Roy and Don waited for their turn to greet their recently misplaced friend. The five had arrived only five minutes earlier, had parked Walt's minivan under a shady oak tree, and had been sitting in shade on adjacent benches near the flower clock at the entrance to Big Spring Park. When the pickup bearing Ann had slowed, the waiting group had moved quickly into the bright sunlight to greet their friend. They were anxious to visit with their friend, eager to deliver good news, and hopeful as to Ann's response.

Neosho is a pretty, thriving little city located on the western edge of the Ozarks in southwest Missouri within forty miles of the borders of Arkansas, Oklahoma and Kansas. The town's physical features include sharp limestone bluffs, an abundance of deciduous trees, natural springs and clear-water streams. The town's square surrounds the courthouse of Newton County. Neosho flourished after the U.S. Army built a World War II camp south of Neosho. When the Army deactivated the post after the Korean War, the city took title to the abandoned property and patiently developed it into a diversified economic base including general manufacturing, agricultural industries, space industries, warehousing, trucking centers, a junior college, and even a nursing home. Neosho was awarded the title of "All-America City" by the National Municipal League in the late 1950s. During the town's campaign for that honor, residents enthusiastically covered their properties with colorful flower boxes. The floral tradition has continued, giving the town its nickname of "The Flower Box City."

Near the little city's central square is an area of Victorian homes that sit among huge trees on sloping hillside lots. Within this area is Big Spring Park, featuring a cold-water spring that discharges nearly a million gallons per day at the base of a rocky bluff. Trout swim in the deep pool formed by the gushing spring and in the rocky stream that channels the water away toward Hickory Creek.

Ann's grandson respectfully waited for his grandmother to finish greeting her friends before he handed her a flat white plastic container, hugged her and drove away. Ann and her friends ambled past the park's spring to a picnic table where Walt and Roy had earlier placed a large basket and a bright blue cooler. As the group re-entered the shade near the table and spring, the air temperature dropped ten degrees.

Ann described the setting. "This is a glorious day in a beautiful park with wonderful friends." She sniffled as a tear slid from each eye, and she again hugged Cyn and Roy, who walked on either side of her.

Ruth responded, "I've been looking forward to this day since Roy called from the guys' road trip and asked me to schedule this outing with you."

"So, I have Roy to thank?" Ann asked, turning toward Roy.

"I just made the call. While we were traveling we decided one of the most important things we had to do when we returned to Ozark View was to come see you."

"Was the vote not unanimous? Where's Abe? He's not ill, I hope!"

Don shook his head. "The vote was unanimous. Abe is at his cottage resting from the trip and planning another one. He had a particular reason not to come today as you will better understand after we visit awhile."

"Oooh! Are you on a secret mission? Are you going to kidnap me and take me back to Ozark View?" Ann's playful questions turned to concern as she frowned and said, "I hope there is nothing badly wrong with Abe."

Walt answered. "Abe's getting along all right. We'll talk more about him later, but I want to know how your life is here in Neosho."

"I have a wonderful daughter and son-in-law who have done everything they can to accommodate this old lady. My oldest granddaughter, now a senior in college, relinquished her bedroom so that I have a view of a beautiful flower garden, as well as easy access to a bathroom and the kitchen. When my granddaughter is home, she sleeps in a room in the walk-out basement that was once a storage room. My grandsons dote on me. I sold my car and love being chauffeured in my grandson's little pickup. He treats me like royalty. The younger grandson, the one who helped move me here, walks with me around the neighborhood. One of my great joys is walking with him to the square and buying him a milk shake or root beer float at an old-fashion soda fountain in one of the drug stores. Life is good, but I miss you, my friends."

Cyn and Ruth had spread a tablecloth as Ann talked. Roy replaced the picnic basket on one end of the table, and Walt placed the cooler on the end of a bench seat. Roy nodded toward the basket, "I hope you still like sandwiches, potato salad, and other picnic fixin's from the Ozark View kitchen. Emma Smith sends her regards."

Ann smiled, "I miss Emma, too. She and her kitchen are special features of Ozark View. I was spoiled by her wonderful meals and snacks."

Cyn kept her hands busy as she said, "Emma loves Abe, Walt, Roy and Don. While they're traveling, they pay for food they don't consume at Ozark View. She says they are a tremendous help to her budget."

Ann's smile hadn't left her face. "Don, you said Abe is planning another trip. When and where are you going next?"

"In July Walt is going to drive us across the big western states to Lake Tahoe, then north to Seattle. From there we'll cruise roundtrip to Alaska. Then, we'll angle homeward across the northwestern states to Branson."

"In the bus?"

Don laughed, "Yes, we've learned that Walt is happiest when he is steering our land-yacht across America."

Ruth paused in placing food on the table. "Don, you said, 'our land-yacht.' Has Abe sold you a part interest in his bus?"

"Abe didn't sell us anything, he gave us equal ownership. He just had the title changed to his, Walt's, Roy's and my names, joint owners with equal rights of survivorship."

Cyn continued to place plastic ware, and said, "I've never understood those title terms. What does 'joint owners...' uh, whatever you said, mean? Walt, you were in insurance. Help me."

"It simply means that all four of us own an equal interest and if one dies, the remaining owners, or 'survivors,' get an equal portion of the dead man's ownership. We now each own 25 percent. If I die this afternoon, Roy, Don and Abe will own 33.3 percent each."

Roy added, "Abe claims he's not giving us anything, but only splitting the ownership among friends who are going to do something for him after he's gone."

Ann tilted her head slightly, "It sounds like the change is in anticipation of Abe's death. You aren't keeping something from me, are you?"

Don took this tough question. "Abe's health is deteriorating, but we aren't anticipating his immediate demise any more than we did two months ago. He instigated this long trip for the four of us because he wants to enjoy Lake Tahoe and Alaska again before he dies."

Ruth mockingly complained, "But the trip is only for the four men. Abe never includes the ladies."

Walt defended Abe's 'men only' travel policy. "Ruth, the bus is not built for privacy. The way Abe had it configured, it's more like a men's locker room and dormitory than a home."

Don stopped further discussion of the subject by suggesting he ask God's blessing for the meal and time together. All agreed and bowed their heads.

After the blessing Ann was the first to speak. "I still feel like there is something ominous not being discussed and that I'm the only one who doesn't know what it is. What's the expression? I'm waiting for the other shoe to fall?"

Four sets of eyes turned toward Don. When Ann saw the others look at Don she did too, and waited.

Don cleared his throat. "Let's get to it. We have good news, and it very much involves you, Ann."

Ann drew a deep breath. Roy reached for his sandwich. Cyn took a very small bite from a potato chip. Ruth and Walt sat very still.

Don continued, "When Abe planned our East Coast trip, the three of us thought it was only to get away from Ozark View because he was so upset that you had to move away. That was partially the reason, but there was more to it. While on the trip, we learned several things about Abe." Don raised his fingers to count the items as he named them. "One, monetarily, Abe is a very wealthy man with a net worth of many millions of dollars. Two, he has no family at all. Three, your situation with the Mid-North fiasco gave Abe a purpose for his wealth. Four, he wanted to make the East Coast trip to meet with financial and legal people in New York to rearrange his financial affairs, and to establish a trust. Five, he asked Walt, Roy and me to serve with him as trustees of that trust." Don had five fingers spread apart on his left hand, and raised the thumb of his right hand. "Six, the trust is to benefit working people whose retirement plans have been wiped out by corporate malfeasance and mismanagement."

Ann sat motionless as she weighed what Don was saying. Don got to the specific reason for their trip to Neosho. "Ann, thousands of people will benefit from the Abe Brown Retirement Assistance Trust. The trustees want you to be the first beneficiary. I think the second beneficiary will also be an Ozark View resident who was likewise hurt by the Mid-North crash." Don went on to explain the benefit amount, and that benefits would stop if obligations to pay Ann's lost Mid-North benefits were to be assumed by government or any other entity.

Don concluded his mentally scripted discourse with, "There is one more thing you need to know before you say 'yes.'" He paused, "Abe isn't here today because he is shy, and would be embarrassed by any attention to him over his kindness."

Tears streamed from Ann's eyes. "Silly ol' man. Why would he be embarrassed? He's doing a wonderful thing." She used her napkin to dry her cheeks, then her eyes. "How did he get rich?"

Roy answered, "Apparently Abe's import/export business was very profitable. He wisely reinvested those profits. And we think he spent very little of his income on himself."

Ruth added, "Abe told the guys that he has no family except Walt, Roy, Don, Cyn, you and me. Apparently he was in love a long time ago, but the lady died before they married. He never sought anyone else."

"How sad! The poor man."

Walt drew on his experience at closing insurance sales, and asked, "What do you say, Ann? Will you be the first to benefit from the Abe Brown Retirement Assistance Trust?"

"How can I refuse? I want to move back and be with you, and Abe has made it possible. Maybe I should say you four men have made it possible because you are all trustees."

In a strong voice Don stated, "Abe has made it possible. But Ann, I want you to clearly understand that the benefit from the trust fund is not contingent on your moving back to Ozark View. You may live wherever you want and receive the trust benefit."

Walt seconded Don's comment. "Yes, Ann. We are hoping you will move back, but you certainly don't have to."

Ruth countered. "However, I will never forgive you if you don't." Ruth was smiling and crying as she looked at her equally tearful friend.

"Nor will I," Cyn echoed.

"Of course I will move back."

The hugging began.

# CHAPTER 25

"Happy Flag Day, Mr. Brown." The greeting lacked enthusiasm and sincerity.

Abe looked upward through his heavy black-framed glasses to the face of the visitor who filled the doorway of Abe's cottage. The middle-aged man was tall, big boned and overweight. "Hello Sid. It's been a long time since I last saw you in Houston."

"Yes, I decided it was time to renew old acquaintances, especially with one of those who disappeared. How do you like your new name, Mr. Thornton."

"I like my new name, and prefer for my friends and acquaintances to use it at all times."

"A good idea, Mr. Brown. Would you like to invite me in?"

"Only if this is a friendly visit." Abe spoke firmly.

"Very friendly. You will be glad I came to see you rather than make public certain facts about your background and recent activities."

"Still trying to tie facts and fiction, are you, Sid?" Abe questioned his visitor as he stepped aside to let him enter the living area of his cottage.

"I think just the facts will do, Travis."

"Please. Abe Brown. Don't use Travis Thornton even in the privacy of my house."

"I'm flexible and negotiable. I can accept your little rule."

"Are we negotiating?"

"Yes, Mister Brown, always."

"I heard you got kicked off the Houston Police Force for negotiatin' with the wrong people at the wrong time. How did you look on the Internal Affairs sting video?"

"I try to always look my best, Tra... uh, Abe."

"I heard the department gave you a choice of retirement or prosecution."

Sid Self dropped his heavy frame onto Abe's low couch, and spread his arms along its back. He sighed and answered, "Something like that. But those clowns would have had a hard time getting a conviction."

"What are you doing now?"

"Funny you should ask. I joined RQB Security Company, the big international firm. Perhaps you've heard of it, Trav . . . or Abe, or whatever you call yourself."

"Not an area of interest for me, I'm afraid. What do you do for the security company?"

"I've been supervising security for big events, such as rock concerts, holiday celebrations, and golf tournaments."

"It must be an interesting job."

"Yes, and some events are more interesting than others. I supervised the Greater Washington Professional Golf Classic. We were very fortunate there. We only had two incidences, two deaths by apparently natural causes."

"Nobody tried to bomb the eighteenth green, huh?"

"No, but imagine my surprise when near the fifteenth green, where one of those deaths from natural causes had just happened, I saw you sitting calmly in the shade near the ball of some golfer or another."

"Yes. I was at a green where a guy fell over. I didn't see him fall. My friends told me about it. I was lookin' at the leader board. I was very impressed with the response of the medical people. Were they part of your responsibility?"

"No. My responsibility was strictly security."

"And for security reasons, you followed me here from Washington?"

"Not exactly. I had to work to identify you as you now exist. Fortunately, two of your buddy's pass cards were clearly visible on the security tapes, and on the television video. I was impressed that your ID was conveniently tucked under your arm."

"Pure accident."

"Right. Do your buddies know your past?"

"They know I was in the import/export business in Houston. That's where I met you."

"That's not the part I'm talking about. I'm talking about your, uh, service business."

"Oh, yes. You're talkin' about the business that is a figment of your imagination; the one you surmised I pursued when you put two and two together and got seven; the one that didn't exist, but for which you tried to shake me down, anyway. You haven't changed, have you, Sid?"

"I want to see your field glasses, Abe."

Abe had moved to a cabinet near his kitchen, and had opened a drawer. He looked at the green glow of an electronic device in the drawer, indicating no radio broadcast activity in the vicinity. His conversation with Sid was not being fed to a remote listening device. "In your current job, is it easier to shake down people, Sid? Does RQB have an internal affairs division? Do you think you might be on video right now?"

"I'm no longer concerned about RQB's internal affairs equivalent. I quit last week in favor of a new opportunity."

Abe moved a couple of items in the drawer. "The field glasses aren't here. I normally keep 'em close to the door to look at the lake. They're probably in the bedroom. I'll get 'em, Sid, but you're still chasing a shadow."

Self rose quickly from the couch and stood facing Abe. "Just get 'em. And, leave 'em in the case. I don't know how they work, but I don't want you to use 'em on me."

"Considerin' what you're thinkin', I should imagine not." Abe was staring intently at Sid Self as he spoke. He raised a hand to each of the thick temple pieces on his glasses. With his right fingers he made an indiscernible adjustment and focused the weapon on Self's heart. With his left thumb and index finger, he pressed a trigger.

Self's eyes widened as he grabbed his chest. He tried to speak, probably something not complimentary to Abe. He fell forward and rolled onto his right side.

Leaving Self on the floor, Abe shuffled toward his bedroom, mentally addressing his old adversary as he went. *I wouldn't want immediate CPR to do any miracles on your behalf, Sid. I'm sure glad I saw you enter the Ozark View office before you saw me. I don't normally wear these glasses. I think I'll put 'em away before I call anybody.*

Abe removed his special glasses and placed them in a sturdy teak box in a dresser drawer. He put on his normal gun-metal wire-framed glasses, and busied himself in his room for two more minutes while he waited for Sid Self's body to complete the death process.

Abe returned to Self's body, and began searching pockets. He found notes and two photos in Self's right inner coat pocket. He found a petite recorder running in Self's left coat pocket, but discovered nothing else that he would not want other people to find on Self's body. Abe shredded the notes and photo, and shuffled to the bathroom where he flushed the shredded paper into the sewer. He then calmly relieved himself after which he again flushed the toilet. Abe placed the recorder in his right trouser pocket before he returned to his living room and pulled the emergency cord.

As the clamor grew outside, Abe knew help was on the way and that the helpers probably thought they were rushing to assist him. He wondered if they would be disappointed when they learned that Abe was fine, but that they would have the corpse of a stranger to work with. Abe had his story ready. An old acquaintance from Houston had come to visit. Abe had gone to the bathroom, and upon returning to the living room found the acquaintance on the floor.

Abe opened the door for the Ozark View emergency responders, and pointed to Self's body. Abe stood by, acting upset, but not overwrought. At his first opportunity, he stepped from his house onto his patio to stand by gathered residents. He thought it was strange that his closest friends were all away from the retirement home at the time of this incident in his cottage. He was still outside when Sid Self was carried away in an ambulance. He thanked the Ozark View staff for their prompt response, repeating his story, "I went to the bathroom, and returned to find him lyin' on the floor. What a surprise! I pulled the cord. My, y'all got here quickly!"

Forty-five minutes later, a social worker from a Branson hospital telephoned, seeking Abe's assistance in contacting Self's next of kin. Abe told the lady, "I can't help you. I only knew Sid Self on a casual business basis, and that was a long time ago. I know nothing of his family. To be honest, I didn't like the guy very well, and had no interest in a friendship. I have no idea why he came to see me after so many years. We talked only for a few minutes, and he hadn't told me why he came to see me. I hate it that he died in my living room." The last statement was honest. Abe would have been much happier had Sid Self died about one thousand miles away.

# CHAPTER 26

Walt signaled departure with two short powerful blasts from the Road Lynx's truck horn. The gathered crowd at Ozark View called, whistled and waved to their vagabond friends now bound for the far West and Alaska, beginning a trip Cyn had labeled "The Great West Adventure."

Preparations for the adventure were accomplished similarly to those for the group's recent eastern trip, but with interesting differences. Abe did the planning, but this time he had more input from Walt, Roy and Don. Walt and Roy arranged for cleaning, servicing, and preparation of the Road Lynx and its trailing garage. Roy took Don's PT Cruiser to the Chrysler dealer for service as a help to Don who was swamped by a heavy travel schedule to visit family plus the demands of his new role as Chairman of the Board of Trustees of the Abe Brown Retirement Trust. Walt parked the Road Lynx in the Ozark View parking lot late Monday morning, and the men had it ready to go by early Monday evening. On Tuesday morning, the four enjoyed a sendoff breakfast with friends in the Ozark View dining room.

There were two other differences from their prior trips. This time, Abe rode his small scooter from his cottage to the dining room, back to his cottage after breakfast, and then to the bus. He stopped at the bus's door where Walt helped him up the stairs while Roy stowed the blue scooter in the garage alongside the other vehicles. A pleasant difference was that in addition to sandwiches, snacking veggies, pies and cookies, Emma Smith provided a two-day supply of Southwest Style Eggs.

As the Road Lynx pulled from the Ozark View parking lot, Cyn looked to her left into the face of her friend, Ruth. Cyn saw big tears. "I'm sad, too, Ruth. Our men friends are going to be gone for over a month."

"I'll miss them for that month, Cyn, but that's not the main reason I'm crying. I have this ominous feeling that not all of our friends will come home alive."

"Are you thinking Abe will die during this trip? He's gotten much weaker lately."

"That's most likely, but I'm not sure my concern is about Abe. I just have a premonition that at least one of them will not get back."

"If it's any comfort, when I say goodbye to someone I love I often feel that I won't see them again. I've even had that feeling when I've said goodnight to you and gone to my cottage. I think it's our age."

"And the fact that every few days someone else we know dies."

"Yes, that, too."

The two watched the Road Lynx move away until it disappeared around a curve. "Cyn, Don left me some of his good coffee. Let's go make a pot and drink it as we stare at our beautiful lake. I don't want to stand here and cry."

What the ladies could not see through the Road Lynx's tinted window were tears flowing down the face of their friend Abe Brown. Abe's friends on the bus did not see the tears, either. Walt was driving and Roy was looking at a map in the front seat across from Walt. Don was pouring coffee and warming a cinnamon roll for Abe.

The four men on the bus were unusually quiet. Walt was concentrating on guiding the bus down the narrow road. Roy's eyes were alternating between the map in his lap and the road ahead. Don was quietly praying for one of his grandsons while watching the cinnamon roll in the microwave. Abe was reflective. He kept his face near the window until he had quit crying and had dried his tears inconspicuously.

The first day's schedule called for little more than driving west and slightly south out of Missouri, across Oklahoma, and into the Texas Panhandle. Roy had suggested they stop at Pampa. He wanted his friends to relish the sampler platter from his favorite Tex-Mex restaurant. He also wanted them to enjoy golf on the high plains of the Texas Panhandle. He had warned them to leave their long woods at home because they would be playing in wind. Don and Walt asked for four strokes for their bets.

The Pampa stop also fit well with Abe's request to visit a bank in Dalhart, Texas.

Through the day, Roy and Don relieved Walt behind the steering wheel more frequently than they had done on any previous trip. Their demand to drive more was accepted by Walt, "Okay. If you really want more time behind the wheel, I'll share the fun. But you know I like to drive this big rig."

Roy countered, "Yes, but the length of this trip could diminish your enthusiasm for driving. When we get back to Branson we want you looking forward to the next trip."

• • •

Don was driving across western Oklahoma when they encountered highway patrol officers, who were diverting all traffic off I-40 due to a grassfire blowing from the south across the highway ahead. The detour consisted of an arrow-straight two-lane section line road running five miles south to an intersection with an equally straight east-west section line road over which the bus would travel eight miles west, then five miles due north to rejoin the interstate. From the detour, the four men could see a huge wall of white smoke rising at a sharp northward angle into an otherwise clear blue sky. They commented about the dry grass and wheat stubble as they discussed that year's drought, which had devastated crops in Oklahoma. Abe commented, "I feel like I'm sitting on a pile of dry straw just waitin' for someone to drop a match."

The detour would have been only a minor inconvenience had it not been for the tight turns at intersections of the narrow roads. To make these turns, Don had to swing the Road Lynx into the oncoming lane almost to the opposite side of the pavement, and steer the left front corner of the bus close to the opposite side of the crossroad. He took advantage of the open view across the wheat fields to time his arrival at the first intersection so that there was no traffic. At the next, a young lady driving a red minivan wanted to turn left and was frustrated by the monstrous westbound Road Lynx sitting at the intersection blocking the lane she planned to use. She finally drove the minivan across the intersection, a pickup truck following her turned right, and Don completed his turn before additional traffic approached. A young man driving a bright blue Camaro was closely following the Road Lynx, and he tested Don's patience by honking his horn without interruption as Don slowly negotiated the turn.

• • •

Pampa, Texas sits on a high plain in the Lone Star State's Panhandle, an extension of West Texas that is bordered by New Mexico on the west and Oklahoma on the north and east. In the summer of 2004, this practically treeless area was also enduring drought and grassfires.

It was late afternoon when Roy steered the Road Lynx off Interstate 40 onto Texas State Highway 273 leading to Pampa. Walt sat in the front passenger seat maintaining conversation with Roy to keep Roy from dozing. Don read in a lounge chair. Abe slept in his bunk.

"I don't think I've ever felt like I was sitting on the horizon like I do now," Walt commented as he looked at the surrounding flat terrain.

"We do have an unobstructed view, don't we?" Roy replied.

"But there's nothing to view except waving grass, wheat stubble, and barbed wire fences."

"I see an old windmill ahead on the left."

"How far away do you think that is, Roy?"

"Let's see. We're sitting in a bus so that our eyes are probably about nine feet off the ground, and we can barely see the base of the windmill on the horizon. We multiply the square root of nine by one-point-one-seven to determine distance. Do you want to do that in your head?"

"Three and a half miles, or so."

"Huh? Did you really figure that, or are you guessing?"

"Guesstimating. We're estimating our eye level above ground to be nine feet, and we think the bottom of the windmill is on the horizon, so our input is an estimate. The square root of nine is three, I multiplied three by one-point-two, and rounded down to three-point-five. Done, but not exactly."

"That formula only works on water and very flat land."

"This area qualifies. Uh, Roy, what's that in the distance on the right side of the road? From here it looks like a huge fence."

"A row of wind turbines, I'll bet."

"This is a good place for 'em. That strong south wind has been blowing all day."

"Yes, it has been! It's not so bad now that we're headed northwest, but on I-40 the wind was blowing directly across the highway."

"Does the name 'Pampa' have anything to do with wind?"

"No, it relates to the surrounding plain. The Spanish word for plain is 'pampas.' The Scotsman that named this place dropped the 's' for the sake of his countrymen."

"So, why is Pampa where it is?"

"It originally was a little water stop for the railroad when there wasn't anything else around but huge ranches. The town boomed when oil and gas were discovered out here. The population has declined for the last several years."

"I'll bet the people around here are good folks."

"They are. I enjoyed living here for several years in my early days in the oil patch. Mae and I had a lot of friends. But none of those friends are still here. They've all moved or died."

Walt looked again at what he had first described as a huge fence. "Those are wind turbines. Watch those blades swoosh around."

"I count ten of 'em."

Except for the wind farm, all Walt could see was ranchland. "Roy, when you lived here did you have a ranch?"

"No. I was always subject to being moved by my company. Besides, all I know about cattle is that a T-bone is my favorite steak."

"Can we get a T-bone in Pampa? And, how close are we to the motel? I'm ready to get off of this bus. We've traveled over five hundred miles today."

"Tonight we'll eat at an excellent steak and barbeque restaurant. We should be at the motel within ten minutes. Tomorrow after golf we'll eat at my favorite Tex-Mex restaurant."

"You like this area, don't you? Did you invest in oil wells while you lived here?"

"Yes I like the area, but no, I didn't personally invest in the oil and gas business while we lived here. That would have been a conflict of interest with my employer. But after I retired and Mae was killed in that car wreck, I guess for something for me to keep my mind occupied, my brother and I started buying little oil and gas royalty interests in Kansas, Oklahoma and the Texas Panhandle. Mineral interests were cheap when the prices for oil and gas were down. Now that the prices are higher and the oil companies are drilling for deep gas, those properties generate a very nice income. My share more than pays my Ozark View bill."

"I didn't know you were an oil tycoon."

"Marginal investor is a better term. Right now the cash flow is good. But history tells us the good times don't last forever."

Walt continued to ask Roy questions, maintaining conversation. He didn't want Roy to run the bus off the road so close to dinnertime, or "supper time" in Pampa parlance.

# CHAPTER 27

"Roy, this Texican Sampler Platter is worth the stop in Pampa. I can't finish it, though. It's bigger than me." Don laid his knife and fork on a bright blue pottery platter on which half of a cheese enchilada, a taco, a pile of rice and a full helping of guacamole remained.

Walt nodded, "I agree with Don, Roy. I'm not a great Tex-Mex food fan, but I liked what I just ate. I hope I still think so later." He looked at Abe's platter which was clean. "Abe, I think you enjoyed yours. Want another platter?"

Abe grinned. "One is enough. Exactly the right amount, but pass those chips over here will you? And, the queso."

"Should we get a bushel of chips and a gallon of queso to take with us? How many times did the waitress replenish them?" Don asked.

Roy was pleased with his friends' positive comments. "You guys remember this is what I want for my last meal. Feel free to drive to Pampa to pick up a platter, if necessary."

Walt suggested an alternative to such a long drive. "The restaurant would probably FedEx a platter to Branson. We'll have to reheat it, anyway."

Roy rolled his eyes. "Don't go to a lot of trouble!"

Don changed the subject." Abe, how late did you sleep this morning? You look refreshed. And, your appetite has obviously returned."

"I slept till ten. Then I cleaned up, ate a nice helping of Southwest Style Eggs, and went for a pleasant ride on my Stella. Thanks for gettin' my scooter out of the trailer for me, Roy."

"You're welcome. What did you see?"

"I saw a pleasant little city and lots of friendly folks. People all over town waved at me as I drove by. I felt like a celebrity."

Roy nodded. "You were. Not many old men ride around Pampa on suave Italian-style motor scooters. You were today's event for local residents."

"It's a quiet little town, huh Abe?" Walt inquired.

Abe acknowledged Walt's deduction. "Yes, it is quiet. The buildings mostly date from the 1950s, 60s or 70s. There are few new ones, and some of the older ones are unoccupied. Roy, is the town's population decreasing?"

"Yes, due to years of reduced oil and gas activity in the Texas Panhandle, plus several recent hard years in agriculture. Drilling activity should be improving with higher oil and gas prices. With the drought, though, the farming and ranching outlook is still weak."

Walt suggested, "Roy, you could find work again as a landman."

"I don't want any work, thank you. I'd rather be involved in trusts, retirement benefits, golfing, fishing and traveling."

Walt tilted back slightly in his chair, and tapped his fingertips on the edge of the table. "Your involvement today in golf was exceptional. This was the first day in recent months that you won all the money."

"Home course advantage. Did you gentlemen enjoy the wind?"

Walt yielded to Don as they both started to answer. Don said, "I was tired of that wind by the time we reached the third hole. Once, when I was waiting to putt, I looked at one of those few trees on the back nine, and wondered if I was bending to the north like the trees do around here."

Walt added, "When I was about to tee off directly into the wind on that long par four, number nine, I thought about those wind turbines we saw yesterday and how strong the wind has to be to turn those big blades. I worried that my ball might land behind me."

Roy replied, "On nine, you hit a three wood straight down the middle of the fairway."

"I chose my fairway clubs today based on your club selection. But I can't hit the long irons like you can."

Abe looked at the big clock in a wooden frame on the restaurant's far wall. "We need to get to Dalhart. Who's the treasurer?"

Don waved the check he had already picked up, stood, and began a zigzagged path through the chrome and Formica tables toward the cash register near the café's front door. The others made their way to the door and out to the Road Lynx parked at the far end of the gravel extension of the parking lot.

Abe sniffed." Our clothes smell like the food we just ate."

"Smells great," Roy happily declared, taking an extra deep breath.

Walt started the bus's engine and air-conditioner, and was ready to pull away when Don entered the bus. Don said, "I didn't want to say anything about our fellow diners when I was in the restaurant. But I noticed we were about the only men in there who weren't wearing jeans, a wide belt with a big buckle, and a long-sleeved shirt with snaps for buttons. I also noticed four hat racks full of western-style hats."

Roy confirmed Don's observation. "This is ranch country. Even if you don't ranch, you dress like your neighbors. When I worked here, I was more effective in securing oil and gas leases if I dressed like a rancher. By the way, guys, I think you'll see more big drilling rigs running today between here and Dalhart."

Walt turned his head slightly to ask Abe, who was in the front passenger seat, "Now that Dalhart is our next stop, how about telling us why we're going there? All I know about Dalhart is that the town has a powerful radio station that can be heard all over the plains."

Abe turned a little in his chair and spoke so that all could hear him. "I have a safe deposit box in a little bank in Dalhart that I want to transfer to y'all. I paid the rent in advance many years ago. It's paid through 2015."

"What's in the box, Abe?" Roy asked everybody's question.

"Two items. One is a sealed flat long box about nine inches wide and three inches tall. The other is a nine by twelve envelope with a letter and other instructions for the executor of my estate. That would now be you, Don, unless you die before me, then it would be Walt or Roy."

Abe did not voluntarily answer the obvious question, and for a full thirty seconds nobody asked it. Finally Roy did. "And, what's in the box, Abe?" As he asked he felt he knew the answer he would get. He got it.

"You'll know that after my death. You're to open the envelope first. It has instructions. In fact, the envelope is marked, 'Open First' and the box is marked, 'Do not open until after reading material in envelope.' It's like Christmas, kinda."

Silence lingered. The bus had left Pampa, and the land looked remarkably similar to the land they had driven through the previous afternoon. Walt, Don and Roy wanted to ask more about the safe deposit box, but contented themselves with quietly gazing across the open terrain. All had concerns about the content of the box, yet they all knew Abe wanted to say nothing more. Walt drove. Roy, Don and Abe sat.

Abe broke the silence. "Okay, what's in the box is from my past. I don't want the information in the envelope known while I'm alive. And I don't want the contents of the box loose until an appropriate time after I'm gone."

Don speculated, "It sounds like a caged wild animal."

"In a way, it might be. Y'all will understand and know what to do after I die, and after you read the instructions in the envelope."

More silence followed which made Roy more nervous than the others. "Keep taking your medicine, Abe. I'm glad I'm number three on your list of executors and contingent executors."

"I just don't want my little secret known until after I die."

Abe's comment ended the conversation. More silence followed until Roy pointed to a huge drilling rig not far off the highway. The four men were pleased to change the subject of their conversation, and peppered Roy with questions about oil and gas leasing, mineral rights and drilling.

Finally, Walt addressed travel plans, "We're stopping at the bank in Dalhart, and then we're busting down the road to Santa Rosa, New Mexico where we'll spend the night. Do any of you have any more surprises for the day?"

Abe knew Walt's question was really directed solely at him. "No, you're safe for the rest of the day."

Don had looked at Abe as Abe responded to Walt's question. "What are you grinning about, Abe?"

"I'm looking at this ranch country and thinkin' what Stuart Range would look like if he was ridin' a horse through that tall grass in that western outfit he bought when he was in Branson last month. I'm thinkin' a mannequin cowboy on a horse." Abe grinned more.

Roy asked, "What are you guys talking about?"

Don explained. "You know the New York lawyers and financial people came to Branson in June while you were in Corpus Christi visiting your daughter. I guess we've been traveling or so busy since you've been back, we haven't told you about it. Well, we took our sophisticated friends to see The Baldknobbers and The Presleys' shows. We also took them cruising on Table Rock, had a mini-golf tournament, and showed them all the sights. After seeing the first show, Stuart decided he needed to dress a little more country, so he bought a couple of pairs of blue jeans, two or three western shirts, a big belt with appropriate buckle, a Stetson hat, and a beautiful pair of cowboy boots. We knew he was not even a little bit country under his clothing, but were pleased he had a great time."

Abe turned a little toward Roy. "We worked and played from early to late. My blue scooter was sure low on power by the time we got home each night. The guys from New York were low on power, too. They were exhausted, but happy as a bunch of squirrels on a nest of acorns."

Don looked at Abe, "A bunch of squirrels on a nest of acorns?"

"I just made that up. Fits, though, doesn't it?"

Don smiled, "I guess. And Roy, one night Walt took the whole group on his boat to dinner at Spuds and Fish, that dumpy little place across the lake that Abe likes so well. Stuart dubbed the boat, 'Walt's Branson Limousine'. The New York guys loved Abe's restaurant. You should have seen them put away the catfish and fried potatoes."

Abe added, "They kept the waitress hopping, bringing more catfish, potatoes, okra and hushpuppies."

Walt turned his head slightly, keeping one eye directed down the road. "That was the night before they left. When I took the group in my minivan to the airport the next morning, they said they were disappointed they couldn't go by boat to the airport, and told me how much they had enjoyed riding across the lake the night before. But I noticed they were pretty quiet. I don't know if it was the fish, the cornmeal, or the grease, but they seemed to be out of energy."

"Even Stuart?" Roy asked.

"Even Stuart," Don answered. "And yes Abe, Stuart would be conspicuous riding across this country. He'd sit taller in the saddle than any horseman I've ever seen."

"Stuart is conspicuous wherever he is," Walt said." In fact, I noticed that all of the guys in that group that came to Branson look to Stuart for leadership, even a couple of the older financial guys."

Roy asked, "Tom Queen did not come?"

Abe answered, "No, he didn't. He wanted Stuart to have the lead. Oh, I learned Stuart is not as young as he looks. He spent four years flying Air Force fighter jets between getting his bachelors degree in economics and going to law school."

Roy was impressed. "Economics, leadership and law, what other background do you want in your trust attorney?"

Abe grinned, "I guess we don't need cowboy experience."

Walt broke in, "Hey, Roy, there's another huge drilling rig ahead on the left."

The conversation changed to oil and gas for a while, and subsequently changed several additional times before Walt parked the bus around the corner from Abe's little bank in Dalhart.

• • •

After completing their business in Dalhart, Roy drove, Abe slept in his bunk, and Don and Walt huddled with Roy at the front of the Road Lynx. They speculated on the contents of the mysterious envelope and box they had just seen in the safe deposit box. Their guesses ranged from a collection of bearer bonds to a horrible history of Abe's past. The three concluded that speculation was worthless, and that they could only accept and comply with the wishes of their enigmatic friend.

# CHAPTER 28

On Thursday morning in the refracted daylight of the impending sunrise at Santa Rosa, New Mexico, Walt drove the Road Lynx out of an overnight recreational vehicle park, and headed west on Interstate 40. Roy sat in the passenger seat with a road atlas on his lap. Abe and Don were still in their bunks in the back of the Road Lynx. It had been Walt's idea to get such an early start, and he had volunteered to drive. He wanted to get a few hours down the road before the heat of the day. As the big vehicle entered the right lane of the nearly empty highway, Roy advised Walt, "You won't need your steering wheel. According to the map, there are no curves for at least eighty miles."

"Fine by me. I'm hoping to get to Albuquerque for breakfast. We have another long road day ahead of us."

The group's destination for the day was Flagstaff, Arizona, five hundred miles to the west. The four would only stop to consume the second day of breakfasts provided by Emma and to refuel the Road Lynx before reaching the Petrified Forest National Park in eastern Arizona.

The four made a quick tour of the park's visitor's center, and then slowly traveled the twenty-two miles through the park, marveling at the colorful display of fossilized tree trunks and other vegetation. Three times they stopped for a closer look at rock displays, but soon found the cool comfort of the bus preferable to the bright sun and heat.

By early evening, the four travelers had checked into a motel in Flagstaff, and were walking, or in Abe's case riding, through the city's 1890s-era downtown. They were looking for a particular restaurant recommended by a friend at Ozark View. By 8:30, the four men, pleased with their friend's recommendation, were well-fed and ready to head for their motel and an early bedtime.

Breakfast the next morning was across the street from their motel at a national chain restaurant featuring "Pancakes and eggs like you want 'em." Don then steered the Road Lynx northwest toward the eastern entrance to Grand Canyon National Park.

For all four men, the big canyon would be a highlight of the trip. They lingered at each observation point. They lingered again over lunch at Bright Angel Lodge as they stared at the beautiful vista before them. They stood at the canyon's edge and looked straight down. They used binoculars and Park Service telescopes to look at distant formations and cliffs. They sat and looked, stood and looked, and leaned and looked. They took photos they knew would not do justice to the expansive vista. At mid-afternoon as they boarded the Road Lynx, Walt spoke for the group, "It is impossible to capture such magnificence on camera, by paint, or in words!"

A 180-mile drive around the eastern end of the canyon took the four men to Page, Arizona, site of Glen Canyon Dam and Lake Powell. There, they enjoyed a view of Lake Powell from a third story balcony off their motel suite. They remained on their veranda while they had a light dinner delivered by room service, enjoyed the pleasant warm evening, and watched the sun set across the lake. The temperature dropped rapidly after nightfall, but the four friends remained on the balcony, looking at the star-filled sky and the lake below. Abe called their activity "passive scenic exposure."

The four old adventurers were out of their motel before sunrise, on board a double-decker tour boat on Lake Powell in time to watch the sun flood brilliant colors onto the high rock walls of the western shore. By the time the canyon was full of sunlight, the light jackets which only a few minutes before seemed inadequate against the cold desert night air had been stowed in the backpack Roy carried for the group. Before 8:00 A.M., the tour boat had returned to its dock and the four men were onboard the Road Lynx headed northwest toward Utah's Grand Staircase Escalante National Monument and Vermillion Cliffs. They stopped at six scenic turnouts where they disembarked with binoculars and cameras. Even as the heat of day approached, the men savored each view.

At Mount Carmel Junction, Utah, Roy parked the bus in a large graveled parking area that showed no sign of ownership or use restriction. Don backed his PT Cruiser from the garage, and Roy helped Don attach a carrier onto the back of the Cruiser to transport Abe's blue scooter. Walt drove the scooter from the side door of the garage and maneuvered it onto the carrier. Don secured the scooter on the carrier with four straps, and Roy used a crank to raise the carrier's platform to the height of the PT Cruiser's bumper. Don put beverages and snacks into the Cruiser, and four guys loaded in for an excursion into Zion National Park.

Don drove over the winding roads and through the low tunnels from Zion's eastern entrance. The four joked about missing the thrill of driving the Road Lynx into the park. The Zion National Park website had warned of vehicle restrictions on the park roads which the Road Lynx exceeded in all dimensions.

Via shuttle bus and the paved scooter-accessible Riverside Walk, the four guys made a limited tour of Zion Canyon, and were back in Don's car within three hours of their arrival. Their return to Mount Carmel Junction was slow, partially because of other tourists and partially because of repeated stops at observation points to better see the magnificent etchings across the faces of huge cliffs. Throughout their tour, Abe kept his Army field glasses hanging from his neck, and frequently used them to better his view of the cream, pink and red walls. Abe's companions had no idea how lethal those glasses could be.

Walt topped off the Road Lynx's fuel tank before he drove away from Mount Carmel Junction, and headed north toward Bryce Canyon National Park, sixty miles away. The four men were surprised that the valley through which they traveled was fertile, a sharp contrast to the arid stretches of hot rocks they had seen for the past two days. Much of the highway followed a pretty stream flowing through grassy fields.

As they rode, Abe surprised his friends. "I wonder if it would be a good idea to ask Ann to join the ABRAT Board of Trustees."

Roy, sitting across from Abe at the table, responded first. "I've had a similar thought. In fact, I've wondered if we should also ask Cyn and Ruth to join the Board."

Don squirmed a little, thinking that Roy's response might scare Abe from inviting any of the ladies to join the Board. He turned in the front passenger seat to look at Abe and Roy as he spoke. "Your ideas have merit. Ann, Ruth and Cyn are compassionate and smart. Any one of them would bring useful experience and ability to the table."

"Y'all are ahead of me, aren't you?" Abe surveyed his buddies. "You've already thought about it."

Don responded, "Yes, but we know of your aversion to ladies in business, and were reluctant to mention the idea."

Roy added, "This is your trust, Abe. You should select the trustees as you see fit."

"It was my trust to start with, but it's our trust now. Before long it will be your trust to manage. I won't be around." Abe emphasized "our" and "your" as he spoke.

Don asked, "You seem to have given thought to the idea of Ann as a trustee, Abe."

Abe acknowledged he had. "She is the nicest person I've ever known. Don, you're exactly right about how compassionate our three lady friends are, especially Ann. That quality itself would be a good one to add to the board. We four guys, 'specially me, sometime miss the point when it comes to compassion. The more I think about it, the more I think Ann has caused a change in me. For most of my life, I wouldn't have given a nickel to relieve victims of corporate malfeasance."

Roy just couldn't help himself. "Ann's had support in the compassion department from Ruth and Cyn."

Abe stared at Roy. He thought. Finally Abe acknowledged Roy's point. "You're right Roy, but I'm afraid the ladies' compassionate natures will cause them difficulty in making tough decisions. So far, the trust decisions have been fairly easy, but at some time, probably soon, we'll have to say 'no' to somebody or group of somebodies. The ability to say 'no' is vital to being a good trustee. I'm afraid of loadin' the Board with compassionate ladies."

Walt had been listening, driving and not talking. He turned his head to talk over his right shoulder." We might have a conflict with Ann. When we went to Neosho to visit her, I left the group for a while and strolled a few blocks to the town square to visit Ann's son-in-law, Jim Rice. We walked from his bank across the square to get a cup of coffee. As we talked, I asked Jim about himself. I concluded he's a candidate for our job of Trust Executive. He thinks it's just a matter of time before his bank is sold to one of the big regional banks. When the bank goes, he'll be out of a job. He has adequate combined years of service and age to qualify for retirement, but thinks he's too young and has too many family responsibilities to fully retire. Without telling him so, I interviewed him for our job of Trust Executive. He has the right priorities, he's smart and has more experience and knowledge of financial markets than I would have thought possible for a small town banker. Just a minute." Walt slowed the bus and turned right off US Highway 89 onto Utah Highway 12. When he had the bus moving again, Walt resumed his comments about Ann's son-in-law. "Anyway, Jim is smart and has a good heart. He loves Ann as if she were his own mother."

Roy added, "Ann thinks the world of him. She told me one time that she thinks her daughter Amy sought a husband with the characteristics of her father, Ann's husband Warren. Ann said Jim absolutely loves and honors Amy and is a wonderful father for Ann's grandkids. He apparently meets a mother's desire for a son-in-law in how well he treats her daughter and grandkids."

"If he is such a good banker and investment man, why did he let his mother-in-law keep so much of her savings in Mid-North?" Abe asked.

"I can answer that," Don responded. "Ann told me that Jim had repeatedly suggested that she diversify from the Mid-North stock. But Warren had always told Ann what a good company Mid-North was, that Mid-North was a very safe investment, and that she would get along just fine if she kept his old employer's stock. She took Warren's advice from a former time rather than Jim's advice based on later concerns."

Abe asked, "So, how are they handling that? Money matters can impact relationships."

Don answered, "Apparently well. Jim knows and appreciates why Ann kept her Mid-North stock, but he feels badly that he didn't convince her to sell most of it before the company crashed. Ann feels badly that she didn't listen to his advice, and doesn't blame him for not being more forceful in his advice. They're both forgiving people, and they think a lot of each other."

"I don't suppose you got his résumé?" Abe asked Walt.

"No. I just used the casual interview methods I used for years in the insurance business. Most of Jim's career has been in that one bank in Neosho. But he knows a lot more about trusts than I know, and I was really impressed with his knowledge of strengths and weakness of various forms of investment. He asked good questions about ABRAT. I think some of those questions were to be sure that Ann is not being unintentionally set up to be hurt again. He's very protective of the lady."

Don looked at Walt as he spoke. "Do I hear compassion with an excellent knowledge of finance and administration?"

Walt nodded. "Yes."

Abe suggested, "Let's get his resumé and do some background checks. We'll table discussion of Ann, Ruth, or Cyn as trustees until we decide if Jim is our man for Trust Executive."

"Ummgh!" Roy's utterance drew everyone's attention from trust matters to the layered columns of rock standing on the north side of the road. Business ceased. Tourism resumed.

A few miles further, Walt steered the Road Lynx into a designated recreational vehicle spot on the parking lot of a huge motel. Don backed the PT Cruiser from the garage while Roy went into the motel's office to check in. As soon as Roy returned, Don drove the foursome into Bryce Canyon National Park.

Don followed signs to Sunset Point where the four enjoyed an impressive vista of the canyon at sunset. They were then ready for a late dinner and bed. They had been awake since before sunrise, and none of them had napped during the day. Don, though, delayed his sleep in order to get thirty minutes in the motel's hot tub.

It was past nine o'clock the next morning, well after sunrise, before the four friends stood at Sunrise Point, the first of a dozen vistas comprising their mid-day viewing of Bryce Canyon. Their common favorite was Bryce Point, which features a colorful amphitheater of hoodoos, or rock pillars. Because it was Sunday, Walt, Don, and Roy thought a short worship service would be appropriate. Don sang "How Great Thou Art," Walt said a prayer, and Roy offered a short devotional in which he summarized the vastness and minuteness of God's creation. Abe remained respectfully quiet throughout the service.

By one o'clock in the afternoon, the four efficient tourists were out of the park, and loading onto the bus for a 200-mile drive northwest to meet U.S. Highway 50 near the Nevada border. From there, they headed west and soon began their journey across the breadth of Nevada. They stopped for the night about sixty-five miles into Nevada at Ely, a town of less than 4000 people and the last town of any size for the next 256 miles.

Highway 50 approximately follows the same course as the original Pony Express route and the Lincoln Highway, America's first transcontinental highway. The highway is touted by the Nevada Tourism Office as "the nation's loneliest road." On that lonely road between Ely and Fallon there are few towns, but one, Eureka, drew the interest of the four old travelers. In 2004, Eureka had a population of less than 800 people, but during the Silver boom of the late 1800s, the town was home to more than 8000 inhabitants. Due to a fire in 1879, much of the town was rebuilt with brick buildings featuring fireproof iron shutters and doors. At Eureka, the foursome took a break for lunch and toured the buildings that had survived from the silver era.

Highway 50 crosses miles of open range. West of Eureka, Roy had to slow the Road Lynx and honk its horn repeatedly in order to clear the road of cattle. As he slowed for this unique road hazard, Roy looked for traffic ahead or behind him. He could see for miles in either direction, but did not see another vehicle of any kind.

The four guys passed opportunities to explore other silver mining relics, but stopped long enough for photos of Sand Mountain, a 600-foot hill of sand stretching for two miles. Abe joked that he was undecided whether to play on the mountain on his blue scooter or on his Stella. None of the four were interested in renting an ATV to cavort on the sand. They pressed on toward Carson City, the capitol city of Nevada, located only ten miles from Lake Tahoe on Nevada's border with California.

After a quick tour of the Nevada Capitol Building, and a slow drive down a few of the oldest streets in Carson City, the foursome headed to South Lake Tahoe, California where Walt had made arrangements to park the Road Lynx at a lakeside resort featuring a recreational vehicle park, marina, hotel, and restaurant on the same grounds.

As the bus approached this intermediate destination, Abe became still. When Walt pulled into the resort, Abe quietly told Roy, "I'm really glad to be here. I'm glad I made it this far."

Roy had no response, except to give his mysterious friend a hint of a wrinkled grin.

# CHAPTER 29

Four old guys, three walking and one riding, followed a boardwalk from their hotel to the adjacent marina. At Abe's request, Walt had arranged a four-day rental of a nineteen-foot low- powered pontoon boat outfitted for scenic cruising. Walt had spent extra time on the telephone with the marina manager making sure that the boat would accommodate Abe's scooter in loading, unloading, and getting around on deck. Today, Walt, Don and Roy would accompany Abe on a lake cruise. On Wednesday and Thursday, the three would leave Abe alone, and would travel to Yosemite.

Don, Roy, and especially Walt were uncomfortable with leaving their older friend in the unfamiliar area, and insisted on assuring themselves that Abe could handle the boat without them. Walt again volunteered to stay with Abe.

"You go on with Don and Roy," Abe told Walt. "After y'all help me check out the boat, I'll be fine. I'll tip the guys at the marina to help me on and off and to provision the boat. I'll have my cell phone with me, and a GPS device. I'll just go real slow, and glide along the lakeshore far enough out to avoid rocks. I may even drift and nap."

"That's when you'll hit the rocks," Walt warned. "You have to wear a life vest."

"What if I drown? It won't make many days difference in how long I expect to live, will it?"

"You're not planning to drown, are you?" Walt emphasized "planning."

"No. I want to make the Alaskan trip and do some other stuff." Abe did not mention his plans for the fourth scoundrel, which came under his category of "other stuff."

Walt was still uncomfortable as the group arrived at the boat. He, Don, and Roy would not help Abe onto the boat. In fact, they would leave all of the arrangements and directions to Abe. What Walt did not know was that Abe had been at the marina when it opened that morning and had tipped the marina's dockhands in advance. Those dockhands were ready for Abe, and Walt was pleasantly surprised at how well the boarding, instructions and provisioning went.

Today, the four guys would gently circle the lake, making several stops for meals, gas, and stretching. Abe sat at the controls, cautiously eased the boat away from the dock, turned it, and slowly headed west along the southern end of the lake. The sun was at the men's backs, they relaxed with the coffee and cinnamon rolls that Abe had made certain were in the provisions. No one suggested they hurry. All four men absorbed the beauty surrounding them. They had field glasses and cameras at the ready, and used them frequently. Abe's World War II Army forward observer field glasses looked distinctly outdated among the modern binoculars worn by his boating companions.

Throughout early morning, Abe provided his cruise mates with a continuous monologue of data concerning Lake Tahoe. "The lake's natural rim is 6220 feet or so above sea level, its deepest point is about 1640 feet, and the lake is the tenth deepest in the world. Tahoe was not formed by a volcano's crater like Crater Lake in Oregon, but was formed by faulting and volcanic flows. It contains enough water to cover California to a depth of 14 inches, or Texas to a depth of 9 inches."

Walt interjected, "Based on those numbers, Lake Tahoe would cover Rhode Island with about one hundred seventy-five feet of water."

Roy smiled at his friend and said, "I think you've been mathematically deprived since you retired."

Abe added, "If you say so, Walt." He continued his data dump. "Tahoe is fed by sixty-three different streams and rivers, but only one river, the Truckee at the north end of the lake, flows out."

"Does the Truckee flow west though California, or into Nevada?" Don asked.

"Into Nevada, and not very far. It ends at Pyramid Lake, a desert lake north of Sparks and Reno."

Roy spoke, "I've heard Lake Tahoe is bottomless, but you said that it is sixteen hundred something feet deep. Which is correct?"

Abe grinned, "I'm correct, and I'm offended you asked. No, the bottomless thing is like other bottomless reports, false."

"Another super story is gone." Roy feigned disappointment.

The data divulgence and banter went on, interrupted from time to time by fantastic new scenes and necessary stops.

As the group neared the northwest portion of the lake, Abe steered the boat a bit closer to shore and paid keen attention to the reading of his GPS monitor. Abe was looking for the Tahoe home of Gilbert Glass, the fourth scoundrel.

"You're paying a lot of attention to that GPS device," Roy asserted. "Are you marking a spot because you see so many fishermen in this area?"

"Yeah, this is the fourth place that I've noticed plenty of fishing going on. I've made a note of each position. These GPS things amaze me. But they don't amaze me as much as these beautiful homes on this beautiful lake," Abe's comment was intended to divert Roy's attention from his GPS activity. Abe raised his field glasses to look at the deck of the house which he mentally calculated sat right on his target GPS reading.

Roy also turned his gaze to the homes, but quickly refocused on the beautiful mountain backdrop.

Abe started a bit when he saw a man walk onto the deck of the house he had pinpointed as belonging to Gilbert Glass. Abe held his field glasses steady, slowly turning the focus knob until he could best see the man's face. He saw the face of Gilbert Glass! Abe did not have to check the photo of Glass in his pocket. He was sure. Abe slipped his finger to the safety of his weapon just as Walt stepped exactly between Abe and his target. Abe put down his glasses. He felt a sense of relief. He had not wanted to do the job in the presence of his friends, but he did not want to miss an opportunity, either. When Walt moved on toward the drink cooler, Abe again raised his old field glasses. Glass was no longer on the deck. Abe sighed.

"What was that sigh about?" Don asked.

"Oh, a long time ago I wanted a place here, but never got around to buying one. I was too busy making money. I don't think I'll buy one now."

Walt speculated, "Just think, Abe, if you had bought a house here you might have retired here and would not have come to Ozark View. You would have a completely different group of friends, and you probably wouldn't have established your trust to help all the people hurt by scoundrels. I'm glad you didn't buy a house here."

Roy agreed, "Yeah, these houses are nice to look at, but I wouldn't want you to live here."

"Nice thought, Walt." Abe replied as he privately wondered what it would have been like to be a friend of Gilbert Glass. Abe shuddered, and Roy noticed.

"Why the shivering, Abe? Cold?"

"Naw. I just thought how much I would have missed if I had not come to Ozark View."

Don changed the subject to a more immediate need. "Abe, I think there's a marina a few miles north of here. We could take a bathroom break there, and have lunch."

Abe slid the throttle handle forward a couple of notches, slowly increasing the boat's speed. Don was right. The group found a marina owned by the same firm that owned the marina from which they had rented the boat on the south end of the lake. Disembarking went smoothly. Abe tipped liberally. Don, Walt and Roy were satisfied that

Abe would not likely be dropped into the lake by a surly dockhand while he used the boat alone over the next two days.

At lunch Abe was quiet. He hoped he had not missed his only chance to hit Gilbert Glass, but he was glad that he had not sent a beam into Walt. Nobody other than a target had ever stepped into Abe's beam. Nobody had blocked his shot the way Walt had accidentally done today. Abe was not sure what would have happened if he had hit Walt with a beam focused for a remote target. He thought Walt would not have been hurt, but he was not certain. Abe shuddered again.

Roy noticed the quiver, but said nothing. He would later speculate to Walt and Don that Abe's trembling indicated their friend's deteriorating health.

After lunch and a pleasant stroll through North Lake Tahoe, the group returned to their boat. The dockhands were again very helpful, and the four men were soon cruising. Abe set the throttle for a "fast crawl" as opposed to the "slow crawl" rate of travel during the morning. As they headed down Lake Tahoe's eastern shore, Abe noticed a squall off to the west. He especially noticed how quickly the squall moved northward, and promised himself to be alert over the next two days for sudden weather changes.

"That lightning in the west is spectacular!" Roy exclaimed as he, too, noticed the squall across the lake." It reminds me of storms I witnessed on the great plains of Kansas, Texas and Oklahoma."

"I'm glad it's over there and moving north," Don voiced. "Abe, keep your eyes open tomorrow. I'd hate for you to get fried while we're gone."

"How would you feel about my being fried in your presence?" Abe countered.

"Well if you were to get fried right now, I'd be fried too. I'm ready to go home, ya know."

"I'll keep my eyes open," Abe mumbled.

# CHAPTER 30

Again the marina dockhands were extra helpful to Abe, and again he tipped them well. Today they had provisioned his boat for an all-day trip, including fishing gear and iced storage for his catch. Abe was not expecting to return with many fish in his well, but he hoped for one or two to serve as a cover for the real purpose of his excursion.

As he set out, he did not tour the southwestern part of the lake as he and his friends had the day before, but headed directly toward a spot about one mile north of Gilbert Glass's house. Only as he drew near to Glass's house did he adjust his course westward so that he was soon several hundred feet off the shore, directly east of Glass's deck. Abe slowed the boat, turned into the light breeze, and cut off the engine. The lake was quiet. He could hear the splash of small waves against his boat's pontoons. Two other boats were drifting nearby. With a wry smile, Abe wondered if people on those boats were standing by to shoot Gilbert Glass. He chuckled to himself, poured himself a full cup of coffee and resolved to finish all of it before he began fishing, placing himself on one of the boat's bench seats facing west, toward his target's house.

From where his boat drifted, Abe was not close enough to accurately use his weapon, but he was close enough to see if anybody was on the deck. Nobody was. He would have to wait.

Abe finished two cups of coffee before he began fishing. When he eventually reached for the fishing rod, he debated whether to use a lure, or just throw a weighted line into the water. He opted for a lure, one similar to one of his favorites many years before when he had spent a little time fishing in South Louisiana. Abe considered the difference between the muddy water in Louisiana's bayous versus the clear water in Lake Tahoe. He didn't care if the lure worked or not. But it did. Within an hour Abe had caught a mackinaw. When he checked his fishing card, he found that two of these pretty lake trout would be the daily limit, and that five fish was the total daily limit. Abe changed his lure, he wanted a fish or two in the well, but he did not want to reach his limit.

From time to time Abe reeled in his line, and moved north or south on the lake. Before noon he twice went into a port for necessary stops. Abe had to guess when to break away. He had not yet seen anyone on Gilbert Glass's deck, and had no idea as to when Glass might appear.

Soon after sunset Abe glided his boat southward past Glass's house. There were lights in the house, but nobody on the deck. Nobody had been on the deck all day, at least not when Abe had been observing. Abe regretted that he had not hit Glass the day before, but shrugged, increased his boat's speed and headed for the marina. He arrived well after dark, and presented his single fish to the dockhand who tagged it with Abe's name and took it to the marina restaurant. For dinner Abe had fresh lake trout, a baked potato, seasoned green beans, and two slices of peach pie. A red light on Abe's scooter warned of a low battery as Abe drove the scooter out of the restaurant and down the board walkway toward the hotel.

In his room, Abe plugged the stumpy cord on the scooter's battery charger into an extension cord that Roy had plugged in before he left. Abe looked around the room as he shuffled to his duffle bag to get clean underwear. He again thought of his three buddies as he had off and on all day. He missed his friends, but was ready for a shower and bed. Abe considered that his most difficult task that day had been to patiently wait for his target. Patience could be very tiring.

# CHAPTER 31

Abe left the marina well before daylight, again well provisioned. This time he had asked for extra cinnamon rolls. He could think of nothing he would like to do more than drift on a beautiful lake while eating cinnamon rolls and drinking coffee.

Lake Tahoe rules prohibit fishing before daylight, which suited Abe. In fact, it was well past daylight before Abe dropped a line into the water one hundred yards from Gilbert Glass's deck. Amazing! Another lake trout! Abe grinned as he looked at it before he dropped his flopping trophy into the fish well. He changed lures to the one so beneficially ineffective the day before and again threw his line into the water. He sat and waited. Neither fish, nor target appeared. Abe was pleased he caught no more fish, but he was not happy with the lack of activity on Gilbert Glass's deck. If he had not seen lights in the house the prior evening, Abe might have thought the house was empty.

The cinnamon rolls satisfied Abe's desire for food. As noon passed, Abe was content to drift and wait. He got a little sleepy, but awoke fast when he saw a man rush onto the deck of the house next to Glass's and raise a small craft lake warning pennant. At the same time, Abe saw four people dash down stairs from Glass's house to a big lake cruiser tied to Glass's dock. Abe looked south, and saw what had spawned the action. A squall was quickly approaching, a storm bigger and uglier than the one he had observed two days before from across the lake.

Abe hurriedly turned his boat north, gave full throttle to the engine, and headed to the marina at North Lake Tahoe. He was sorry that he had asked Walt to rent a low-powered boat. Other boats seemed to be moving much faster than his.

The big cruiser from Glass's house left its slip, entered the lake and also headed north. Abe started to raise his glasses, but as he did so, realized he needed both hands on the boat's steering wheel. Even at the low top speed of the pontoon boat, his arthritic body hurt from the boat's bumps, and his weak hands ached as he held the wheel. The cruiser was not long in range. It was much faster than Abe's little boat, and it stayed close to the shore, taking the most direct route toward North Lake Tahoe.

By minutes, Abe's boat beat the storm to the same marina he and his buddies had visited two days before. A dockhand waved Abe to a space well away from the marina's entrance, in the shallower area. As Abe entered the marina, he spotted Gilbert Glass's boat, and saw that it had drawn the attention of the dockhands. He could see Gilbert Glass himself ducking in and out of the cabin. Abe would likely have to sit on his boat until the crew finished its work with Glass's boat.

Glass and his friends had tarried on the big cruiser, and only left it as Abe slid the pontoon boat into its assigned slip. The four, two men and two women, apparently were making a dash for a restaurant across the street from the marina, trying to get to their chosen luncheon spot before the storm hit. Their timing would be close. Wind and waves were pounding the marina as Glass's group disembarked. Large drops of wind-driven rain began making two-inch wet ovals on dock planks as the four people struggled along the rolling runway.

Abe's boat rocked and the entire marina heaved with the sudden waves from the storm. The thunder behind the storm was deafening, and the air was filled with bright bursts of lightning and the odor of ozone. Abe watched as Glass, with his friends in front of him, ran along the heaving dock to a short stairway leading to street level. Abe raised his glasses and focused on the third step of the stairs, but he doubted he could get a shot as his boat pitched and rolled in the storm. He held onto the steering wheel with his left hand, letting go just as Gilbert Glass got to the stairs. He aimed at Glass's back. Abe's boat was rolling and he was reluctant to fire erratically. Abe steadied his aim, but couldn't press the trigger.

A huge bolt of lightning struck the flagpole next to the stairway Glass was climbing, shaking everything in the marina, including Abe. The brightness momentarily blinded Abe. The sound hurt his ears. Abe fell or was knocked to the deck of the pontoon boat. He thought he had been hit by lightning, but did not feel burns or pain, only the overwhelming feeling that he had been hit by something many times bigger and stronger than anything he had ever experienced. *Now what?* he thought.

Abe's boat was banging in the slip as lightning continued to crash nearby. He couldn't get up. *Hell, if I were at Ozark View in my cottage, I could crawl to a bell cord and call for help. There ain't no bell cord on this boat.*

Abe could not hear a youthful dockhand as he called for Abe to stay on the deck, and he didn't see the young man jump onto his boat. He only saw two feet land near him as the boat banged the side of the slip and dropped downward. The dockhand on the boat caught a rope from another dockhand, and the two of them lashed the boat's aft port side to the slip. The first dockhand crawled toward the bow, where he and his partner lashed the forward port side to the slip. The boat continued to surge, but within the constraints of its lines.

The dockhand crawled to Abe. "Are you hurt, mister?"

"Mostly my pride. I think I'm okay. First I thought I had been hit by that lightning."

"You weren't?"

Even though Abe could see the young man within two feet of him, through Abe's ears his voice seemed to be distant, a product of the overwhelming lightning strike. His own voice likewise sounded distant when he replied, "No, otherwise I think I would be burned somewhere. It knocked me to the floor, though."

"Yeah, I saw you go down. It knocked down the guy on the stair, too. Mr. Glass."

"Oh?"

Another huge crash of lightning made both the young man and the old man hug the deck.

Abe wanted to get up and to look to where Gilbert Glass was probably on the ground. But he didn't dare, concerned lest he fall again and get hurt. As he lay on the deck with his new young friend, Abe questioned himself, *I wonder if Glass went down because of the lightning or because I jumped and triggered my weapon? I don't even know that I triggered my weapon, but I might have. Even if I did though, my shot was probably wild.*

Although the boat slip was covered by the marina's Plexiglas roof, the wind was driving heavy rain almost horizontally onto Abe's boat, filling the deck with water, and soaking Abe and the young dockhand.

The dockhand yelled to Abe over the noises of the thunder and the groaning marina, "When the storm lets up a little, we can make a run for the marina office."

"I haven't made a run for anything in years. I can't even get up without help. I'm already wet. You can make a run for it as soon as you dare. I'll be all right, and if I'm not, it's okay because I'm old and ready to go." As Abe said this, he wondered if he was really ready to die. According to Don's test, Abe wasn't.

"I'll go see if they need help with Mr. Glass and his party. Are you sure you're all right?"

"No, but I don't want to get up! Not until this storm passes!"

Abe watched his young friend jump quickly to the marina dock and disappear in the direction of the street. As he did so, Abe heard the wail of a siren intermittent with crashing thunder, which was no longer as loud as earlier. In fact, he noticed his boat was not surging as much as it had been. Abe heard the siren stop nearby, and saw flashing red and white lights.

Abe reached for his field glasses. He wanted to turn on the weapon's safety. But where were they? He could not find the glasses as he groped around the area of his head, shoulders and upper body. Finally, Abe quit hugging the deck and propped himself up on his elbows. He looked around the deck for his field glasses, but did not see them.

*I guess I could have thrown them when that big bolt hit,* he thought.

Another big shot of lightning nearby made Abe hug the deck again. This time, though, Abe kept his arm between his head and the deck because the water was more than an inch deep. *I need to remove the scupper plug,* he told himself.

Abe raised himself enough to crawl to the edge of the boat's platform and pulled loose a scupper cover, allowing the water to flow overboard from the deck. He thought about trying to pull himself onto a cushioned bench seat, but thought better of it as another bolt of lightning struck nearby. It seemed to be farther away and less ferocious than previous bolts, but it was still a force to be honored.

"Mister, where are you? Oh, there. You opened the scupper. Good for you. The storm's letting up. Are you ready to run for it?" The young dockhand had jumped onto the boat.

"No. I don't run. But if you'll help me up, we can walk. How's...." Abe started to say "Glass," but caught himself. "How's the guy on the stairs."

"Bad! Real bad! He's burned. He looks like he's blind. His head is hanging funny. Not funny. Strange. He can't move anything, and he's having trouble breathing. My manager gave him CPR until the ambulance came. I couldn't do anything to help, so I came back to check on you."

"Did you tell them about me?"

"No, but maybe I should have told the EMTs. They could check you out."

"I can check myself out. You did the right thing. I'm not hurt. There's no need to distract the emergency people. Let's get into that office. What's your name?"

"Don."

"I have another good friend named Don."

Don helped Abe get up, step off the rocking boat and walk down the swaying dock. Within two minutes, Abe was sitting in the marina office. Don got Abe a towel and a cup of coffee, and got himself a towel and soft drink.

Don was shaking when he returned to Abe. "Mister, I thought you were dead when you went down."

"Me too, but it turns out not to be so. You're shakin'. Are you cold?"

"I'm still scared."

"Me too, but I'm more cold. Can I buy some dry clothes in the store?"

"Shorts, tee shirts, sweat pants, and sweatshirts. All of them have 'Lake Tahoe' written on them."

"That's fine. I'll give you some money. You go buy me a pair of sweat pants, tee shirt, and sweat shirt. Oh, and underwear if they have it. Also get me a windbreaker jacket and a dry bucket hat. Get dark blue for everything if they have it. If not, use your judgment. Just don't get me something girlie like pink or purple or something with butterflies on it. All of it should be men's small. Get yourself a dry outfit, too, whatever you want. Here are three hundred wet dollars. If that's not enough tell 'em they want too much and negotiate the price down." Abe grinned. "Is that a restroom over there? I think I'll go strip."

Abe pushed on the chair arms to raise himself, tested his ability to stand, and with Don walking at his elbow, shuffled to the restroom.

"I saw your scooter on the boat. I don't know what the water will do to it." Don said.

"I don't think it will hurt it. The manufacturer makes its scooters capable of carrying people through rainstorms."

"I'll dry the scooter for you and help you with your boat after we get dry clothes. Thanks for thinking about my wet clothes, too."

"Thank you, Don. Now get going. I'm cold."

Abe wasted no time getting his wet clothes off even though every movement hurt. By the time he had dried himself, Don was knocking on the door.

"Mister, I have dry clothes for you. Picking "dark blue" and size "small" made it easy. I got you a laundry bag for your wet clothes, too." Don handed a plastic bag full of clothing to Abe through the partially opened door. "Oh, and here's your change. I didn't need it all."

"Keep the change. You're doing me one favor after another. Do you work here year around, or do you go to school somewhere?"

"I go to UC Davis. Uh, I don't know where you're from, but that's the University of California at Davis."

"Yes. It's a great school. What's your major?" As he asked, Abe was slipping into his new dark blue, very brief undershorts with "Tahoe" across the back.

"Biochemistry. Or, it will be. I just finished my first year. I mostly worked on general requirements, like most freshmen."

"Do you like chemistry? Did you have a class in high school?"

"Yes, and biology, too. I liked them both and got A's"

"Are you going to use this place to change when I finish?"

"No, we have a locker room."

"You go ahead and change. I'll wait for you in the office. I don't hear rain now."

"Yes sir. I'll see you in a few minutes."

Abe hurt all over as he dressed himself faster than he normally would. He did not want to linger around the marina and be asked questions he did not want to answer. But before he left, he wanted to learn more about the status of Gilbert Glass. *I don't know if this situation is gonna have a great outcome or a lousy outcome,* Abe thought to himself as he slipped a blue sweat shirt over his blue tee shirt. He was still cold.

The marina manager rushed into the office just as Abe exited the restroom. "Are you the man that was knocked down on the pontoon boat?"

"I don't know that I was knocked down. I was startled by the big bolt of lightning and fell. I stayed down because I don't get up very easily and because it just seemed like a good idea with all of that lightning flying about." Abe paused. "Don told me somebody got hurt bad."

"Yes, one of our regular customers got hit by the lightning. The paramedics took him to the hospital along with the three people with him. The three others seemed to have only minor burns. I think they're lucky that's all they got. Dashing across a street in an air-to-ground lightning storm is not a good idea. But are you hurt at all? Don said you were not, but I wanted to check myself."

"I'm fine. And thanks to Don, I'm now dry and wearin' new clothes from your store. Don helped me a lot. He's a good hand."

"He's one of my best hands. But he's only here in the summer and over college vacations."

"I hope you don't mind. He was so helpful to me that I bought him some dry clothes, too. I don't know what you pay him, but you can give him a raise as far as I'm concerned. While you were lookin' after the most serious problem, he was lookin' after me."

"I'm glad he did. I'm not surprised. He's a good kid. He was raised by his grandparents who both work for the county. He needs to work for school money, and he does a good job."

"About the guy that got hit by lightnin', what kind of injuries did he have?"

"Bad. He was burned all over, blinded, looked to be paralyzed, and his head hung at an awkward angle to the side. He couldn't hear, but appeared to be conscious because he kept moving his shoulders. It looked like all he could move were his shoulders."

"Could he talk?"

"No, and he could barely breathe."

"You said he's a customer?"

"Yes, he docks his boat here when he wants to eat at a nearby restaurant or when he wants the boat serviced. Otherwise, he uses the yacht club marina up that way. He lives south of here in one of those places that could fund my retirement along with a several others."

"What's his name?"

"Gilbert Glass. He's been a part time resident here for a long time. He gives a lot of money for things like the Fourth of July celebration and other civic stuff. He's some kind of big-time financier."

"Think he'll live?'

"I doubt it. Even if he does, he might not want to. He won't be like before."

"Nope, it sounds like he won't. Oh, here's Don. He's gonna help me get my boat underway. I don't want to miss any time on this beautiful lake of yours."

"It was an ugly lake a few minutes ago," the marina manager admitted.

"No. It was a beautiful lake with an ugly storm. I want to get going." Abe headed to the door with Don falling in behind him wearing dark blue shorts and tee shirt.

"Our shoes are still soggy," Don said as they headed to the boat.

"Well, I can slosh in mine. I guess you can, too. Huh?" Abe responded.

"Yes sir." Don had a handful of towels with him, and immediately set about drying Abe's scooter. He then dried the console, the two swivel seats, and began working on the bench seats.

As he did so, Abe looked over the boat deck, and over the side. He was looking for his field glasses. He asked Don, "You haven't seen an old pair of field glasses have you? I musta lost mine."

"This may be them. The strap caught on the cleat below the line I used to secure your boat during the storm. Just a minute. It looks like they almost went into the lake."

Don untied the line, and raised the innocuous-looking old field glasses. They dripped water as he raised them. He handed them to Abe, saying, "These look like old favorites. I'm sure you want to keep them."

"Well, I've certainly gotten my money's worth from 'em. Those glasses and I have done a lot together. Thanks for finding them."

"You're welcome. Did you lose them when the lightning hit?"

Abe lied. "I don't know exactly when I lost them. I was intent on getting off that lake. I could have lost them at any time between when I first saw the storm coming and when you tied the boat."

Abe picked up his coffee cup from the helmsman's chair, and looked around for his pump pot containing coffee. It must have gone overboard. He looked over the sides of the boat, looking directly to the lake bottom, but did not see the pot.

"What are you looking for?" Don asked as he finished toweling the boat's railings.

"This morning your sister marina down south put two pump pots on the boat, one with water and one with coffee. I found the one with water, but haven't found the one with coffee."

"I'll get you another pot, and refill or replace the water pot while I'm at it. Do you need anything else?"

"No. I got gas earlier. Everything in the waterproof lockers is dry, like it should be. I'm ready to go. Abe slid another one hundred dollar bill into Don's hand.

Don thanked Abe warmly, and soon returned with a fresh supply of coffee and water. "The manager said there would be no charge for the new pot and coffee. He's really glad you weren't hurt."

"Me too, and I'm ready to go thanks to you, Don. Study hard at Davis. Cast off my lines, please."

Abe eased from the slip, and slowly moved away from the marina. He spoke softly to himself as he did so. *Well, my last hit was a dandy, and I don't even know if I did it. Maybe there is a God.* He thought about what he had just said to himself. *Maybe I should think about that.*

When Abe was well onto the lake, he picked up his field glasses. He wanted to check on the "special" features. He switched on the safety, and checked his battery charge. It was low. He had probably triggered his weapon when the big lightning bolt hit. *But even if I did, I don't know if I hit Glass or if all the damage is from lightning.* He grinned, *Maybe Glass got a double whammy, from me and the lightning. Justice for the main scoundrel, maybe.*

Abe headed straight for the point he had left when the storm approached. He was pleased to see floating in the area some of the same boats that had been there before the storm. He cut the boat's motor and drifted, poured himself a cup of coffee, found a cinnamon roll in the food locker, and slipped onto a bench seat for a quiet celebration. Later, he would put his favorite lure on his line, and try to bring in a second lake trout. "My buddies might like fresh fish tonight," he mumbled. However, he caught no more fish, and an hour before sunset he headed for the south shore.

• • •

Walt, Roy and Don had returned from Yosemite, and were on the dock waiting for Abe when he glided into a slip. The marina manager had told them about the storm on the north end of the lake, and that Abe had made the North Lake Tahoe Marina just in time. He also told them Abe had been knocked down but not hurt by lightning, and had been soaked by the rain. From a dockhand they had learned that another man had been hit by lightning at the north shore marina, and that he was in the hospital.

"Had enough excitement for one day, Mr. Brown?" Walt called to Abe who was still in his boat. "They've told us about your adventure."

"Yeah, I was in a plenty scary storm! I guess news travels fast between company locations. Did the marina people tell y'all about it?"

"I don't know if it's 'all about it,' but it's interesting," Walt answered. "Were you hurt when the lightning knocked you down?"

"No, but I stayed flat on the deck for a while. Lightning was flashing all around. A nice kid working at the marina helped me. We both hugged the deck for a while. One of the marina's regular customers got hit by lightning."

Roy boarded the pontoon boat and pointed to Abe's shirt. "That's a nice new outfit you're wearing Abe. Did you go shopping today, too?"

"I hit the deck as it was filling with rain water. I got soaked. Well, the way the rain was blowing in waves, I was getting' soaked anyway. I have a bag full of wet clothes in one of these lockers. By the way, Don, the kid that helped me so much was named Don. He reminded me of a young version of you. He's studying biochemistry at UC Davis.

"If he's studying biochemistry, he's not a young version of me." Then Don smiled as he asked, "Other than a ferocious storm in which you were almost killed by lightning, how was the rest of your day, Abe?"

"It was really good, an excellent day. Thank you. How was your trip to Yosemite?" Abe did not elaborate about the event that made his day so great.

# CHAPTER 32

Walt, Don, and Roy played golf during the morning while Abe went for another boat ride. Abe cruised along the southeast shoreline, and spent much of his time looking at the backdrop of mountains. He felt as if he were soaking in memories of the beautiful scenery. It seemed good for his soul.

Abe also thought more of his last hit, or if it was in fact his hit at all. Had he really sent a beam into Gilbert Glass, or was Glass hit only by the lightning? He thought of something he had heard Walt say one time, that we sin not only when we take physical action, but also when we think about wronging our fellowman. Abe wondered why he should worry about the difference. Even if God only counted recent physical sins, Abe knew he had at least four big ones within the last ninety days.

Abe thought more about the specifics of the incident with Glass. *I was aiming my weapon at Glass's back, but was not able to push the trigger! I probably hit it when I jumped because of the big lightning bolt. So was that an accident or a willing act impelled by trauma?*

Abe concentrated on his real question. *Why was I unable to trigger the weapon when I had it aimed at Glass? Even though he was jogging and I was moving up and down on my heaving boat, Glass was a fairly easy target. There was a difference about yesterday. I was unable to shoot. Never before have I been unable to push the trigger. Something is different. I suspect I know why. My heart has changed. Or has it?*

Something else bothered Abe. He felt no joy when he thought of Glass lying blind, deaf and paralyzed in agony on a hospital bed. His initial pleasure at the apparent success of the hit had faded.

But Abe wasn't sad, either. He was glad the fourth scoundrel could no longer hurt people, especially large numbers of people. Abe calculated that he had no more passion about Glass's condition than he would have had for a weed pulled from a garden.

Abe returned to the main question. *I just couldn't push the trigger. Why?* He groped for a source to help answer his question. *I can't exactly tell my buddies that I was literally aiming to kill a man, but couldn't quite do it, but maybe I did do it when the lighting bolt startled me. Now I have no joy or remorse. I can't ask 'em to explain this to me or if the Bible covers this situation. They don't even know there was a fourth scoundrel, and I don't think they suspect I knocked off the three scoundrels they knew about. They would tie it all together if I told them about my weapon.*

Abe continued to sit, think, and stare at the beautiful scenery as he let his boat glide slowly through the water. *Don would tell me to pray about it. But I don't know how. Don also says that prayer is just talkin' to God and listenin' to him. I wouldn't know if God told me somethin'. I guess I could talk to God. Maybe I should. I guess it can't hurt. I'm out here all by myself.* Abe paused. *Somethin' about me has changed!*

Abe switched off the boat's engine, letting the boat drift. Abe compared the quiet around him now to the noise of yesterday's storm. He compared the light splash of small waves against the pontoons to the crashing of thunder and the noise of the banging of boats against docks during the squall. *This is kinda like a big outdoor chapel,* he thought. *I wonder if I should pray audibly or silently. That is, if I do pray.* He knew the answer. It would make no difference. *Should I get on my knees or sit here like I am?* He thought of a comment Walt had once made, "Getting on your knees to pray helps you get your attitude right and helps you concentrate on your prayer, but you can also pray as you drive a car."

Abe braced himself on the bench seat as he slowly lowered his aching body to kneel. He put his elbows and forearms on the seat, and looked at the majestic mountains in the distance. *God, if you are really ther. . . no, I don't question that anymore. God, I don't know if I caused some or all of Gilbert Glass's injuries yesterday.* Abe paused. *No that's not what this is about. I don't understand why I was not able to push the trigger yesterday. Somethin' has changed about me. I don't know what. If it is you, please let me know. If there is somethin' I should do or say, let me know. If you don't let me know, I'll just know I'm a tired old man who has lost his spunk for livin', and for killin'. My friend Don says I'm supposed to listen to you, but I don't know what to listen for. Do you whisper or yell? Do I simply get the right thought all of a sudden and know it's from you? How will I know what the right thought is, or do you take care of that, too? I want some peace, God. Now, I guess I'm supposed to shut up and listen.*

• • •

A horn blast from a nearby fishing boat abruptly woke Abe. "Hello on the pontoon boat! Wake up! You're about to go onto the rocks!"

Startled, Abe looked about. He had been asleep with his head on his arms on the bench seat, his body leaning against the boat's forward railing. He felt pain shoot all over his body as he grabbed the boat's rail and tried jerking himself to a standing position. He couldn't. He turned on his knees and crawled to the helm. He raised himself as much as he could while still on his knees, located the rocks and picked a clear path to deep water. He started the engine, turned the wheel, slipped the transmission into forward gear, and moved away from shore. He didn't go far. He could not see well. He put the engine in neutral, and slowly lifted his sore body into the helmsman's chair. He waved at the fishermen who had warned him. He noticed that one of them was still holding an anchor, which Abe presumed he had planned to throw onto Abe's boat if he and his partner had not been able to rouse Abe. "Thanks, fellas," Abe called." I musta dozed off."

"You're welcome. You looked peaceful. Are you all right?"

"Yeah, fine." Abe thought about his prayer, the fisherman's comment, and that in fact he did feel peaceful. "I'm more than fine now. Thanks, again."

"Glad to help. You scared us."

Abe looked at his watch, and called to the fishermen, "I have to go. Good luck fishin'!"

As he shifted into forward gear, Abe whispered to himself, *And the answer is: It is not important that I know whether I hit Glass or whether the lightning did all the damage.*

# CHAPTER 33

"Mail call, gentlemen!" Roy announced to his three traveling companions as he strolled from the office of the RV park toward Don's waiting PT Cruiser. Roy was carrying a box measuring approximately twelve by twelve by fifteen inches. It bore a FedEx label and had been sent from Branson by Cyn Smith. The contents should be their mail, personal mail and mail for the Abe Brown Retirement Assistance Trust.

Don could not open the hatchback of his little red car because of Abe's scooter on the carrier, so Roy dropped the mail box over the back seat into the storage area beside Don's blue cooler. Roy then turned in the seat to sit beside Walt. Abe was in front. Don was the driver.

Today, their last day at Tahoe, the four men would circle the lake by automobile. Other than taking in the scenery, their plans included shopping for quality souvenirs for their friends in Missouri and New York, lunch at the prettiest spot they could find, and a meeting of the ABRAT Board of Trustees. The foursome now considered it to be Board policy to meet whenever possible in a pretty outdoor setting.

Abe showed signs of fatigue, but seemed to be in high spirits. He announced as Don shifted the PT Cruiser into drive, "Dinner is on me tonight! I suggest that specialty steak place in that huge brown hotel just down the road from the RV park."

His offer was readily accepted by Walt, Don and Roy. They had no idea that they were accepting an invitation to a celebration of another scoundrel's downfall.

Don drove eastward into Nevada. He soon turned north along the east edge of the lake. The group's late morning start and counter-clockwise route around the lake would take full advantage of bright sunlight on magnificent scenery. It was not long before Don picked a spot for lunch and mail call.

While Don and Walt set out the food, Roy used his pocket knife to open the FedEx package. He and Abe began sorting the mail into five stacks. They eventually needed a sixth stack for two large envelopes and one small envelope addressed to all four men. They opened the large common envelopes and found greeting cards. One, which was signed by numerous Ozark View residents, proclaimed the four were missed at home and wished them well in their travels. The other, a note from the Ozark View staff, featured a standard wish for good travel and included notes from staff members. Emma Smith's memo caught their attention. "Following announced yesterday: Due to decline in demand for Southwest Style Eggs, this menu item will be discontinued until enough residents beg or bribe Emma to re-instate it." The smallest common envelope was from Cyn. She reminded the group that the box's contents complied with their instructions in that obvious advertising had been left in their cottages, but everything else was included. She also included a wish for a good trip and good health.

Don's stack of mail was highest. It ranged from very formal mail from financial firms to bright red, yellow and purple envelopes made of construction paper and bearing the handwriting of young grandchildren. Walt and Roy had a similar mix of mail, but less in total than Don. Abe had the smallest amount of mail, all of it related to business.

Mail for the trust rivaled Don's in quantity, and it was all formal-looking. Walt re-sorted this stack, with anything specifically addressed by position or name handed to that person, and the balance given to

Roy, secretary of the ABRAT Board of Trustees. Most interesting in the ABRAT mail were forty-four applications for benefits, and twice that number of requests for application forms. Awareness of the trust was spreading.

Roy raised the stack of applications, and commented, "I'll bet eighty percent of these are from Mid-North retirees." He then added, "I'll log these when we are traveling again on the Road Lynx. I'm going to discipline myself to log in each application before we read it. Otherwise, we'll have a control problem one of these days."

"We appreciate your consistency, Mr. Cole," Walt commended.

Don first opened an envelope containing a note from Ruth. She asked him to share her news with his traveling buddies, so after scanning the note, he read it aloud. It contained news of other Ozark View residents, including a report that the health of one of Ozark View's long time residents had diminished to such a point that he had permanently transferred to the center's nursing care facility. His family had come within the past week to vacate the cottage, and Ozark View maintenance people were busy updating it for its new occupant. Ann Walker would soon be moving into the cottage!

"When are you going to mail the first checks, Walt?" Abe asked after hearing Ruth's news.

"Well, neither of our first two recipients will actually get checks. Both asked for automatic deposits. This month, there are only two payments, and I asked the bank to have the payments in its system no later than the twenty-third for payment on July thirtieth, the last banking day before August first. We get on the ship on the twenty-fourth, and I may not be able to get back online until we get back to Seattle on the thirty-first. I want to be sure the first payments arrive on schedule. Remember, we decided to make monthly payment on the first of each month or the last banking day before, if the first is not a banking day? The short answer to your question is July thirtieth."

Roy grinned at his big, orderly friend. "You gave Abe both the long answer and the short answer."

Abe offered, "Thanks for both. It's gratifying to think we're about to make the first payments. And, thanks for gettin' it done right the first time."

"My pleasure," Walt answered.

"When are you going to have new applications ready to review, Mr. Secretary?" Don asked Roy.

"I'll get them logged in tomorrow, and I'll look over them to see if additional information is needed. We'll be able to review all complete applications after that."

"Okay. Let's plan on having a review session at Crater Lake, or somewhere sooner if we find a beautiful spot for a meeting."

All agreed. Abe's question to Walt concerning payments had begun the meeting of the Abe Brown Retirement Assistance Trust. Don had two other items of business, both of which regarded Board authorization for banking and legal services.

The four were soon again in the PT Cruiser headed north, jovial and relaxed. At North Lake Tahoe, Abe bought a newspaper to check Gilbert Glass's condition. He learned that Glass had been flown by helicopter to a Los Angeles hospital where authorities were not releasing information. However, one of Glass's estranged sons was quoted, "The old man is a vegetable. He can't hear, see, talk or move. He can barely breathe. He's as good as dead. Not many people care. Gilbert Glass is the ultimate jerk of all jerks."

# CHAPTER 34

Don Stone called to order the meeting of the Board of Trustees of the Abe Brown Retirement Assistance Trust. In conformance with the Board's policy of meeting in beautiful locations, the trustees were seated in four Ozark View high back rocking chairs arranged in a semicircle under the shade of whitebark pines and Shasta firs at the rim of Oregon's Crater Lake.

Abe wanted to memorize every detail of the lake. He loved to see the lake's nearly perfect reflections of puffy white clouds floating overhead. He could have sat all day and done nothing else, but there was work to be done, and the four trustees had been sitting for almost an hour before Don began the meeting.

The only item on the agenda was to consider thirty-two applications for retirement assistance that Roy had deemed to be complete and ready for the Board's consideration. Roy had worked diligently for the past two days to log and review all applications for completeness and accuracy. To assist him, Walt and Don had shared driving the Road Lynx through Northern California with occasional stops at points of interest.

The work did not take long. Of the thirty-two applications, twenty-nine were from Mid-North retirees. The other three had retired from a small meat packer in Iowa that had gone broke after being taken over by the founder's irresponsible son. Apparently these three applicants

217

had learned of ABRAT from friends who had retired from Mid-North. With the help of Stuart Range, Don had verified that the situation of the meat packer retirees met the requirements for assistance from ABRAT.

The Board approved all thirty-two of the applications, and instructed Roy to notify the applicants and to authorize payments. Roy then answered questions about other applications for which he had requested additional information. Don, Walt and Abe thanked Roy for his efforts, and agreed that the trust must soon hire administrative help in addition to the secretarial service in Branson.

After Don adjourned the meeting, the four continued to sit and enjoy the view. Abe chose this time to astound his friends. "Like you guys thought Bryce Canyon made a good chapel, I think this place makes a good chapel. It seems like a good time to tell y'all I'm ready to confess my sins and accept God's grace. That is, if y'all are sure of what you've told me about God's grace being greater than the worst of sins."

"Praise the Lord!" exclaimed Walt, sitting next to Abe. Walt restrained his desire to hug Abe hard. Instead, he gently placed his left arm over Abe shoulder and squeezed slightly.

"Thanks for containing your exuberance, Walt. My arthritis doesn't like strong hugs."

Don arose from his chair, and stepped in front of Abe, where he knelt on one knee, his better one. He spoke with a strong reverent voice, "I agree with Walt. Praise the Lord! Are you ready to pray a prayer of confession and acceptance?"

"I am."

Roy, normally first to speak, still had said nothing. He also left his chair and knelt beside Don, placing his right hand on Abe's left hand, and his left arm over Don's shoulders. Roy cried quietly.

"Pray something like this Abe, 'Dear God, I am a sinner, and I accept your grace offered through your son Jesus Christ. Please forgive my sins and accept me as one of your own.'"

Abe bowed his head and prayed exactly the prayer Don had suggested, "Dear God, I am a sinner, and I accept your grace offered through your son Jesus Christ. Please forgive my sins and accept me as one of your own."

As he raised his head, Don looked to see if Abe was crying. He was not, but his tired old eyes were sparkling.

Abe asked his friends, "Do I confess each of my sins to you guys and to God, or do you just accept that I am a sinner in general terms."

Roy could finally speak. "Acknowledgement in general terms is fine by me. God knows the details."

"Does it bother you guys to know that my past has lots of sins, some big ones?"

Don shook his head. "I can't imagine your sins are worse than the sins of the guys that put Jesus on the cross, and for whom Jesus asked God's forgiveness."

"I can't imagine it's any worse than the hatred I had for my former brother-in-law, the ex-husband of my sister," Walt offered. "I've trusted the Lord to forgive me that hatred."

Before Roy could offer his comparative sin, Abe responded, "Mine mostly fit somewhere between your two examples. Now, tell me, how do I know I have God's forgiveness? Do I have to wait a few days until I die and see pearly gates or a pit of fire, or just nothin'?"

Don answered, "You don't have to wait for the pearly gates. A man named John, one of Jesus' closest disciples, spoke about assurance of forgiveness in a letter he wrote to the early Christians. In the Bible his letter is referred to as '1 John.' Here's what he wrote: 'If we confess our sins, he—"he," meaning Jesus—is faithful and just and will forgive us our sins.' Other passages in John and in other books of the Bible tell how Jesus proved that he does in fact have power to forgive sins."

"So you're telling me that I can be assured because this John said so when talking about Jesus?"

Don nodded. "Right. And, if you read the examples of how Jesus forgave men, performed miracles and always honored God, you will better understand John's assurance."

Roy added, "That will help. But also I think soon, if not already, you're going to find a new spirit within you that will also give you that assurance."

Abe wrinkled his face. "Spirit?"

Walt picked up the conversation. "It's known to Christians as the Holy Spirit. He comes to you when you accept Christ, or God's grace."

"How do I know when I get that?"

Roy answered through a kind smile. "You'll just know, Abe. You'll just know."

It was Abe's turn to smile. "I may already know. I haven't told y'all, but I was really troubled by somethin' while we were at Lake Tahoe. On Friday, while I was floatin' in the boat while y'all played golf, I got down on my knees and prayed about it." Abe smiled as he looked at the astonished faces peering at him. "I said what I had to say, then shut up and waited for an answer like Don had told me to do if I ever prayed. While I waited, leanin' on a bench seat, I drifted off to sleep. A couple of fishermen woke me just before my boat drifted onto the rocks." Abe smiled broadly at Walt as he said this. "I couldn't get up fast, so I crawled to the controls, started the engine and moved the boat and me away from the rocks. Then I crawled into the helmsman's seat. That's when I realized that I knew the answer to the question that I had asked God. It was an answer beyond any that I had thought of. And, maybe here's the part about the spirit: I was peaceful. I've been peaceful ever since. But I felt like I should confess that I am a sinner even though God knows it. I accept what you said, Roy. He even knows the details."

Roy confirmed the thought. "Yeah, the ugly details."

Abe smiled at Roy. "But does it make sense that God cares about the sinners if he knows the details of their ugly lives? Why wouldn't he stick to the religious folks, and let the rest go to hell, or wherever?"

Walt answered. "Jesus repeatedly is quoted as saying that he came for sinners, that is, to reconcile sinners to God for eternity. All men have sinned. Unless a man recognizes that and confesses his sins, he continues apart from God. If he never confesses and accepts God's plan for salvation, he is apart from God eternally."

Roy felt as if he needed to help Abe. He offered, "One of my favorite stories of Jesus is when a Jewish man who was chief tax collector for the Romans made an extra effort to see Jesus, Jesus had dinner with him. During dinner, the tax collector repented. The religious leaders at the time were irate that Jesus had dinner with the tax collector who they despised. But Jesus was delighted that the man had repented and accepted salvation."

Abe smirked slightly. "That story might fit me. I could say I've collected some taxes . . . in my own way."

Walt suggested, "Abe, during the rest of our trip, we'll have plenty of time for you to ask questions. We'll answer them as best we can, but more importantly, we will show you how to use the Bible to answer your own questions. We can make good use of our time."

Abe was solemn as he asked, "What's that word in the Bible for foretelling? Prophecy? And, doesn't this spirit, this Holy Spirit, somehow help people see the future sometimes?" As his friends nodded, Abe continued, "Anyway, a part of this peace is that I know I don't have many more weeks on this earth, but I'm not concerned."

Roy was blunt. "You think the Holy Spirit is telling you that you are going to die soon?"

Abe nodded, "Well, at least to life as I've always known it. Y'all just assured me that I will have eternal life now that I have accepted God's salvation."

"And you do have, Abe," Don affirmed. "I want to pray a prayer of thanks for your salvation. Let's all put a hand on Abe, as I pray."

"You guys pray a lot."

"Happy or sad, glad or mad is the rule I was given a long time ago by a young minister," Roy advised as the four men bowed their heads.

Don prayed, "Dear Lord, Thank you for giving salvation and grace to your child and our friend, Abe Brown. We, his friends, have been very concerned for him. Now he tells us that he may not be with us much longer. We would like to have him a while longer, Lord. But not our will, but yours be done. Now that we know he will spend eternity with you, we can better accept you calling him home, if that is what you are going to do. We accept your infinite wisdom. And, for our friend's salvation we are more thankful than we can ever express! Thank you, Lord. In the name of Jesus, I pray. Amen."

All four raised their heads. Abe was crying. He said, "Few people have ever called me 'friend.' Over the last three days, I've been repeatedly thankin' God for you, my friends."

# CHAPTER 35

Early Tuesday, four happy friends prepared the Road Lynx for departure from Crater Lake. Before heading north and east out of the park, Walt stopped the bus near a favorite vantage point for one more view of the beautiful lake. Satisfied, the four men reboarded their vehicle, and headed toward Portland via a recommended scenic drive that would take them over forest roads through the town of Bend and the Mount Hood National Forest. The group would stop at four points to photograph Mount Hood standing tall and alone to the northeast.

In Bend, Don bought Abe a large print Bible. Abe then alternated his time between viewing scenery and reading Bible passages as suggested and found for him by Don and Walt. Abe read all of the passages mentioned the day before by Walt, Don or Roy. After several more verses selected by Don to help assure Abe of God's grace, Abe's salvation, and the presence of the Holy Spirit, Don suggested that Abe take his time and read through the Gospel of John. After reading for a while, Abe told Don, "I see why you picked this book. It was written for guys like me!"

Abe had selected a hotel in Clackamas, Oregon, just off Interstate 205, which skirts Portland to the east, because Abe liked the sound of the town's name, and because the hotel's reservations clerk had promised an unobstructed view of Mount Hood from the balcony of the suite Abe reserved. The view was all that was promised, and better than

Abe had expected. After a dinner of steaks and salmon, the four friends sipped coffee on the balcony and beheld the view. It was well after sunset before the four retired from the balcony and went to bed.

From Portland, the group took a wayward course around Mount Rainer to their high-rise hotel in Tacoma, Washington, where Abe had also reserved rooms with "a fantastic view from the balcony." Throughout Wednesday Abe continued to read his new Bible and view beautiful scenery. As he asked questions, they were answered by the friend seated closest at the time.

Don was frequently the closest. As he answered Abe's questions, he gave Abe a short course in basic Bible study. From time to time Don wondered just how long his friend would be around to read his new Bible. Whenever he had this thought, Don offered a short silent prayer of thanks for Abe's salvation and his new thirst for God's word.

Abe had reserved the suite at Tacoma for three nights, even though the foursome would not use it on the second night. On Thursday, the four packed into Don's PT Cruiser for a tour of the Olympic Peninsula. They took a western route across the bottom of the peninsula, then turned north to ride along the Pacific Coast. At the northern end of the peninsula, Don turned east along the Strait of Juan de Fuca. In a seaside restaurant at Dungeness, the four enjoyed famous Dungeness crab. They spent the night at Port Townsend in a bed and breakfast located in a home built during the late 1800s by a lumber baron.

Roy had to wake Abe Friday morning in time to have breakfast and begin their drive south along the Puget Sound. Abe was slow to respond when Roy awoke him. He seemed disoriented as he showered and dressed. He was very quiet at breakfast. Abe's lethargy continued in the car. Abe was soon asleep again as he leaned against the right corner of the back seat.

Abe continued to sleep when the group stopped at scenic points for refreshments or for other reasons. His buddies were concerned that Abe was missing the experience of the tour, but accepted Abe's sluggishness, suspecting that during the night he had taken one of his "Houston Pills" to relieve pain. To accommodate Abe's slumber while they lunched, Walt, Don and Roy bought hamburgers at a drive-through window of a local eatery, and found a picnic table at a state park overlooking Puget Sound. They left Abe sleeping in the car parked nearby with all four windows opened, while they enjoyed their meal and the scenery.

At three o'clock in the afternoon as Don drove through the town of Purdy, Abe awoke with a start. "We gotta find a bathroom soon."

"You've been sound asleep," Roy said." Did you take a Houston Pill last night?"

"No, and I slept all night. What time is it?" Abe asked as Don pulled the PT Cruiser into a fast food parking lot.

"3:00 P.M.." Roy answered." You've slept about seventeen hours with one hour awake for dressing and breakfast. Are you okay? How do you feel now?"

"I feel like I gotta go," was all Abe answered as the P. T. Cruiser glided to the curb and Abe sprung open the door and left the car. Walt followed him while Roy and Don went to the restaurant's order line for coffee.

Back at Tacoma, all four men chose a salad entrée for dinner delivered by room service to their balcony. Abe's choice was a surprise to his traveling buddies who knew Abe had eaten little for breakfast and nothing for lunch, eating only a cinnamon roll soon after he woke in the afternoon. Through dinner and coffee, the four again enjoyed their view of Mount Rainer before going to bed soon after nine o'clock.

Early Saturday, Walt retrieved luggage from the front of the Road Lynx's trailer before Don drove his PT Cruiser into the traveling garage. The group normally traveled in the big bus without bags, but luggage would be needed to transport their belongings onto and off the cruise ship. Roy and Don had earlier carried to the bus four fresh laundry bundles from the hotel's valet service. In the Road Lynx, the three men packed for their cruise.

Roy packed Abe's big bag and a small carry-on, allowing his old friend to sleep late. As Roy was placing Abe's passport into the carry-on, he dropped it. When he lifted the opened booklet from the floor, Roy noticed the document had no entries even though it had been issued four years before, about when Abe moved to Ozark View. Roy concluded Abe had made a big adjustment from a life Abe had described as constant international travel to one of no international travel for the past four years.

Roy woke Abe at ten o'clock, one hour before the hotel's required check-out time. Abe was groggy, but not disoriented as he had been on Friday morning. Roy stayed in the room as Abe dressed in the shirt and trousers Roy had chosen for him when he had earlier packed his friend's clothes for boarding the ship.

Abe thanked Roy for letting him sleep and for packing for him. "I'm sure you did a good job of packin'. I may let you do it all the time. Uh, did you put my field glasses and extra glasses in the carry-on bag? Where's my passport?"

Roy assured his friend that all three items were in the carry-on as he zipped the bag when Abe was ready to go. Roy followed Abe and his blue scooter from the hotel, and helped Abe board the Road Lynx for the short trip to Seattle and the cruise dock.

# CHAPTER 36

The embarkation and disembarkation of a cruise ship is a big event. Within relatively few hours, two or three thousand people with a mountain of luggage get off a ship, clear customs, and depart the terminal in vehicles ranging from private automobiles to fifty-passenger buses. The passengers always vary widely in their ability to negotiate the process, with a few being totally self-reliant and others being completely dependent on directions from cruise line and port personnel. Before all of the arriving passengers depart the port area, the first of an equal number of out-bound passengers arrive at the port by various means, equally independent or dependent on directions from cruise line personnel. Especially dependent are those who are beginning their first voyage.

At some ports, a cruise ship's embarkation or disembarkation can be pure havoc. However, the Colorful Seas Cruise Line and the Seattle Port Authority are well practiced at the operation, and well organized. As Walt pulled onto the cruise terminal property, a port policeman directed the big Road Lynx into a special line for recreational vehicles. Near the terminal building entrance, a porter met the bus for the luggage, Roy recovered Abe's blue scooter from the trailer, and Abe, Roy and Don proceeded to a departure lounge just inside the building. There they waited while Walt drove the Road Lynx to a remote parking lot designated for recreational vehicles. A small shuttle van returned

Walt to the terminal entrance within fifteen minutes of the group's arrival. The four friends then moved through the check-in and border control processes, and were soon onboard the *Color Emerald* for their round trip voyage to Alaska.

Once on board, the group rode an elevator to deck seven where their adjacent staterooms were located on the ship's port side near mid-ship. Abe and Roy were again roommates in a room designed to accommodate wheel chairs and scooters. Abe maneuvered his scooter through the door, drove to the nearest bed, stepped off his scooter, and stripped to his underwear. He then pulled back the bedcovers, and lay down, slipping his legs under the sheet. "Roy, I don't know what's goin' on with my body, but I need more sleep. I'm gonna take a nap. If you'll take one of the walkie-talkies, I'll call you when I wake up. You and the others go about explorin' the ship. I gotta rest." He closed his eyes.

Roy responded quickly, knowing Abe's ability to go to sleep within seconds of lying down. "Before you go to sleep, I'll tell you the safe's combination will be 8673, your age and mine. I'll put our passports and extra cash in the safe before I go. I'll leave your walkie-talkie on the bed stand. Uh, and, I'll put the do-not-disturb sign on the door."

"Good. Thanks." Abe went to sleep.

Roy stared at his aged friend, noting Abe's breathing was more labored than it had been over the past two weeks. Roy knew Abe had routinely rejected medication for his failing heart. He guessed Abe's condition to be worsening, and wondered if his friend would awaken from his nap. "He's in your hands, Lord," Roy prayed. Roy sighed as he thought of Abe's recent confession of faith.

Roy unpacked the few items he had carried for Abe and himself in their red and yellow duffel bags. Roy put most items in drawers in the nightstand separating the beds, reserving the larger drawers in the room for clothing that would arrive later in the big bags. He placed toilet articles and medicines on shelves in the bathroom and put two envelopes containing cash along with his and Abe's passports in the safe. He set the safe's combination, locked the safe, turned off all but one of the room lights, took the do-not-disturb door hanger, and slipped out of the room.

As he placed the hanger on the door lever, Roy heard, "Welcome to the *Color Emerald*. I am your room steward, Ivan." Ivan pronounced his name "E-Von."

"Hello, Ivan. I'm Roy Cole. My roommate, Abe Brown, is already napping on your restful ship. Do you need to do anything in the room?"

"No, not if you found everything in order. Is Mr. Brown feeling ill?"

Roy chose not to answer that a passenger who had just boarded was feeling ill. "I think he's just tired. We've been traveling for a while. He is old, and requires a lot of rest."

"Very well. I will leave your luggage in the hall when it arrives. I will not disturb Mr. Brown. I am here to be of assistance. Let me know of anything you need. My pager number is on the card I left on the desk. Do you have it with you?"

"No, I left it in the room."

"Here is another. If I may be of assistance, please call."

"Thank you, I will." Roy had moved to the door of the adjacent room as he spoke to Ivan, and was about to knock.

"I understand that Mr. Stone and Mr. Wilson are traveling with you?" The statement was in the form of a question.

"Yes. We are all friends."

"And you are from Missouri in the United States?"

"Yes. Have you been there?" Roy knocked on the door of Walt and Don's room as he asked.

"No. I've heard of Branson from many of the passengers that I have served. It has country music, I think?" Again the statement was in the form of a question.

"Yes. It also has many other types of music and other entertainment. It's a favorite place for families and for senior citizens. We live just outside of Branson."

"Do you go to a music show each evening?"

"No, but we go frequently. We have our favorites."

"But Ivan, we have different favorites, so we have to compromise." Walt entered the conversation as he opened his stateroom door.

"You've met Ivan, I assume?" Roy asked.

"Yes, Ivan is from Romania, and tells me we should plan our next trip there."

Ivan smiled and looked to Roy for a response, which was slow in coming.

"Uh, yeah. That's someplace I haven't thought about, but maybe we should plan to go there." Roy's response was made to cover his deeper thought. *With Abe, we haven't traveled outside of the United States. But he may soon not be with us. I wonder how our travels and our lives will change without him.*

"Where's Abe?" Walt asked.

"In bed. He's very tired."

Ivan sensed he was not needed for the conversation. "I shall go. While you are dining, I shall remove the partition between your balconies as you requested, Mister Wilson. If you need anything else, page me."

"Thank you, Ivan," the two friends responded in near unison.

"What's going on?" Don asked from behind Walt.

"Abe's napping, and I'm ready to explore the ship," Roy said. "We had an early breakfast, and haven't had lunch. Let's find the Top Side Buffet."

"When do you want to open the box?" Walt referred to the FedEx package from Cyn they had picked up on their way to the cruise terminal. It was the same size as the box received in Tahoe, but heavier.

Roy grimaced. "Well, this is Saturday. Let's take the weekend off and not open the trust office until Monday."

Don spoke firmly. "We've already taken most of the week off. If you were an applicant for retirement assistance trying to survive from day to day, you'd want that box opened before lunch."

Walt suggested, "Let's have lunch, explore a little bit, and then open the box."

"Agreed."

• • •

Walt was first to complete his selections from the Top Side Buffet. He found a table overlooking the cruise terminal. He saw that buses were continuing to arrive, probably from the airport or from pre-cruise excursions arranged by the cruise line. Roy was next to the table with a completely different selection of food on his plate, and Don soon followed with yet a third variety.

Walt commented, "From our plates, it looks as if we're eating in three different restaurants. I went for breads, cheese and lunchmeats, Roy chose pastas, and Don has fish and salads. To our credit, we showed restraint. None of us needs a sideboard on our plate."

"I told myself to take small portions. I can go back for another plate," Roy confided.

"I guess that's an effective means of self-control," Don observed. "The test will come in a few minutes when you finish what you have and decide whether to be sustained by your first plate, or whether you must have a second."

"I plan to go back only for dessert."

"More self-control. What a man!" Walt chided.

"What's in the box?" Roy suddenly changed subjects.

"Our mail." Don answered.

"Not in the FedEx box. What's in the box in the safe deposit vault at Dalhart?"

"Where did that come from?" Walt asked, leaning back and staring at Roy as he did so.

"The back of my little brain," Roy answered. "The question has been there since we learned about that box, and every so many hours the thought pops forward to the front of my brain, or to my consciousness . . . wherever that is."

Don spread his napkin on his lap. "I thought we had agreed that we wouldn't be concerned about the contents of that safe deposit box until it's time to be concerned. Why raise the issue?"

"Our friend Abe gave us a box full of something he doesn't want disclosed until after he's dead. He recently accepted Christ and thinks he is about to meet his Maker. He slept two-thirds of the day yesterday, and is now taking a nap after sleeping thirteen hours last night. He might be dead in his bed right now. We may suddenly be concerned about the box, the one in Dalhart."

Walt responded. "Even after Abe dies, we don't have to rush to Dalhart to see what's in the box. Abe only told us not to open the envelope until after he's dead. He did not say we should open it immediately after he dies."

"Are you worried about it, Roy?" Don asked.

"More curious than worried, I think. But I don't like the idea that he put an envelope and box in a rural area safe deposit box, paid the rent in advance, probably by cash, passed title to us and told us not to open his surprise until after he's dead."

"You think he's hiding something really bad?" Don pressed.

Roy looked Don straight in the eyes. "Yes and no. He might be hiding something bad." Roy emphasized 'might,' indicating his uncertainty. "Remember he has told us repeatedly that he was a great sinner."

"We're all great sinners," Don reminded his friend.

"Yeah, but Abe has been using the human standard to classify himself, not the godly one. The human standard ranks sins."

"So you think Abe has a Number One sin like murder or something on his list of sins?" Walt asked.

"Walt and Don, I suspect Abe has a long list of high-ranking sins in his background. Abe normally understates. He doesn't exaggerate. But he's repeatedly said that his sins, plural, were really bad."

Nobody at the table was eating. The meals that a few minutes earlier had seemed so appetizing were sitting untouched on their plates.

Don spoke. "Abe's comments could also stem from the fact that Abe's sins are Abe's sins. Many people see their own sins to be worse than those of others."

"Abe doesn't exaggerate," Roy repeated.

Walt offered a different view. "Guys, we're working on the low end of the scale. We're assuming that whatever is in the box is bad. It might be good. It might be control of a half billion dollars that Abe wants us to use for good purposes after he is gone. You remember he was too shy to personally tell Ann about the trust and his desire to help her and other people likewise hurt by scoundrels? Well, maybe he doesn't want to be around when we learn that he has provided for an even greater good."

"A positive thought," Don acknowledged. "But whatever's the truth, what could we do with the information if we had it right now?"

"That depends on the information," Roy answered.

Don nodded, "Yes, but we can do nothing until we have the information. Our friend has asked us to wait until after his death before we see the contents of the box. We're wasting our time speculating, and our food is getting cold. Let's drop the subject and eat. Walt, will you ask God's blessing?"

Before Walt could pray, Roy asked. "What about the big list of bad sins?"

Walt, like Don, had grown testy with Roy's worry. "Whoa, buddy. We've only heard Abe say his sins were bad. We don't know what they were. We can only speculate, and that's of no value to us, Abe, or to anybody else. I agree with Don. Let's drop this conversation and eat!"

"Okay, okay! I just don't want to some day suddenly learn that we are accomplices before the fact, during the fact, or after the fact on some big crime that we would have known about and stopped had we asked the right questions."

Don had lost patience with his friend, "Roy, dang it, Abe's an old man with no capability to do great sins like you seem to fear. If he has done something really bad, it was long ago. If the big bad sins are documented in the safe deposit box, we won't know about it until we open the box after Abe has died. I can't think of anything suspicious that I've seen Abe do since we've known him. He has only been secretive about his early life."

Roy quietly stated, "Three Mid-North scoundrels died while we were nearby."

Walt countered, "One died when he ran in front of a speeding taxi. Another died of a stroke while he played golf. Another died of a heart attack while eating breakfast, little different than the guy that had nothing to do with Mid-North that died while we sat at the fifteenth green at Basswood. We had nothing to do with any of them, nor did Abe. He was standing right beside us when the third guy died. What was his name? White? No, Whitby."

Don added, "Roy, the Mid-North guys all died of natural causes. Or at least natural causes if you count a traffic accident to be a natural cause in our modern society. Let it go!"

Roy calmly smiled at his two friends. "I'll let it go, but you guys have thought about it, haven't you?"

Walt confessed, "Yes, I was bothered by the coincidences. I especially thought about it soon after the scoundrels died. But they all died of natural causes. I dropped my worries weeks ago. Do you think our friend Abe has the ability to trigger death by natural causes? Is that his secret in the Dalhart safe deposit box?"

Don admonished, "Roy, you need to drop these silly thoughts. Our friend Abe, a tired old man, can't cause a man to have a heart attack, or a stroke, or to fall in front of a cab."

Roy took a deep breath, forcefully exhaled, and shook his head. "You're right. But even if our food is cold, I'm glad we had this discussion. I needed to hear from you guys that you've had similar concerns, and that it's silly to think there is a connection between the deaths and Abe."

"May I pray now?"

"Please."

• • •

Soon after lunch, Walt, Don and Roy opened the box from Cyn. It contained roughly 40 percent personal mail and 60 percent ABRAT mail. The favorite items were the cards from grandchildren and others wishing the guys a great cruise. For Walt, the trust's financial advisors had sent investment ideas and financial reports for his review. For Roy, forty-six candidates had submitted applications for benefits. For Don, the mail brought a variety of trust management issues. By Tuesday, certainly not later than Wednesday, a trustee meeting would be necessary. The combined balcony of their staterooms would be and excellent place for such a meeting, conforming to the four friends' policy of meeting in beautiful locations.

# CHAPTER 37

Abe joined his friends for dinner in the Colorful Collage Dining Room. He said little as he dismounted his scooter and slid into a barrel-back chair brightly splotched with color, which Mario, the table's assistant waiter, slipped forward as Roy parked the scooter nearby. Abe remained quiet as their waiter, Vedran, welcomed them and announced the theme for that evening's dinner. Abe asked for "just water" when Mario took drink orders.

"Your friends appreciate your pulling yourself from your bed to join us for dinner," Walt kidded.

"I had to attend the safety drill, anyway," Abe responded with a slight smile.

"How are you feeling, Abe?" Don asked.

"Weak. Tired. Worn out. I'm not lookin' forward to the effort of liftin' my fork, and that's bad." Abe's soft voice reflected the weakness he felt.

"We're glad that you're with us, though." Roy added.

Vedran reappeared at their table. "Again gentlemen, tonight's theme is North Atlantic. I think that is because we are in the North Pacific. But not to worry, Colorful Cruise Lines has many ships. One of them must be cruising tonight in the North Atlantic."

Three men at the table smiled. Abe did not. Vedran presented menus beginning with Abe, and offered his personal recommendations.

Vedran then announced that he would give the gentlemen a few minutes to peruse the menu before he returned to answer their questions. He hurried away to greet guests being seated by Mario at another table.

The dining room in all aspects was colorful. The walls, floors and ceilings formed a polychrome collage, complemented by vivid table coverings, napkins, chairs and flowers. The mixture of bold dinner jackets worn by the wait staff further added to the amalgamation of color. The only drab objects in the room were passengers in "country club casual" attire of blues, grays, blacks, tans, off-whites and tweeds. Don summarized the effect. "To stand out in this room, one should wear all white."

"If an angel comes to collect me during dinner, we should see him comin'," Abe mused.

"How would you feel about that?" Don asked.

"If I saw an angel comin' to get me, I would tell my friends goodbye, and use my last strength to stand to meet the angel. I'm ready."

"Good," Walt responded.

"Yes, it's good," Abe agreed. "I'm as happy as I've ever been in my life. Much happier than I was for 95 percent of my life."

"I would like to hear more about that 95 percent." Walt said.

"I don't like to talk about my past," Abe stated as firmly as his weak voice would allow. "Besides, here comes Vedran. I want to order and eat soon. Y'all let me skip lunch, ya know."

Throughout the meal, conversation centered on the features of the *Color Emerald*, the discoveries Walt, Roy and Don had made that afternoon, and upcoming ports of call. Abe mostly listened, but he seemed to enjoy his friends' enthusiasm for the ship. As his friends discussed excursion plans at the five cruise stops, Abe stated, "I hope I'm strong enough to get off the ship at Ketchikan. I want to pick out rain jackets as gifts for my friends. There should be a good selection, considerin' the rain forest there. Otherwise, I'll be happy to sit on the balcony and be a scenic sponge."

Befitting the name of the cruise line, dessert was colorful and scrumptious. After coffee, Roy recovered Abe's scooter, and the four men wished Vedran a good evening.

As they left the dining room, the four noticed the movement of the big ship. The *Color Emerald* had departed its Seattle berth and was sailing at a very low rate of speed northward through Puget Sound.

Abe suggested the four men enjoy their balcony. "I'll stay out as long as I can hold my head up, but I'll probably give out soon. Y'all can then cavort around the ship."

The men paused in their rooms long enough to grab jackets or sweaters. Abe wore both. The temperature of Puget Sound's surface water in July was only slightly more than fifty degrees Fahrenheit, and that water temperature directly affected the air temperature. The guys expected a very cool breeze on the balcony. Don ordered coffee from room service.

Roy was first to step onto the balcony, and braced himself as he encountered the chilly wind. He said to Walt who followed closely, "People around Dalhart right now would love to feel this cool breeze."

Walt agreed. "Yeah. Those wind turbines we saw near Pampa must all be running full blast to chill homes in the Texas Panhandle.

"Those homes won't have the fresh aroma of this sea breeze."

"You're right. Refreshing, isn't it?"

"Chillin'," Abe countered as he shuffled out of his room and onto a deck chair." But it feels good." He turned his face directly into the wind. "I feel like a dog with its head stuck out of a car window. I understand dogs better now. It's really pleasant."

"For a while," Don warned. "We don't want you getting pneumonia out here in the fresh air, Abe."

"Yes, Doctor Don!" Abe countered with his face still directed into the breeze.

Roy asked Abe about a thought Roy had pondered all day. "Abe, when you were in your import/export business what countries did you travel to mostly, and why did you get a new passport just before coming to Ozark View?"

"You noticed my fresh passport when you packed for me today, huh?" Abe was still looking into the wind. Finally, he turned his head and looked straight out from the ship as he spoke. "I went to almost every country in the world at one time or another. Some of them, the big tradin' partners of the United States, I visited frequently. How frequently depended on the business at the time. When Japan was just gettin' restarted after the war, I went there twice monthly. Sometimes I was in a country for a couple of months straight. There was every kind of business to be done. Later, when Korea started to become a competitive producer, I spent plenty of time there. I also went to Europe a lot. I didn't get to Africa much. Those people on that dark continent just couldn't get themselves stabilized enough for me to risk my time and money." Abe paused. He hadn't yet answered Roy's second question. Roy waited.

"As to my new passport: Well, I could tell you that the old one was about to expire, and I renewed it. A few weeks ago I might have said that, but I've been readin' this new book that Don bought for me. The book discourages lyin'." He saw grins on Don's and Walt's face, but not Roy's. Roy wanted an answer.

"The truth is I haven't always been Abe Brown." Now he had everyone's attention. "I got that new passport when I had to become somebody new and hide. Ozark View is a nice place to hide from some rough people that would like to find me. So far, they don't know about Abe Brown." He didn't look around. He continued to stare directly out from the balcony. "I made some serious enemies in my past life. Remember, I said that I have sinned bad. Well, some of my enemies have sinned worse, and are still at it. They would enjoy killin' me before my time to die." Abe smiled a triumphant smile. "They had better hurry now if they're going to do it."

Abe continued, interrupting Don as Don started to ask a question. "Do you think God's forgiveness applies to me before I was Abe Brown? As you said, Roy, God knows the ugly details."

Don said quietly, "God looks at the heart, the true individual. It doesn't matter what you are calling yourself at the time."

"I kinda thought that."

Roy blurted, "Were you with the CIA or something? Is that why you had to get lost?"

Abe looked away from the view and down to his feet. "This is the last question I will answer tonight about my past. Sometimes I worked for the CIA as a contractor. My line of business gave me a good cover. I could get into places the CIA couldn't."

Walt asked a question about the current circumstances, but related to Abe's past. "Is there any chance ABRAT could suffer if someone or something comes out of your past?"

"No. The trust is safe. The money is legitimate. It took several years and a bunch of transactions to move it to the name of Abe Brown. But that was to hide me, not the money. I didn't want the money to lead my enemies to the new me."

Don picked up on Walt's question. "So, you don't think there's any chance the trust assets could diminish or disappear, causing us to break promises to the trust's beneficiaries?"

Abe shook his head. "The assets are safe. The only thing that has been at risk and is still at risk is me. However, my personal risk is about to die with me."

Nobody said anything for a full two minutes. Finally, Roy asked. "The guy who died in your cottage was from your past. Was he an enemy?"

"That guy was a stupid treacherous enemy to everybody he ever met. Yes, he was an enemy to me. I'm glad he's dead, but I wish he had died somewhere else."

Don asked, "Might his death in your house draw other enemies?"

"Probably not. He was a loner who always had several schemes workin'. His trip to Branson was probably on his own and shouldn't raise any questions about me."

No one spoke. They sat.

Abe broke the silence. "Besides, I may not get back to Branson anyway. My fatigue is from my failing heart."

Walt questioned, "Have you seen the ship's doctor, or are you self-diagnosing? If you haven't seen the ship's doctor, why don't you?"

"I'm gonna wait until we make the turn and start back from Glacier Bay. After that, the ship's doctor is not likely to put me off the ship. If I approach him too early, he may want me to be taken off and put in some hospital. I don't want to do that."

Walt countered, "You could die before Glacier Bay."

"So could you. But if I die, just put me in a meat locker and get my body back to Branson. Don knows where I want to be buried."

None of the three responded to Abe's declaration. The four men were content to stare across the water at the lights on shore. The ship slowly slipped through the water, small waves splashed quietly against the ship's hull, and stars began filling the early evening sky. The four sat, stared, and absorbed another fantastic sight. Three of the men thought deeply about what they had just heard from their older friend, but none wanted to discuss it.

His three buddies could not see Abe's eyes twinkling as he announced it was time for him to leave the balcony. "I've accepted God's grace and I'm ready to die. I chuckle when I cogitate what my old enemies would think if they knew I moved to Branson, met y'all, and got reconciled to God. They wouldn't understand it, and probably wouldn't believe it, but they would hate the possibility that I could have eternal life! On that happy thought, gentlemen, I'm going to bed."

# CHAPTER 38

When his three friends returned from a morning tour of Ketchikan, Abe was ready to disembark. The four men headed directly to a large outdoors store near Creek Street. They wandered around the store for fifteen minutes before Abe approached a sales clerk. Abe assumed the clerks worked on commission, and wanted his commission to benefit someone nice. He had watched a very pleasant lady in her sixties assist an indecisive customer with a bratty child in tow. Abe would reward the clerk's patience. He asked her to show him the rain jackets, and confirmed the store had an ample selection before he signaled his buddies for their assistance.

Abe bought nineteen jackets. He let each of his three friends select his own. He designated jackets for Ann, Cyn and Ruth. He picked jackets for four staff members at Ozark View. He let Roy pick a jacket for Ivan, their room steward. He asked Walt, Don and Roy to help him pick jackets for Tom Queen, Stuart Range, two other attorneys, and four financial people from New York. He asked the clerk to individually wrap and box the jackets for his New York friends, and provided addresses for each. In each box Abe placed an envelope containing a personalized thank you note. He asked Walt and Roy to bag and carry to the ship the jacket for Ivan along with all jackets bound for Branson.

When it came time to pay, Abe asked, "Who is the treasurer for today?" Walt stepped forward, and produced his credit card. Abe smiled, looked up into the face of his big friend, and said, "Obviously, this is on me." The size of the purchase triggered the credit card company's security alert. Walt had to identify himself by telephone to an agent of the company before the charge cleared.

"Lunch is on me, too." Abe announced as the four left the gift shop. "We should find good seafood chowder here."

Don pointed to a restaurant he had spotted earlier not far down the street and in the direction of the ship. Don noticed Abe was breathing heavily and sweating. He wanted his friend back on the ship as soon as possible.

By the time the four returned to the ship, Abe was exhausted. He went directly to his bed, and did not get out of it again until the next morning. For the next few days, Abe did nothing more active than sit on his balcony. He ate small meals in his room, and did not again join his friends in the Colorful Collage Dining Room or the Top Side Buffet.

As the *Color Emerald* cruised out of Glacier Bay, Abe kept his earlier promise to Walt. Accompanied by Don, he rode his blue scooter to the ship's medical center. During the short ride down one hallway the ship rolled slightly. Don braced himself between Abe and the bulkhead to prevent Abe from toppling from the scooter. Abe was growing weaker.

The ship's Chief Medical Officer, a doctor from Scotland, confirmed Abe's self-diagnosis. He listened intently as Abe explained and reaffirmed his earlier decision to refuse extensive medical procedures or medication to prolong his limited painful life. The doctor then bluntly stated, "That being the case Mister Brown, you had best get your affairs in order, but I don't think you will have many more waking hours in which to do so." The doctor prescribed medicine and oxygen to ease Abe's efforts to breathe and to improve his rest when he slept, thereby allowing a few more hours of wakefulness. He gave Abe the choice of medical evacuation at the next port, staying in the medical center or staying in his stateroom. When Abe chose to stay in his stateroom, the doctor told Don and Abe that he would be by from time to time to check on Abe, and gave them his pager number.

Even with oxygen, Abe slept most of each day propped up by five pillows. Ivan was extremely helpful. He provided extra linen changes, exchanged pillows, serviced the room at odd hours to avoid disturbing Abe, brought beverages, replaced oxygen containers, and cleared room service items. He kept the room nearly spotless while working around the sleeping patient.

Roy, Don and Walt took turns sitting with Abe. All three kept a book from the ship's library in Abe and Roy's room. They read for hours during which Abe showed little activity other than breathing and occasional mumbling.

During one wakeful period, Abe asked his old friend Don to establish a special fund to provide for Abe's young friend Don, the dock man who had helped him during the storm at North Lake Tahoe. "Young Don reminds me of me at that age. He was raised by his grandparents because somethin' happened to his parents, kinda like what happened to mine. He's a good kid, a hard worker, and he's thoughtful. He oughtta get a break. I can give it to him. Create the fund from my money not yet in ABRAT. But don't give him too much, and don't give it to him all at once. I want to help him, not ruin him." As soon as Don told Abe he would take care of his request, Abe drifted back to sleep. He did not raise the subject again.

Because of Abe's condition, his three friends limited their time ashore, and made maximum use of their balconies to enjoy the beauty of Alaska. On their balconies and over dinner they often discussed in hushed voices the hodgepodge of their emotions. In the Colorful Collage Dining Room one evening, Don confided, "My emotions are similar to the collage on the walls of this dining room. My collage includes elation over Abe's salvation, exhilaration from the fantastic scenery, concern with Abe's condition, indulgent comfort from the ship's amenities, and also anxiety toward the coming road trip home."

Roy immediately agreed, "I think I'm trying to make the best of several situations at once, unable to fully engage with the emotions of any of them. The most important are Abe's salvation, and our faithful service to our friend."

At night, Roy slept in his bed four feet from Abe's, always alert to the presence of his dying roommate. Roy slept lightly, and lay mostly on his right side facing Abe. He awoke when Abe moved or made noise, but Abe moved infrequently and only mumbled in his sleep. Rarely were Abe's mumbled words distinguishable, but two nights before returning to Seattle, soon after Roy had gone to bed, Abe moved sharply in his bed and rasped with his scratchy voice, "Roy, don't open the box."

Roy slipped off his CPAP mask and asked, "What box?"

"The box at Dalhart."

"Why?"

"It's dangerous. Nobody should know about it, unless."

"Unless what?"

"Unless somebody else makes one."

"One what?"

"Weapon. It's awful."

"What kind of weapon?"

There was no further response from Abe. He moved softly on his pillows, and seemed to relax.

"Is it a bomb?" Roy asked.

Abe did not respond. Roy could not see movement in his friend's bed. Startled, Roy swung his legs off his bed and sat up. He stared at Abe, looking and listening for breathing. First he heard, and then he saw shallow but regular breathing. No, his friend had not uttered a final message and then promptly died, as Roy thought he might have done.

*That damned box.* Roy thought to himself. *How much danger is there with that damned box?* Roy considered what kind of weapon was most dangerous. *Does Abe have a nuclear bomb or plans for one in that box? A chemical weapon?* Roy continued to stare at his friend. Roy was tired, but now he was wide awake. *What do I do with this information? Are Abe's words reliable or just irrational babbling by an old man in a near-coma?*

Roy sat quietly on the side of his bed for thirty minutes, repeating the same thoughts and questions he had had since first learning of the envelope and box in the safe deposit drawer in Dalhart. Finally, fatigue took control of Roy's mind and body. Roy put his CPAP mask back on and stretched out on his bed. He slept until morning.

• • •

When Roy awoke, he immediately looked at his friend, and found him awake, staring at the ceiling. "Abe, are you okay?"

"Do you mean, 'Abe, are you dead?'"

"Are you better than dead? Are you feeling better?"

"I feel about the same, but I'm awake. Will you help me to the bathroom?"

"Sure."

While Abe used the bathroom, Roy ordered from room service a fruit plate, two boiled eggs, orange juice and coffee. He straightened Abe's bed, fluffed his pillows, and got a clean set of underwear from Abe's drawer.

When Abe finished in the bathroom, Roy helped him change underwear, which also served as Abe's bed clothing.

"I want to sit on the balcony." Abe stated firmly.

"It's cool out there. You'll have to wear some clothes."

"Ya don't think I should expose myself to the British Columbia coastland, huh?"

"No. I'll get your robe, coat and blanket."

"Get my big hat, too. Thanks."

When Roy opened the sliding glass door to the balcony, he startled Walt, who was reading his Bible and drinking coffee on the balcony.

Walt moved quickly to help Roy get Abe into the closest chair.

Walt pointed to the pump pot sitting on the table. "Bring your cups, Roy. I got this coffee this morning at the Top Side."

Roy went in, took a few minutes to get himself dressed, including jacket and hat. He returned with two cups. He also brought sunglasses for himself and Abe.

Abe refused the glasses even though the water seemed to magnify both the light and heat of the sun. Abe closed his eyes and raised his chin, simultaneously enjoying the warm sunlight and the cool ocean breeze.

Walt pumped coffee into Roy and Abe's cups. Abe took his without opening his eyes. Roy wrapped both hands around his cup and took a big swig. The three sat in silence as the big ship slipped through the cold blue water.

"Do I talk in my sleep?" Abe asked, his eyes still closed and face directed straight into the sun.

"Yes, and you scared me last night."

"How?"

"You normally mumble in your sleep. I normally can't understand anything you say. But last night, you suddenly almost shouted, 'Don't open the box, Roy!'"

Abe tightened the muscles in his jaw, but said nothing.

"I asked, 'What box?' and you answered, 'The one in Dalhart in the bank vault.'"

Abe took advantage of Roy's pause to ask, "Did I say why?"

Roy changed from inexact quotes of Abe's conversation to paraphrase. "Yeah, you said there was a dangerous weapon in the box, one that nobody should know about unless someone else makes one."

"What kind of weapon?" Walt asked.

Abe's hand shook. He spilled coffee onto the white terry cloth bathrobe covering his right leg. Walt moved to assist Abe, but Abe waived him off. "It's all right. The ship's laundry can get this robe clean, and my leg is only warm, not burned."

Roy had left the sliding door opened enough to hear the room service waiter knock on the hallway door. The knock was untimely, coming just as Abe spilled his coffee. Roy moved through the stateroom, took the breakfast tray and returned. He set the tray on the balcony's tea table, moved it in front of Abe, removed the plate covers and plastic wrap from the top of the orange juice glass, and spread strawberry preserves on a piece of toast. Service tasks done, Roy bluntly asked, "Tell us about the weapon."

"Not now. There's a lot to tell. I either must tell you nothing or everything. Don should hear it." Abe had placed his coffee cup on the tray. His hands were trembling. He was crying slightly.

"It's bad?" Walt asked.

"When I tell you, you decide." Abe sat motionless except his hands were shaking. He placed them on his lap to stop the tremor.

"So it may not be as bad as Walt and I are speculating."

"You can decide."

"Do you need help with your breakfast?"

"No. I need the exercise." Abe grinned slightly. "Don't y'all normally pray before meals? Will one of you thank God for my breakfast, this wonderful sunshine, the cool air, good friends, and our lives as they now are?"

Walt offered the prayer, but added, "And Lord, please give the four of us peace about whatever is in the box. Let us be open, loving and forgiving with one another."

Before Abe finished his breakfast, Don joined the group on the balcony. As Don pumped coffee for himself, Roy stared at Abe.

Abe answered Roy's unstated question. "No, not now. Let me tell you the next time I wake up. I'm tuckered out right now."

"Huh? Have I missed something?" Don asked.

Abe squinted as he looked at Don. "Walt and Roy can tell you later. I'm just gonna eat a few more bites and go back to bed."

As he finished those "few more bites," he gave his friends additional instructions. "Y'all don't have to sit with me all the time like I think you've been doin'. If I die, I die. I'm ready. Just get me back to Branson. Don knows where to put me."

"You're not planning to help yourself to an early death so you don't have to tell us about the box, are you?" Roy asked.

"No, I'll try to survive long enough to tell you about the box . . . and some more things."

When Roy had brought Abe's breakfast to the balcony, he had again left the glass door partially open. The room needed airing, and Roy reasoned if Abe could handle the cool air on the balcony, he could later handle fresh air in the room. It was good that Roy had done so. He heard a knock on the hallway door.

"How's Mister Brown?" the ship's doctor asked as Roy held the door open for him.

"He's on the balcony finishing his breakfast."

"It's amazing how many older men surrender everything in their life before they give up their breakfast," the doctor responded.

On the balcony, the doctor took Abe's vital signs. He also listened to Abe's heart with his stethoscope. "The cool fresh air must be good for you. Your heart rate and blood pressure are higher. I can't compare it to the resting rates that we've been taking in your bed over the last few days. The measurements simply are not comparable. However, I'm glad to see you enjoying the sunshine and fresh air."

"I've had about all of the enjoyment I can stand. I'm ready to go back to bed."

"We'll help you get there, and I will take more readings. They still won't be exactly comparable because of your activity this morning," the doctor answered.

"He says there is no need for us to sit with him," Roy mentioned to the doctor as he and Walt helped Abe to the bed.

"There isn't a need for someone to be with him continually if Mister Brown is comfortable with that."

"I'm comfortable. I don't want a code blue, or whatever you call it on your ship."

"On the *Color Emerald*, we don't use colors for medical situations, we use numbers. But our numeric codes are super secret, and shared only with staff so that passengers don't worry when they hear the calls. Have you gentlemen had breakfast?"

"We're going to the Top Side in a few minutes." Walt answered.

"Keep yourselves nourished, but stay away from the gravy. It's full of stuff that will kill you. After I finish here with Mister Brown and visit another patient, I'll find you in the Top Side. I want to make arrangements with you for Mister Brown's disembarkation. And, I will check your plates for gravy."

• • •

The three friends later met the friendly doctor's gravy test. Before the doctor arrived, the three had limited their conversation about Abe's ominous warning, talking in quiet voices and using abstract language. When the doctor joined them, they did not look happy.

"Are you extremely concerned about your friend?" the doctor inquired when he sensed the hushed mood at the table.

Don nodded, "Yes, but he's ready to meet the Lord. We're ready to let him go."

"Good. That seems to be very important to many Americans."

Walt asked, "Do you know the Lord?"

"I don't know," the doctor responded. "Not the way so many Americans seem to think they do. I believe there is a Creator. I don't see how one who deals with the complexity of the human body can argue with the concept of supreme intelligence. I just don't know about this Jesus stuff."

"Well, I'm very sure about 'this Jesus stuff'," Walt returned." I'll give you a book that tells you about it. It's called John. It was written a long time ago by one of the guys who were with Jesus."

"St. John?"

"Yes. 'Saint' is a term for believers."

"So the word 'saint' used with John would indicate he was a believer in Jesus?" The doctor asked.

"Yes, and he accompanied Jesus constantly from the early days of Jesus' ministry. He had firsthand information."

"Well, get the book to me. I shall read it. But I want to talk about your friend, Mister Brown."

"Go ahead," the three said almost in unison.

"He's going to die soon. He might be dead as we sit here, but I don't think so. I think he will last a few more days. His passenger record says that he is traveling with independent transportation. I assume that is with you?"

Walt and Roy deferred to Don who would be the administrator of Abe's will, and who had power-of-attorney to act on Abe's behalf while Abe was alive. Don answered the doctor's question. "Yes, we are traveling by motor home. We traveled extensively before boarding the ship, and had planned to leisurely wander back to our home near Branson, Missouri. But Abe's health suggests we hurry home. I think he wants to return to Branson before he dies."

"Some people set such a short term goal when they reach Mister Brown's point in life. Many are able to accomplish their goals. If you think he wants to return home before his death, I suggest you help him."

"We will." Don responded as Walt and Roy nodded agreement.

"That's very good. Now, let's talk about an exact plan to disembark Mister Brown and the three of you. I will see that you are disembarked as soon as the ship clears pratique and meets other port and government requirements. I will arrange a pass for one of you to drive your motor home directly alongside the ship, much as we would do for an ambulance. By the way, there will be two ambulances awaiting the ship, and one other private vehicle. You won't be able to push those vehicles off the dock to minimize the distance we transport Mister Brown."

The three friends appreciated the doctor's levity. "We can accept that," Walt replied.

"I thought so." The doctor did not smile, but clearly enjoyed lightening the conversation. "We will also arrange for your baggage to clear customs immediately and to be carried directly to your motor home. It will be your job to arise early, have breakfast and get your luggage ready for special handling on the day we arrive, tomorrow. Do not allow your room steward to put your luggage into the normal process. I will arrange special luggage tags. Soon before we dock, I will send crew members with a wheelchair for Mister Brown and with luggage carts to handle your luggage. You will accompany those crew members. Oh, there is Mister Brown's scooter. Can one of you drive that? Good. The crew will bring you, your luggage and Mister Brown to the Medical Department by elevators and hallways that you don't even know exist. That will avoid the crowd of people who have enjoyed the cruise so much they want to be the first to disembark." The doctor smiled as he thought of the normal unnecessary rush of passengers leaving their cruise ship.

"We will disembark you directly from the medical department. The first will be whoever is to go for the motor home. Oh, we will also arrange a priority shuttle to take that person to the parking lot. The motor home is in the special RV parking at the Seattle dock, is it not?"

"It is," Don answered." Walt, will you go for the Road Lynx?"

The doctor raised his head, "Oh, a Road Lynx! I've seen those. They are very nice. You have a land yacht."

"Abe bought it," Walt thought the doctor's appreciation should be passed to Abe. "Oh, and it has a trailer. That won't cause a problem, will it?"

"No, but I shall so note on the paperwork. I will need the registry number . . . correct that, the license plate number and state of registration before I prepare the paper work. Can you give me that today?"

"Right now, Walt answered. He pulled a note card from his billfold and wrote the information from memory.

"I'm impressed you know the numbers, Mister Wilson."

"Walt loves numbers," Roy interjected.

"We use him for a calculator," Don added. "By the way, Doctor, what's all of that gravy doing on your plate?"

"It enhances the biscuits, actually. It's one of my favorites from the American killer diet. But I only allow myself to partake about once a week."

"And, this is the day!" Roy exclaimed.

"Yes, my gravy day. What an exciting life I lead at sea!"

# CHAPTER 39

Disembarkation went exactly as planned. Two hours after the *Color Emerald* docked, Walt steered the Road Lynx onto eastbound Interstate 90. Roy sorted mail from another box from Cyn which had been held for them at a FedEx service store near the ship terminal. Abe slept in his bunk.

Don was sitting in the passenger seat with a map on his lap directing Walt. "Walt, let's stop at Issaquah to replenish the bus. I'd like to shop in a full-line grocery store, and the bus needs fuel."

"Okay. Now that we're on land and underway, how do you feel about our plan?"

"Still good. We want to hustle Abe back to Branson, but we don't want to kill three old men doing it. We can drive all day every day, but we must stop for the nights. Sleeping in the Road Lynx is the best plan for Abe. Besides a break for sleep, the rest of us also need to stretch our legs."

"I like Roy's idea of eating light snacks in the bus. We could kill a lot of time in restaurants."

"Yes. I think it's a good idea. That's why I want to stop soon. By the way, the drinks we left in the refrigerator are cold. It's great that the port's RV parking has hook-ups."

"I hate to think of the cost of keeping our drinks cold all week," Walt quipped.

"But I'm glad the refrigerator is cold and ready for our snack foods. I'll also get something for a more substantial meal one evening. I want to get small T-bone steaks for a special meal for Abe."

Walt took his eyes from the road, glancing at Don. "His last meal, huh?"

"You remember our conversation from the eastern trip, don't you? Yes, but we won't know which meal will be his last. I want to honor him with his favorite meal while he can enjoy it."

"I doubt he can eat much of it, Don, even if he's awake at the right time."

"You're right. He doesn't have strength to eat much of anything. I'll buy diet supplement for him, too. Maybe that will help sustain him."

"Do you think he'll be awake long enough to tell us about the weapon?"

"I already know more than I want to know. But your guess is as good as mine about how much, how often and how long Abe will be awake."

Walt noticed a road sign. "We're making good time. Watch for an Issaquah exit and food store signs."

After their stop for food and fuel, the three men rotated driving duties every hour. They timed fuel stops for driver changes, and made a quick pullover for all other driver changes. They refused the temptation of changing drivers while underway. Except when refueling, within two minutes from the time one driver brought the Road Lynx to a full stop, the next driver had the big rig underway. Roy began timing all stops. He normally got the bus underway faster than Walt or Don. Walt defended his time, stating that he always had to adjust the mirrors, whereas Don or Roy did not have to adjust the mirrors when following one another.

Abe had asked his friends for two favors during their hurried trip home to Branson. The first was to divert through Yellowstone Park to see Mammoth Hot Springs and Old Faithful. The second was to stop at Mount Rushmore. The three assented, noting among themselves the stops would add several hours to their trip, but felt they could accommodate their friend whose failing health was the reason for the hurry.

• • •

Walt was driving his fourth shift when he followed Roy's directions to a state park in Montana, not far from Butte. As soon as Walt had the Road Lynx parked, Don pulled the charcoal grill from the trailer, and started a hickory fire in it. He had made a salad and sliced potatoes for frying while traveling over the last hour. To expedite frying the potatoes on the campfire, Don had partially cooked them in the Road Lynx's microwave.

Abe awoke, and was helped from the bus by Walt and Roy to a high back rocking chair Roy had retrieved from the garage. He looked around at the towering lodge pole pines, took as deep a breath as he could, coughed, and said, "You guys sure pick nice spots. Whatcha cookin' Don? I'm starved."

"Your favorite: T-bones, fried potatoes and salad. You want your steak medium-well like always?" As he spoke, Don spread the burning hickory chunks, and placed the potatoes in a black cast iron skillet on the grill.

"What would y'all have done if I had slept through dinner?"

Roy answered, "I would have eaten your steak."

"It's great to have friends," Abe laughed.

"What do you want to drink, Abe?" Roy asked.

"Don's coffee, please. I smelled it brewing before we stopped."

"Coming up," Roy said as he headed to the bus door.

"Oh, Roy. Will you bring me my field glasses and my extra glasses, the ones with big black rims?" Abe's spoke softly and slowly with a raspy voice.

"Uh, sure."

Walt was setting plates, bowls, forks and steak knives on a dark green plastic tablecloth he had spread on the campsite table. "What are you going to do with your glasses, Abe?"

"Keep a promise," Abe answered.

"Huh?"

"You'll see in a few minutes, Walt," Abe answered, then turned his attention to Don, "You can get a hot cooking fire burnin' faster than anybody I've ever seen, Don."

"I don't like to mess around waiting on the fire. But the fire has to be right to cook properly."

Walt was hungry and asked, "How long before we eat?"

"With this fire, which is not perfect, I'll guess seventeen minutes."

"Could you be more precise?" Roy kidded as he stepped from the Road Lynx.

"Best I can do on my outdoor range," Don retorted.

Don's estimate was short by two minutes. He had not allowed time for Walt to say grace.

Don helped Abe by cutting his steak from the T-bone and by cutting a portion of the slightly pink meat into small bites. Abe surprised his friends by eating as much of his meal as he did. He asked for a second helping of potatoes and ate every tomato chunk from his salad even though he left a substantial portion of his lettuce. He ate over half of his small thick steak.

The others were still eating when Abe laid down his knife and fork. He rasped, "I promised y'all I'd tell you about the weapon. It's a long story that I'll summarize, and only part of it is about the weapon. It starts with me." Abe's friends continued to eat, but at a much slower pace. Their eyes and ears were directed to Abe.

Abe paused for breath before he continued, "For all but the last few years of my life, the years that I've known y'all, I was Travis Thornton. I used to say I was born an orphan. Maybe I was. I never knew my parents. I was raised in an orphanage in Galveston. I could see the ships go and come, and I got interested in geography, politics and business. In high school I worked part time for an import/export company as a runner. I was a good one. Then I became a clerk, then a manager. When the war came along, I joined the Army and got sent to Africa and Italy. I was lucky and survived, and I learned a lot along the way. I got sent to the Pacific just in time for the war to end, but I learned some stuff there too. I was especially interested to see how those two devastated areas would recover. When I came home, I got a college degree in economics, but I also took all the history, political and geography classes I could manage. I worked while I was in college . . . . Hell, I always worked my fool head off. Soon after, I bought, really just took over with no money, a little no-account import/export business in Galveston. I moved it to Houston and turned it into a tradin' company. That's when I really started travelin'. International communication was difficult in those days. Travel was, too, but it was better than waitin' on letters and telexes to slowly go back and forth. Anyway, by goin' to the devastated areas, I found plenty of tradin' opportunities. People in the war areas maybe could make somethin', but they didn't have anyplace to sell whatever they made. And people in those areas needed things, but didn't have the wherewithal to get what they needed. I met the needs, and took some risks. Before long I had a sizeable business. I was getting' rich, but not too fast. I was careful not to gig those poor people whose lives had been blown apart by war.

"When I traveled I met lots of people, and liked or at least got along with most of 'em. Some, though, I hated intensely, and at times thought about sellin' my business because of a few jerks I just hated. The jerks I hated most were people who demanded bribes before I could deliver food and other goods to people that really needed stuff I had found for them. Sometimes the jerks were petty bureaucrats, sometimes they were the dictators of countries. I hated those people. I bribed a bunch of 'em, but kept looking for a better way to deal with 'em." Abe paused while he took a sip of coffee and regained his breath. "Finally, I just shot a few of 'em. Killed 'em dead. Cleverly, of course. Uh, I was a sniper in the Army. It's a wonder I survived the war. Most snipers didn't.

"But back to my story. Somehow, I took on a couple of contract killin's. Then, I developed a nice little side business. Only one guy ever had reason to believe it was me that was doing the killin's that I did. He was my go-between. I paid him well. Oh, I always checked out my contracts to make sure I wasn't killin' somebody I shouldn't. I turned down some jobs."

Abe halted his story in favor of breathing and coughing. After a few minutes, he continued. "My import/export or tradin' business made a great cover for my second business. Oh, before y'all ask: None of the money in the trust came from that second business. I gave all of it away. In fact those payments mostly went directly to orphanages like the one that raised me, and didn't even come through me. But I couldn't kill everybody that got in my way, and my frustration with scoundrels, as I came to call 'em, was just part of my business for years.

"In my spare time, minutes per day, I liked to read about and play with new technology. In the fifties some people were working on light stimulation, which eventually led to the laser. I got my hands on some of the early work as a part of a complicated trade that I put together. With a very smart German friend, a physicist, I started experimentin'.

"My friend and I darned near burned down his house once when we accidentally compressed a bunch of light down a tube. We hadn't invented what we now call the laser, but we had somethin' similar. With a little more work, we had somethin' usable. Before we could give our discovery a name like laser or light ray, my friend got killed in a car wreck. I soon figured out the best use for our discovery was as a weapon. With my new weapon, that's what I called it, 'my weapon,' I could send a concentrated mass of light down a tube out through the air, and from fifty feet away cut a steak like these we are eatin' tonight. As a weapon, the cuttin' range was about two hundred fifty feet." Abe took another sip of coffee, and then breathed in and out for two minutes. Nobody else moved.

"My weapon frightened me. The United States and Russia were going though the atomic weapons race then. We had air raid warnin's, and emergency provisions were bein' stored in public buildings. Both countries kept buildin' bigger bombs. I could imagine our government developin' my weapon to cut flesh from a distance of four miles or more. I got even more scared when I thought what the Russians might develop if they ever got their hands on my weapon." Abe had an attentive audience.

"I decided to keep my weapon a secret. I originally put the plans and calculations in a safe deposit box in Uvalde, Texas, but moved 'em to Dalhart when I became Abe Brown. Of the four weapons I made, I put two in the safe deposit box with the plans. The other two are layin' right in front of you, the field glasses and the plastic frames on the old eyeglasses. The field glasses have the longer range, about 250 feet in the right atmosphere. The eyeglass frames have a short range, across the room, about 35 feet.

"My weapon helped me overcome frustration in my tradin' business. I used it to eliminate some of those jerks that demanded bribes. I also was able to handle more activity in my secondary business. I had to change my contract terms in that second business to provide that payment was due if the target somehow 'got dead' within a certain time frame. The light could cut internal human tissue without damagin' outer tissue. Targets of my weapon appeared to die natural deaths such as a strokes, heart attacks, or aneurysms. Sometimes, if I was dealing with a first-class jerk, I would cut his bowel and the guy would die a miserable death of internal infection. I also could cut knee or ankle ligaments and cause bad falls."

Roy's eyes widened. *The three scoundrels had died of stroke, fall in traffic, and a heart attack.* Roy said nothing, wanting Abe to continue.

"I quit my contract business in the mid-1980s. It was too much work and had too much risk. I also quit killin' people just because of normal greed. But I knocked off a few really bad characters, some prominent, some not. In the nineties, I probably didn't kill more than a dozen people."

Don gasped. "How many did you kill in total?"

"I don't know. I lost track, and decided I didn't want to count 'em anyway. Since 2000, I haven't killed anybody, until lately."

Walt thought he knew where Abe was going. "Until lately?"

"Yeah. I retired from all of that activity in 2000, when I became Abe Brown."

Walt asked again, this time turning his better ear a bit more toward Abe. "'Until lately'? So what do you mean by that?"

Abe took several deep breaths. He was sweating. "Okay, here comes the confession: Walt, Don and Roy. I used you guys to transport me to knock off three scoundrels, and to try to kill off a fourth scoundrel I learned about later."

Don saw the pattern, "While we played golf at Chesnut Hills, you killed the former President of Mid-North on the green at Glistening Springs."

Walt added, "While we played Bethpage Black, a guy fell in front of a cab in Manhattan. The guy was a Mid-North scoundrel."

Roy stated, "You got Gus Whitby at Basswood almost while we watched. You used those field glasses to cause a heart attack."

"Right in all cases. By the way, I did not kill that guy that had the heart attack at Basswood the day before I got Whitby."

Don asked, "So who's the fourth that you tried to kill?"

Gilbert Glass at Tahoe.

"Who is Gilbert Glass?" Roy asked.

Abe clarified, "The man who got hit by lightning at the marina while I watched. Only I wasn't just watchin', I had him in the sights of my field glasses, but my boat was heavin', and I was afraid to push the trigger. Then the huge lightning bolt startled me, and I pushed the trigger. I don't know that I was pointin' the glasses exactly at Glass when I triggered the beam. The field glasses went flyin' almost overboard, I fell on the deck, and Glass went to the ground. I don't know if I hit him or not. The lightning could account for all of his injuries without any help from me. On the other hand, I was aimin', or tryin' to aim, at the back of his neck. I wanted to paralyze him. He was the worst scoundrel of all."

Walt guessed, "You wanted him to suffer."

"Exactly, but somethin', maybe that Holy Spirit y'all told me about, is workin' on me. I don't feel good about Glass lyin' on a bed like a vegetable, even though I think he is a very evil man." All sat quietly for a few seconds before Abe continued. "Here's the interestin' part. I want him to accept God's grace like I did. I'm acknowledgin' God's grace is bigger than our biggest sins, like y'all have told me over and over. And, I occasionally feel remorse that I cut off the other three scoundrels' lives before they accepted that grace."

"You know enough about people to know that many never accept God's grace. You can't assume any of those men would have ever come to Christ," Don advised Abe.

"I guess I won't have to see 'em in heaven." Abe's straight face showed no emotion. He had merely stated his supposition.

Roy suggested, "Abe, you can pray for this guy, Glass. Pray that God will continue to offer his grace, and send a special messenger."

"You're tellin' me to ask God not to give up on Glass, but you've been tellin' me that God never gives up on us, anyway. Isn't that a waste of prayer time?"

"Such a prayer might bring peace to you. Praying in God's will, it's called. I don't understand all there is to know about it. I only know it is helpful for the person you're praying for and for you, the prayer," Roy explained.

Abe didn't understand Roy's comments. He was feeling very tired, but he wanted to further discuss an earlier conversation rather than explore Roy's advice. "Speaking of prayer, I told y'all about my experience on the boat on Lake Tahoe when I went to sleep after praying. Well, my prayer was askin' God if I had caused Glass's injuries or if the lightning had. The answer I got was that I don't need to know."

Walt had been sitting silently. He wasn't participating in the conversation about Gilbert Glass. His mind was still spinning with thoughts of how many people Abe had killed over his lifetime, and that Abe had recently used his closest friends without their knowledge to kill three more people and to try to kill a fourth. Abe had deceived his friends from the start of each trip. It hurt. Walt tried to formulate a question to make him better understand Abe. "Abe, how many people have you killed altogether, a hundred?"

"More than that. It's more than a hundred, but closer to one hundred fifty than two hundred."

"So one hundred seventy-five or a few less?"

"Yes, around that. I killed many of them a long time ago. I hated officials that had to be bribed to help their people."

Walt pressed. "How about the guy that died in your cottage? Did you cause that heart attack with one of your weapons?"

"Yes, with my black-frame glasses. He was onto my field glasses and wanted to see 'em. He qualified for my list of guys that just oughtta be killed. He knew what had happened as soon as I hit him with a beam. He knew he had just been outsmarted. Being outsmarted probably bothered him more than knowin' he was dyin'. I don't think he liked his life much. I wish he had died somewhere else, though."

"No regrets?" Don asked.

"Not really. I don't think he would have ever accepted God's grace. But now I know that I made sure he didn't. I feel a little bad about that. Should I feel really bad?"

"You're on your own. I can't answer that one. Ask God," Don advised.

Over the last several minutes, Abe's voice had weakened further. His breathing was labored, and he was sweating heavily despite the coolness of the evening. Abe knew he must close the discussion of his past and get to his main reason for telling his friends about his murderous activities. "Fellas, I'm wearin' out again. Before I go to sleep permanently in this chair, I need to do two things. First, Don, thank you for fixin' my favorite meal. I hope it's not my last with y'all."

Don nodded, whispered "You're welcome, Abe," and waited for Abe to state his other pressing issue.

"Number two is tough for an ol' goat like me, because I'm not good at makin' apologies. I never practiced that activity much in my former life. But here goes. Walt, Roy and Don I have lied to you, used you, and drawn y'all dangerously close to crimes that I should not have committed. I have also hidden my past, but have asked you to be my friends now and after I'm gone. I thank you for helpin' me find God's grace. I ask y'all to forgive me, your foolish old friend, of my sins against you. I would appreciate it if you would." By the time Abe got "appreciate" out of his mouth, he was exhausted. He sat with his head against the chair back, breathing heavily.

Roy was first to respond. "Sure, Abe. But you've scared the pants off me."

Don next assured Abe. "In God's grace, I forgive you. I have a raft of thoughts, in some of which I appreciate you, but in some of which I'm mad at you. Mostly though, I love you, my action-oriented old-but-new brother in Christ. I forgive you."

Walt rose from his chair, stretched himself full height, drew a deep breath and said. "I'm bewildered about what to say. Yes, I can forgive you, and I do. But I'm still hurt. We trusted you, but you used us. We made your last round of murders possible. Does that make us accessories? Should we have seen what you were doing and stopped you? In my human nature I appreciate what you've done. But I thought I had put that nature behind me. The fact that I sort of approve of what you've done disappoints me in myself, because I really want to think and act like Christ taught us to. I guess I have to forgive myself for my thoughts. I'm very tired and confused. You must be exhausted. Let me help you to bed."

Abe nodded his head. He looked at his friends, let a tear slip down his cheek, and whispered, "Thanks."

While Walt and Roy helped Abe, Don cleaned up from the dinner. He put everything away except for three of the rockers. He wanted to talk to Walt and Roy about what they had just learned. He guessed they would want to talk about it, too.

Roy emerged from the Road Lynx wearing sweats, which he wore as pajamas on cool nights.

"Walt went to bed," Roy announced.

"I'm surprised. I should think he would want to talk. I do."

"Me too. Walt said he was too tired to think. He drove more than we did today, and I think he really feels betrayed by Abe. He's hurt." Roy dropped into the rocker beside Don.

"I'm hurt too. And, I wonder if we yet know the whole story."

"I wonder if you, Walt and I are legally accomplices to murder, and what, if anything, we should do with our new knowledge of Abe."

"I'm sorry he told us. His secret would have died with him if he hadn't told us."

Roy speculated, "I guess he thought we should know about the weapons in case America's leaders suddenly start toppling over with heart attacks and strokes."

"Don't forget bad falls and sliced intestines."

"Yeah, those too. But if we give the secret to our government, the best that can happen is for enemies to unexplainably die. This is a weapon, not a cure or protection against someone else's weapon."

Don saw the point. "We could be instrumental in another round of weapons escalation."

Roy asked, "If Abe had told us at the first of May about his weapon and asked us to help him kill the scoundrels, would you have done it?"

"No, but I'm glad they're dead," Don confessed.

"Same here. We're not exactly perfect are we?"

"No."

"Do you think anybody believes the scoundrels' deaths are suspect?"

"No. Everybody seems sure they're dead."

"That's not what I meant, Mister Stone."

"Somebody probably suspects that three deaths within a few days, and a near-death not long after, is more than unusual."

"I didn't know there was a fourth scoundrel. Did you? How did Abe find out?"

Don shook his head. "I didn't know and I don't know how Abe found out. Do you think he knew all along? He only talked to us about three."

"He spent a lot of time on his computer after Ann moved. I thought he was dealing with his business matters. He was probably researching the Mid-North deal. Somehow he learned of the fourth guy. What's his name? Glass? Abe just didn't bother to tell us about him."

"Remember, Roy, he only told us what he wanted us to know when he wanted us to know."

"If he finally told us because I asked too many questions about his background or about what's in the box, I'm really sorry I asked."

"I think he wanted to confess his offense and to ask our forgiveness. He was sorry he had used us to do something we would not have condoned had we known what he was doing." Don paused, and added, "In a way that's a good sign. It shows remorse and love of friends, something Abe spent most of his life without."

"I'm glad you've generated a positive idea for this mess, Don. I'm going to bed." Roy picked up the field glasses and the black-framed eyeglasses. "In the bus, Abe gave me instructions for these. I'll take care of them tomorrow."

# CHAPTER 40

When the Road Lynx rolled past the gates of the state park early the next morning, Don was driving. Roy and Walt sat at the table. Abe was asleep in his bunk. On the floor beside the table, Abe's big tool chest sat open. Two small boxes from the tool chest sat on the table. One contained jeweler's tools. The other contained a strange collection of tiny tubes, lenses and panels.

Roy used the small tools to disassemble Abe's black-framed eyeglasses. He followed step-by-step directions he had found per Abe's instructions folded in the bottom of the box of tiny parts. The directions were deceptively labeled as being for Model A-15 Warm Tone Hearing Aid Glasses.

On the table was another sheet of directions labeled Sight Modifications for Forward Observer Field Glasses. The top edge of this sheet was ragged, giving the appearance that the page was missing important product identification information. Both documents were yellowed and bore dark fold marks.

Roy was doing the first of the tasks Abe had asked him to do as soon as possible. Roy was to disassemble both weapons, smash the critical pieces, and dispose of all parts and pieces. Abe had asked Roy to disperse the weapon parts among trash receptacles at various stops the friends would make on the way home. Abe had confessed he had thought about dropping both weapons overboard in the Pacific, but was afraid that by some amazing string of events one of them might be recovered by a curious fisherman. In a trash can near the men's room in the park they had just left, Roy had made his first deposit, which included batteries from each of the weapons, one eyeglass earpiece and a small selection of screws and fasteners.

Walt watched Roy work and said, "I've seen Abe wearing those glasses a few times. I wonder if he wore them from time to time in case he might have to use them at Ozark View."

"No 'might' to it," Roy shot back. "He told us last night he used 'em to kill the guy in his cottage."

"I guess he knew somebody from his past would eventually find him."

"I'm glad I didn't accidentally kill myself when I packed Abe's bags in Seattle and on the ship."

"Me too. Otherwise I might have the job of disassembling those things."

"I'm glad you were not so inconvenienced, Mister Wilson."

"Thank you. Seriously, may I do anything?"

"Feel free to work on the field glasses. Here are the directions."

Roy changed the subject. "Have you thought any more about our dilemma now that we know Abe killed those guys?"

"Yes, and considering Abe's condition, that he will die soon, and that we will reveal the existence of Abe's weapons if we say anything to anybody, we have no choice but to keep quiet. I don't want to start another arms race. Abe has boxed us up like he did the weapons in the Dalhart bank!"

"Don and I came to that same conclusion when we talked this morning while you were showering. We don't want to start an arms race, and the implications of Abe's weapons getting into the wrong hands are terrifying."

Walt shivered. "I'm uncomfortable with those weapons in the 'right hands,' ours. What if we discover there is a fifth scoundrel. Will we be tempted to drive to Dalhart, get a weapon, and finish Abe's work?"

Roy quoted from the Lord's Prayer, ". . . and lead us not into temp-tation. . . ."

"Yeah, I hope I'm not tempted by a fifth scoundrel, or somebody else of similar character."

Roy motioned to the parts on the table. "What if all of this is another lie?"

"You mean the weapons aren't really weapons, and Abe didn't kill anybody?"

"Yeah, and what if Abe's confession of faith is a bunch of hooey, too?"

Walt nodded. "Abe has deceived us so much that we don't know what to believe."

"Of everything, I hope the confession of faith is real. But, why would he make up a story about the weapons and the murders?"

"He could be covering up something else. And, maybe he felt he needed to tell us about the box in Dalhart."

Roy stopped the work of his hands, and looked directly at Walt. "He had already told us, even showed us, the box."

"We saw the box, but we did not see what's in the box. And, we don't know how to use the weapons. Abe didn't tell us that."

"Yeah, all we know is how to take 'em apart. Abe didn't tell you how to trigger the weapons?"

"No. He didn't tell me anything he didn't tell you." Walt began twisting on a binocular lens. "We don't know what to believe. I hope for Abe's sake his acceptance of God's grace is real. I think we just have to accept it is."

"Well, he has shown some fruit of the Spirit during the last couple of weeks, but Abe's a well-practiced deceiver. I agree we just have to accept his confession of faith. It's really between him and God."

Don spoke from the driver's seat, "Will one of you refill my coffee mug, and tell me what you've decided in your hushed conversation?"

• • •

At Bozeman, Montana, Don pulled into a convenience store parking lot for a driver change. Roy made a deposit in the store's outdoor trash can, and Walt slid into the driver's seat of the big bus. Roy's deposit took less time than the driver switch, and the Road Lynx was rolling again within two minutes.

Thirty minutes before the guys reached the Montana-Wyoming state line, Don woke Abe. "Abe, we aren't far from Yellowstone and Mammoth Hot Springs. You should get dressed and have a bite to eat."

Abe opened his eyes, and asked, "Are y'all still speakin' to me?"

"Yes, Abe, and you're still our friend."

Abe smiled broadly. "Thanks, Don. Will you help me up?"

• • •

The stops in Yellowstone added more time to the group's travel than Walt, Don and Roy had estimated. The park was crowded with tourists. Parking the Road Lynx and trailer very close to either Mammoth Hot Springs or Old Faithful was not possible. Walt let Abe, Roy and Don off the bus as close to the hot springs as he could get, then found a parking place for the big rig. They followed a similar process at Old Faithful. The big issue at each stop was to get the scooter out of the trailer and Abe off the bus without stopping traffic more than necessary. After looking at each attraction, the four made a long journey to the bus with Abe sitting on the scooter and two friends walking exactly beside him to prevent him from toppling off. All four were pleased that they did not have to repeat the process at a third location. By the time they boarded the Road Lynx near Old Faithful, Abe wanted to return to bed. Abe slept through the balance of the drive through Yellowstone, but he was happy. Roy dropped four small bundles of parts in Yellowstone, one each at the park's north entrance, at Mammoth Springs, at Old Faithful and at a park store and gas station.

Roy drove the Road Lynx from Yellowstone by the southeast exit, and followed Wyoming highways eastward. Shortly after dusk, the guys stopped at a campground southwest of Buffalo, Wyoming where they would rejoin Interstate 90 the next day. Don made a quick fire in the grill, and grilled skewers laden with chicken chunks, mushrooms, bell pepper slices, tomato wedges and potato chunks. Abe did not join his friends outside for the meal, and only nibbled on a few bites of chicken and potato when Don took a plate to his bed.

Roy noticed a message on his cell phone, which had been showing "OUT OF RANGE" all day. He returned a call from Cyn, who quickly got Ann on the phone. Ann asked to speak to Abe. When Abe scratched a weak hello into the phone, Ann announced that she had moved into her cottage at Ozark View, and she wanted to immediately thank the guy that made it possible. Abe could not answer. He trembled, cried, and let his hand with the phone drop to the pillow. Finally, he lifted the phone to the side of his face, and simply said, "Ann, it is my joy. Welcome home." Abe spoke so softly that Ann could not quite hear all he said. Roy repeated Abe's statement after he stepped outside, leaving Abe crying softly in bed. The conversation with Ann, Cyn and Ruth continued for forty-five minutes, with Walt and Don taking turns on Roy's phone. All of the men were careful to say nothing about their recent revelations.

With another early start, the group reached Mount Rushmore before noon. During the morning, Abe had gotten out of bed only briefly to use the bathroom. His short walk required the assistance of both Roy and Don. Abe was not awake when Roy steered the bus off Interstate 90 near Rapid City for the short drive to the monument. Abe shook his head when Walt suggested he get dressed to visit the monument, but agreed when Walt suggested Don and Walt could help Abe to the captain's chair by a big window from which he might view the monument without leaving the bus. Roy found a space in a large parking lot from where Abe could see all four famous faces. Abe stared at the monument for a few minutes, then dropped his head and indicated he should return to his bed. The bus was in the parking lot at Mount Rushmore for no more than ten minutes.

Roy returned to Interstate 90, and headed east across South Dakota. Roy did not slow down for the famous Wall Drug Store or the Badlands National Park. He kept the Road Lynx moving at the speed limit across the grasslands, as did Don and Walt when they took their driving shifts. Thirteen hours after leaving their campground that morning, Walt pulled the Road Lynx into a commercial recreational vehicle park near Sioux City, Iowa. Walt, Don, and Roy stretched their legs with a slow walk around the RV park while they waited for a pizza delivery from a nearby outlet of a major chain. They were in bed by nine o'clock. The next day they would be home. They had to hurry. Abe seemed weaker.

• • •

Roy made his last weapons parts disposal at a convenience store north of Kansas City. Throughout the morning, the three drivers had held their coach's speed at the highway's limit. Abe was no longer able to walk to the bathroom, but had to use a bedpan brought from the *Color Emerald*. When Abe first used it, he smiled slightly and whispered to Don, "Helluva cruise souvenir, huh?"

As the bus approached Springfield, Don called ahead to the Ozark View medical department to let the staff know that the Road Lynx should be arriving in about one hour and that Abe was extremely weak. Don told the nurse that Abe did not want to go to a hospital, but wanted to spend some time in his cottage before being moved to the Ozark View skilled nursing facility. The staff called the Ozark View attending physician. He would meet the bus when it arrived. Don also called Ruth, who alerted Cyn, Ann and other friends.

# CHAPTER 41

A subdued crowd met the Road Lynx at Ozark View. Two nurses and a doctor were standing beside a gurney in front of Abe's cottage with Ruth, Cyn and Ann. Others stood or sat in wheelchairs, high back rockers, and folding chairs along the wide sidewalk near the parking lot. Everyone who could stand rose when the big rig entered the parking lot. Unlike when the group departed almost a month before, there was no blast from the Road Lynx's horn, nor was there any cheering from the crowd.

Roy brought the bus to a stop in a space cleared for it in front of Abe's cottage. The three ladies in front of Abe's cottage simultaneously broke into tears as the medical staff boarded the Road Lynx. Others cried or steeled themselves for bad news.

The nurses and doctor examined Abe in his bunk. One of the nurses stepped off the bus, grabbed respiratory equipment, and rushed back on board. Eventually, the medical staff, with help from Walt and Roy, carried Abe, strapped to a transfer board, down the steps of the Road Lynx. They placed Abe on the waiting gurney and rolled him toward his home. The nurses slowed the gurney as it passed by Cyn, Ruth and Ann. Abe opened his eyes and acknowledged his friends by firmly blinking twice. He could not speak because of the oxygen mask over his nose and mouth. He opened his eyes again as he was rolled into his house. He surveyed what he could see of his living room, and slowly closed his eyes.

Don surmised Abe had reached his goal, but Don was wrong. Abe had a greater goal. He wanted to talk to Ann, Cyn and Ruth before he died. But he must sleep first.

Abe was slipping fast, and the physician confirmed to Don that Abe's death was imminent. Don passed the information to the friends. All hoped for one more chance to talk to Abe. With Don's approval four hours after Abe's friends had delivered him to his home, Abe was moved to the skilled nursing unit.

Early the next afternoon Abe told his nurse he wanted to speak to his six close friends. They soon assembled around Abe's bed.

With a gravely weak voice and with interruptions for breathing, Abe individually thanked his friends for the characteristic about each that he most enjoyed. He told them they were good friends, and that he had had few friends in his life. He told the men how much he had valued them as friends, traveling companions and as trustees of his trust. He told Ann that her loving personality was the kindest that he had ever seen. He told all three ladies that they had helped him come to Christ, and that he appreciated their prayers for his salvation.

Then he said, "I have a special request. I want y'all to pray for three people. Pray for Stuart Range, whom you've met. He's a young man who should have a better life, including his eternal life. Pray for an old friend, Tom Queen. He's a good man but hasn't accepted God's grace. And, there is a fellow named Glass, Gilbert Glass, who was hit by lightning and is lyin' like a vegetable in a hospital in California. Pray for his salvation like you prayed for mine. He is a serious sinner like I was."

Abe's six friends were surprised but pleased by Abe's thoughtfulness. They promised to honor Abe's requests. The friends continued to visit for almost thirty minutes, during which Walt and Roy handed the ladies the gifts Abe had bought for them. When Abe's consciousness began to fade he asked, "Roy, did you get that last task completed?"

"I did. It's done."

Abe closed his eyes.

• • •

Abe lingered for two more days with only a few minutes of consciousness. Don was sitting with Abe when one of those conscious moments occurred. Abe said nothing, and showed no recognition of Don before he drifted back to sleep.

On Friday evening, Walt left Abe's bedside to find Don, who was sitting with Roy on Roy's lakeside patio. "Don, the doctor would like for you to be near when Abe dies, which will be very soon. Let us know when it happens. I'll be here with Roy."

Twenty minutes later, Don returned to the patio, and looked down the sidewalk toward the row of cottages. Don took a deep breath, exhaled, and finally spoke. "Walt and Roy, our friend Abe, who I think only we three know was a man who struck down scoundrels, has passed on. Let's go tell Ann, Cyn and Ruth. We can tell them Abe finally solved his biggest issue, and is now with his newly found Lord."

# BIBLE REFERENCES

*But do not forget this one thing, dear friends: With the Lord a day is like
a thousand years, and a thousand years are like a day.
The Lord is not slow in keeping his promise as some understand slowness.
He is patient with you, not wanting anyone to perish,
but everyone to come to repentance.*
2 Peter 3:8–9, New International Version

[Jesus is speaking to the repentant thief on the cross]
*"I tell you the truth, today you will be with me in paradise."*
Luke 23:43, New International Version

# A WORK OF FICTION

*Striking Down Scoundrels* is a work of fiction. Yes, it is set in real places, mentions real trade names and describes real scenic views, but the work is fiction. All of the characters and all businesses except those listed on the following page are fictional, and all actions involving the trade names are fictional. Similarity of fictional characters, businesses, or actions to real people, businesses or actions is strictly coincidental.

I don't think what I've described in this book really happened, but it could have. That's the fun of writing and reading fiction. With enough real background, sometimes modified for the convenience of the story, the reader can envision the fictional characters thinking likely and unlikely thoughts, making likely and unlikely statements, and taking likely and unlikely actions.

What's not fiction is God's grace. It is my sincere hope that by reading this fictional story at least a few readers will come to know and enjoy the true grace of God.

--- Jerry D. Harrison

# Trade Name
# Acknowledgements

Trademarks and copyrights are hereby acknowledged for the trade names listed below. These are well known businesses and products broadly available to the public. Their use in this book reflects that public availability which has made them a part of the society in which the story is set. Their inclusion does not indicate sponsorship or endorsement.

## Name(s) Used / Owner; Headquarters Location

Stella / The Genuine Scooter Company; Chicago, Illinois

PT Cruiser, Dakota, and Chrysler / The Chrysler Group, LLC; Auburn Hills, Michigan

U.S. Open Golf Tournament / United States Golf Association; Far Hills, NJ

Biltmore Estate / The Biltmore Company; Asheville, North Carolina

Pro Football Hall of Fame / Pro Football Hall of Fame Corporation / Canton, Ohio

Illinois State University / Illinois State University; Normal, Illinois

Lincoln, Lincoln Town Car / Ford Motor Company; Dearborn, Michigan

Downtown Hospital / New York Downtown Hospital; New York, New York

New York Times / The New York Times Company; New York, New York

Rockefeller Center / Tishman Speyer Properties; New York, New York

Trans Tahoe Regatta / Tahoe Yacht Club; Tahoe City, California

The Washington Post / The Washington Post Company; Washington, D.C.

The University of Virginia / The University of Virginia; Charlottesville, Virginia

Camaro / General Motors Company; Detroit, Michigan

The Baldknobbers Jamboree Show / Baldknobbers, Inc.; Branson, Missouri

Presleys' Country Jubilee / Presleys' Country Jubilee; Branson, Missouri

FedEx /FedEx Corporation; Memphis, Tennessee

"How Great Thou Art" / Manna Music, Inc.; Pacific City, Oregon

University of California, Davis / The State of California; Sacramento, CA

# ACKNOWLEDGMENTS

When I retired from an oil company, I inquired of the Lord, "What do you want me to do? Where may I serve?" My paltry suggestions were ignored, and I heard almost spoken words, "Write the book."

Therefore, I first give thanks to the Lord for directing me into the fascinating retirement activity of writing novels, and for continuing to lead me. Secondly, I give thanks to my wife, Evelyn, who has been a constant source of encouragement and support from her first reading of the first chapters of the first book. Next, I give thanks to family and friends who have encouraged and supported me in every way, including their critical reading of error-filled drafts in which action sometimes dragged. Special thanks to Rebecca and Dennis Currington at Snapdragon Group Editorial Services for their wonderful professional help.

You, the reader, should be thankful for these people, too. Without them, the story you have just read would not have been nearly as good. I hope you enjoyed the book!

---JDH

# ABOUT THE AUTHOR

A friend commented that Jerry Harrison always begins his prayers with "Gracious Lord." There is a reason. Jerry appreciates God's patience with man's imperfection. Jerry appreciates God's grace.

Early in his life, Jerry developed his enjoyment of reading. But he also enjoyed baseball, football, and many other sports. He worked on student publications in high school and college and took more English classes than required. During his career in the oil industry, Jerry often had a book available for time in the airliner seat or in a hotel room. During those years in business Jerry would occasionally comment about unusual events, "When I write my book this will be chapter . . ."

*Striking Down Scoundrels* is Jerry's second book. It reflects Jerry's appreciation for God's patience and Jerry's disgust for corporate raiders.

Jerry and his wife Evelyn live in Tulsa, Oklahoma, are active in their church, travel extensively, and enjoy their adult children, "children-in-law", and grandchildren. Jerry's voluntary community service ranges from picking up litter on the trail during his daily two mile walk to serving with an organization that provides free consulting services for small businesses.